The Orphan Band of Springdale

The Orphan Band of Springdale

ANNE NESBET

CANDLEWICK PRESS

Copyright © 2018 by Anne Nesbet

First edition 2018

Library of Congress Catalog Card Number pending
ISBN 978-0-7636-8804-2

18 19 20 21 22 23 LSC 10 9 8 7 6 5 4 3 2 1

Printed in Crawfordsville, IN, U.S.A.

This book was typeset in Berling.

Candlewick Press
99 Dover Street
Somerville, Massachusetts 02144

visit us at www.candlewick.com

For my mother, Helen,
whom I miss as much as she missed Maine,
and
for all who love a hill or a town or a view somewhere
that made them who they are

ᘒ 1 ᘙ

What Happened in Portland

G usta Neubronner hadn't expected to be on a bus in Maine when she lost her father. She hadn't expected to be sitting alone scrunched up next to the dark blue coat of a woman she didn't know, or to have her French horn case balanced between her ankles, or for the weight of a night's worth of not sleeping to be pulling at her eyelids and making her mind slow and stupid just at the moment when she needed to be even more alert than her usual quick-brained self.

Things never happen the way we imagine them ahead of time.

"Sit here," her father had said, hardly a moment ago. They hadn't meant to come late to the

Portland–Springdale bus, of course. But they had been riding buses all day and all night—New York to Boston, and then waiting in Boston, and then Boston to Portland, and then in the waiting room here in Portland—and the truth was they must have both nodded off, even her father. That must have been what had happened. So then there was a hurry to the bus, and other people already on board, and her father had pushed her scruffy suitcase onto the rack above her head and said, "Sit here," so she had done so, next to this woman with the scratchy blue coat, and then he had said something else, something urgent and hard to hear, and dashed right back off the bus again—why?

He had said something, so it must have been an explanation. Had he gone to grab a cup of coffee? He was tired out—they were both so tired out—and he did like the bitter taste of coffee. But coffee wasn't worth risking missing their bus, was it?

Gusta took a ragged breath and squinted toward the front of the bus, willing him to come bounding up the steps again. She would know him anywhere, just from the way he moved, with impatience like springs in the soles of his feet and his shoulders always tense, ready to push boulders aside if boulders appeared. *Hurry up, Papa*, she told him.

Two men did come swinging up the steps then, but neither one of them moved like her father. Their eyes looked like mysterious dark pools to Gusta. They stood at the front of the bus looking at all the tired people sitting there, waiting to be on their way to Springdale, and they said in terrible, hard voices, *"August Neubronner!"*—which was Gusta's father's name.

Then they started moving down the aisles, looking at all the men who might be August Neubronner, and as they brushed by Gusta, paying no attention to her because she was just a scrawny eleven-year-old girl tucked up next to a woman in a blue coat, she saw that the dark pools were actually dark glasses, and the men were in uniforms, and that was how she knew the thing they had been dreading and expecting all these months, even years, was actually really happening. Not in some shadowy future, but right now, for real, in 1941.

"When they come for me—" her father used to say at the dinner table in New York, and her mother would say, "Now, August," and he would say, "We've got to have a plan, always. When they come for me—"

There were things to be hidden and things to be done, and if they were in a place with a back window, maybe Gusta's mother could even talk to them to give Gusta's father time to climb out and run, and in all of these plans, Gusta's job was to *not say anything.*

But never in any of those imaginings of the terrible moment when they would come for her father had Gusta been alone at dawn on a bus in Portland.

Every part of her started to tremble, waves of trembling that rose up from the horn case between her feet and made her stomach tight and her arms shaky.

There were grumbles from the people on the bus as the men asked for identity papers here and there in the back.

There was no August Neubronner at the back of the bus. The men from the government retreated back down the aisle.

"Sorry, folks," they said. "We've got us a fugitive to track down."

Now Gusta's *teeth* were beginning to tremble. In a moment they would be making some kind of chattering noise, and that would give her away.

The men left the bus.

Maybe her father had seen them coming? Maybe that was why he had left her so suddenly? Maybe while those men were checking papers on this bus, her own papa had been able to slip away?

Her heart shuddered like a small creature, hiding behind her ribs.

The bus driver made a discontented sort of noise, revved the engine, and closed the door behind them.

"Portland–Springdale line," he announced with that booming, ceremonial voice all bus drivers seemed to use.

Gusta grabbed the handle of her horn case and half stood up. Suddenly she was flooded with the urge to run off the bus while there was still time, to run after her father, to call his name, to run, to *not be left behind*—

"What's the trouble? Aren't you going to Springdale, dear?" said the woman next to her. "Let me see that ticket of yours."

It turned out that Gusta was holding her bus ticket. The woman took it from her to check. Her father must have put that ticket into her hand when he had said "Sit here" just those few minutes ago.

"No, you're fine," said the woman kindly, patting the ticket back into Gusta's hand. "Portland–Springdale bus. What is that thing you have there?"

She meant the horn in its case.

Gusta leaned sideways instead of answering so she could peer out through the windows past the woman in her coat, but of course there was no way to make sense of anything: the smears of blue must be the terrible men in their uniforms, the smears of gray other people outside—beyond that she couldn't see what was happening. She couldn't see.

Did they have him by now? Had they caught him? Or had he seen them coming in time and escaped, running north, north, north toward Canada, where the Americans couldn't touch him anymore, where he could join the Canadian Air Force and help fight the Nazis over in the European war?

She had no way of knowing. All she could do to help him now was to *not say anything*, which meant acting like nothing in the world had just gone wrong— which meant going on by herself.

It was the hardest thing she had ever had to do, thus far in her life, to sit back quietly while inside her skin she was shouting after her father and wanting to jump off that bus and run, run, run to find him, wher- ever he was headed, off to Canada or off to prison in chains. Inside her skin, there was a great struggle going on. There was a war. That's what her father said the whole world was: *struggle*. He liked to point at quiet things, at plants, at people sitting on a bench, and whisper to Gusta, "What's going on, do you think, in their inside? Struggle and contradictions. Even in you, my calm little thingling."

That's how Gusta knew it must be true about plants and other people, because it was certainly true about herself, Gusta. She was very good at being calm on the outside, but inside her there was always a struggle raging. She was all secrets, struggles, and contradictions.

For now she kept those contradictions packed away inside. She pressed her lips tightly together, so that the sounds of doubt and fear could not possibly squeeze their way out, and as the bus shook itself and roared, she fell back against that not-very-friendly seat, the seat that was moving, every minute, farther from her father.

❦ 2 ❧

Almost as Good as Courage

The seats of the bus seemed half-starved, they had so little padding on them. The woman next to Gusta, wrapped up in her sturdy body and thick blue coat, wasn't so much bothered, or at least she didn't let her botheration show, but Gusta kept finding herself shifting a little thisaway, and then a little thataway, trying to keep her poor bones comfortable. The winter must have been picking at the scabs of that road for months. Every time a wheel of the bus hit a missing bit of road, every person riding that bus rattled a little, and Gusta's teeth clattered, and the French horn case between Gusta's knees flung itself from one shin to the other one, as if it couldn't decide which leg needed bruises most.

A plan, her father liked to say, *is almost as good as courage.* He believed in having plans for every possible disaster—for raids, for strikebreakers, for those bad moments when you've disguised yourself as an assembly-line worker to pass around leaflets and one of the bosses gets suspicious and starts walking over your way.

A plan was what would tell your feet where to go and your hands what to do when you got there.

But once the bus had lumbered into what must be Springdale, and the driver had helpfully handed down her ragged little suitcase from the upper rack, and the other passengers had hurried off so confidently toward their homes and destinations, Gusta found that for a moment her feet hardly knew how to move at all.

"Is no one coming for you, little girl?" said the woman in the blue coat, lingering for a moment. She clearly disapproved of Gusta's being all on her own, which was a kindness on her part, maybe, or nosiness, or both.

Gusta tried to look like a person with a plan.

"I'm to go to Mrs. Hoopes's home," she said, and then she recited all she had of an address: "Mrs. Hoopes on Elm Street, Springdale, Maine."

"Oh!" said the woman. "Bound for Mrs. Hoopes's Home! Well, then! But I never heard of a state child showing up all on her own this way, and with such outlandish packages in hand."

By "outlandish packages" she meant the French horn, apparently. Gusta bristled for a moment, out of love for that horn. Then she wondered what a state child was. It didn't sound like a pleasant thing to be.

"And with the sky smearing in, too," said the woman, with a click of the tongue that said she disapproved of bad weather. "Another storm coming, sure as sure."

That made Gusta blink, because it was something her father said almost every day: *the storm is surely coming.*

But this woman meant an actual storm, not a war.

"Well, Elm Street's across the Mousam River, over that way," said the woman, waving forward with her hand. "Nobody with you and no instructions! Who ever heard of such a thing? Poor girl."

"I've got a letter for Mrs. Hoopes," said Gusta. "So I guess I'll be fine."

And to show that it had not (like some fathers)

suddenly disappeared, Gusta fetched the letter right up out of the extra-deep pocket her mother had sewn specially into her skirt, the pocket that was lumpy with all the things that must not be lost, like that letter and handkerchiefs and mittens.

"Well, then," said the woman doubtfully, and after squinting at the address spelled out on the envelope (since Gusta's mother was a firm believer in spelling things out), she began to head off wherever she was heading to.

The air had gotten another notch or two colder. Gusta put the letter away and fished out her mittens.

Strange! There was something tucked right into her ordinary old right-hand mitten. Gusta felt a flush of love for her always-thinking-ahead mother, because of course her first thought was that this must be the emergency quarter. It was important, her mother believed, for a child on her own to have an emergency quarter.

But this object, although round like a quarter, was bulkier than any quarter Gusta had ever met.

She began to figure it out, to tell the truth, even as she brought the thing close to her eyes to see. Her fingers, cold as they were, recognized what it was—and then a second later, her brain finally caught up.

It was not any kind of money after all. No. It might look like an old-fashioned round pocket watch, but in fact what it was, as Gusta knew, was all that was left of a broken Wish.

❦ 3 ❧

The Wish from the Sea

Here's what you need to know about Gusta's mother, Gladys Hoopes Neubronner:

Gusta's mama was another one of those quiet people with contradictions rattling around inside.

She had grown up on her parents' farm in Maine. She could sew up a shirt, which is not the easiest kind of sewing, with blurry-fast hands. She could make a decent supper out of not much, and she knew all sorts of things about cows and pastures and planting and hay. She was the sort of person who liked to get things done without fussing.

She was also the fastest reader in Manhattan or maybe anywhere. She could read a whole book faster than most people could light the lamp and pick out a story. It could be a really hard book, too: all economics, maybe. She could whip through it and then tell it all to you in her own way, which was clearer than most books.

Reading like that had gotten her all the way to college, the first of the Hoopes family to go. She had won herself a scholarship. And then at some point in the city where her college was, she had met a fiery young union organizer from Germany named after the equally fiery month of August. She typed up flyers and pamphlets for him on a typewriting machine, and he fell in love with her quick way with words.

What he didn't realize at first was that Gusta's mother liked all sorts of words, not just the kind that would eventually change the world (as Gusta's father saw things) by being so logical and true that the powers that be would hear them and tremble and fumble and eventually crumble.

Gusta's mother was omnivorous when it came to words.

She could write a pamphlet or a letter asking the Working Man to think about whether he was really being paid his due. But that was not all: Gusta's mother could tell a story—any story—like nobody's business.

According to Gusta's mother, she had learned about telling stories from her own grandfather, Captain William Griffiths, who had come far enough inland once to glimpse Gusta's great-grandmother Prudence, to fall in love quick as a shipwreck, and then settle down in the surprising place that shipwreck had left him: Springdale, Maine, so far from the sea that it would take a very good telescope and good weather up on the highest hill for a person to see even the largest sail out Portland way. It was a different Maine than the one he'd been used to.

"Our corner of Maine," said her mother. "A fine sort of place, but with cows instead of lobsters. Could be, he missed the salt in the air, but he loved my grandmother enough to keep coming back—and then, eventually, to stay. And he bounced us little ones on his knees and told us the adventures he'd had out on that ocean we mostly never saw but once a year, when we went all the way out to Old Orchard Beach."

Gusta learned about Captain Griffith's various shipwrecks from her mother, all the stories, true and more-than-true, that clung to a sea captain like barnacles to a boat, and that he could then pass down to his children and his children's children, far as they might live from salt water.

The stories came to Gusta like gleaming pieces of eight, and she stowed them safely and secretly away — because her papa didn't like them.

Some nights, Gusta's mother would sit on the edge of Gusta's cot and murmur the most incredible tales to her, fairy tales and adventures. Not just about ships and oceans, but about poor children who got lost in the woods and found gingerbread houses. Heroes hiding under the water in marshes and breathing through reeds. Kings who accidentally turned their own daughters into gold. Captain Griffiths sharing a tree with a real orangutan. Magic tablecloths that conjured up feasts for a poor man's table. She had to whisper, of course, so that Gusta's father wouldn't get mad.

He was firmly against the passing on of that nonsense. He said it was all designed to keep the people living in ignorance and the dark.

"A magic table that covers itself with food!" he said, when he caught Gusta's mother in the act of smuggling fairy tales. "You know why the rich people want you to tell that story? To keep the starving ones from asking for real wages so they can buy actual food, and not just dream food."

Gusta's contradictions inside pummeled each other when he said that, because some of her could see how right he was (real food was unquestionably important to have, no?), and yet the wicked rest of her could not help wanting to feed itself on dream food, too.

Some stories are realer than others, though.

"Mama," she whispered. "Tell me again about my great-grandpa, the sea captain. Was he really truly shipwrecked?"

Her mother nodded. "More than once," she said. "But the most important wreck was the one off the coast of Madagascar. . . ."

Gusta sighed happily. *Madagascar!* There was magic in that word, but it was the name of a place that was so real you could find it on the globe on the teacher's desk at school.

"My grandfather's strangest story," said her mother. "And it starts with him finding a little chest full of things he had thought at first were coins, in some harbor market, very far away—"

"Treasure!" said Gusta, imagining a pirate's chest, the kind that hides under a nice dark X on old maps. If they had a chest filled with treasure, they could surely pay the landlord the rent they owed. (They were always having to move to new places, the Neubronners, when the rent came due.)

"So you'd think," said her mother. "But listen: he bought them for the price of a parrot, twelve lemons, and a really good pipe from some trader on the other side of the world who claimed they weren't actually coins, they were wishes."

Wishes!

Gusta snuggled closer to her mother. She hadn't known that wishes were actual things you could keep in a chest.

"Mama, were they? *Real wishes?*"

"Well, as you can imagine, I asked him that myself. And my grandfather laughed and said sure enough, he wasted a bunch of them the first day, just convincing himself of what they were. He wished for this and that—for sugar in his tea! For a really good sardine! All such foolish little cravings—and each time the wishes came true, one way or another: someone turned out to have some secret lump of sugar stashed away, and then felt moved to share it with my grandfather, for no particular reason. That sort of thing. He said that after a day or two, he suddenly realized the seriousness of the situation. These were *actual wishes*, and he was *wasting them*. He would pick up one of those odd little coin things and wish for his sardines (for example), and after that, he said, he could tell that

Wish was all used up. It didn't sparkle anymore, he said. It just looked empty."

"How can a coin be empty?"

"I don't know. That's how he described it. And of course that made him realize he couldn't keep wasting those Wishes; he needed to think it all through more carefully, make wishes that counted. And then—right that very day—something really terrible happened: the ship he was on hit a reef and sank."

"The shipwreck!"

"One of his several shipwrecks, yes. One of the worst. It sank, but my grandfather clung to a mast and lived. Only the chest with the Wishes in it was gone."

"Oh!" said Gusta. "But Mama, he should have wished for the boat to be unshipwreckable."

"Maybe he should have," said her mother. "But he didn't know ahead of time that he would be shipwrecked, did he? It's so hard to know ahead of time what danger you should be warding off. And then there was the problem of making the *right* sort of wish. In fairy tales, magic things are very clever. You have to be cleverer even than they are. Imagine: What if he had wished for his ship to be 'entirely safe from shipwrecks'? What if—oh, I don't know—what if *lightning* then struck it, and it burned to ashes right there, bobbing on the sea. That might be worse than a shipwreck, mightn't it?"

"There might be no mast left to hang on to," said Gusta. She thought it over. "So you'd have to wish for no bad thing to happen to that boat—make the boat always absolutely safe and disaster-proof."

"And then the sailors might all get a case of fever and die, even if their boat's *absolutely safe*. That wish might not be the right one, either."

"So you have to wish for the boat to be safe and sound, *and* all the people in it to stay well, and—oh, but they could still break their legs, if they fell from up where the sails are. So no broken bones. No accidents. And then . . ."

Gusta started thinking of other things that could go wrong. Pirates, for instance. Sea monsters. And her words petered out after a moment.

"See?" said her mother. "It takes a great deal of care to make wishes properly. And anyway, it was too late for him. He washed up on a shore with his arms around that mast and only the clothes on his back. The little casket filled with Wishes? It must have sunk right to the bottom of the sea."

"Oh, no!" said Gusta. All that magic, drowned!

"Except!" said her mother. "When he reach
into his trouser pocket, guess what he found?"

"A Wish?" breathed Gusta.

"A single Wish," said her mother. "One last Wish
left. He kept that Wish safe, and he brought it back
home with him. And you know what? He never used
it, his whole life long. That's what he told me, anyway,
and I knew him when he was very, very old."

"So why *didn't* he use his Wish, Mama?"

It seemed to Gusta like a clear case of wasting.
And usually her mama was firmly opposed to all wasting of things.

But now her mother made a funny sort of face —
as if her inside contradictions were bumping against
the edges so hard they were nearly beginning to show.

"Well, now, I don't know," she said. "Maybe making wishes gets harder the older you are. You know
too much about how tangled up things are. You worry
about what the right wish might be. And anyway, it's
just a story. He told such wild stories!"

"But what happened to the one last Wish in the
end?" said Gusta. "What happened, what happened,
what happened?"

"Settle down, Gusta. You don't want to be

bothering your papa. Anyway, I remember my grand-father calling me over to where he was sitting in his big chair one day — oh, he was immensely old by then — and I could tell he was anxious about something. He had his old sailor's pocket watch in his hands, the one that eventually he left to me. You know: this one."

It was a funny old half-broken thing with two small dials that used to tell two kinds of time at once, captain's time and "home time," which was the time in his home port of Castine, on the rocky coast of Maine.

Gusta and her mother admired the captain's watch for a moment together.

"He was so proud of this watch, even if half its little mechanisms no longer ticked along as they were supposed to. But that day he called me to him, he was looking at it and saying, 'It's gone, it's gone, I put it away.' I was confused, of course. The watch itself wasn't gone; that's why I didn't understand at first. Then I saw he was showing me the *other* end of the watch chain, where a link was broken right off — see it here? It looks as if there used to be something there. So when he pointed that out to me, back then, of course I was trying to remember whether I'd seen something there in the past. I thought maybe there had been, sometime in the past, a medallion or something. In any case, now he wanted it back, whatever it was. It was in a box, he said. He had put it away in a box. A box about so big."

Gusta's mother sketched out a little box in the air, as long ago her grandfather's hands must have also done.

"A box on a shelf. 'Go find it, Gladdy,' he said. 'Bring it here.' So of course I looked and looked, in all possible boxes on all possible shelves. Oh, I brought him spoons and thimbles and nails and plenty of other roundish things, and every time he just shook his head and pushed it away and said, 'No, Gladdy, in the *box*, on the *shelf*!' But he couldn't tell me what box on what shelf."

"So you didn't find it?" said Gusta.

"No," said her mother.

"Oh!" said Gusta. "But you *think* it's still there somewhere?"

She was sitting straight up in her cot now. The tips of her ears were tingling. The tips of her fingers were alert, too. New ideas were spilling through her blood vessels and changing her view of the world.

Her mother must have seen how trembly she had gotten, because she laughed.

"Oof. Now I've gone and riled you up, when what

I meant to do was settle you down. Lie back and shut your eyes now. It's time to sleep tight, Gusta."

But it gave Gusta the shivers, thinking about that unused Wish, still loose in the world somewhere. And then her thoughts turned a sharp corner, just as her mother was slipping out past the blanket wall that separated Gusta's cot from the rest of that room.

"Does Papa know? About the Wish hiding away in your family?"

Because she was thinking about all the things that were so important to her father—all the ways a Wish might come in handy. The times when workers went out on strike; the rent getting paid; the war that, like a storm, was *surely coming*. Couldn't a Wish fix all of that once and for all?

"Goodness, Gusta," said her mother, all the laughter in her vanishing at once. "You know your papa isn't the kind of foolish person who believes in wishes."

But maybe, thought Gusta secretly and guiltily and with the hint of a tingle in the tips of her ears, *maybe my mother and I—or at least part of me and part of Mama—maybe we're secretly foolish in that wish-believing way. . . .*

❦ 4 ❧

Gusta, in the Light of Trouble

A watch that was maybe all that was left of a broken Wish turned out to be no use at all to a girl trying to get herself more than a mile down Elm Street in chill weather.

Gusta had to walk with care—*gingerly* (which was a word her mother liked to use)—because her poor shins were already so bruised from the horn case. It turns out that when you're carrying a raggedy old suitcase in one hand, you can't do much to defend your legs from awkward horn case–shaped edges dangling from the other hand. Eventually her shins kind of gave up complaining, and then it was easier.

She crossed the bridge over a dark, cold smear that must have been the mill river. Vague buildings loomed along the road, holding secrets.

She counted her steps to jolly herself along: fifty more! Good! Fifty again!

And now and again, when she really couldn't stand it anymore, she put her suitcase down on one side and her horn on the other, to rest her arms, and pretended she needed to check the address on the letter her mother had sent along with her, the one she had shown to that woman in the blue coat. It still said exactly what it had said half an hour before: *Mrs. Clementine Hoopes, Elm Street, Springdale, Maine.*

Gusta rolled the envelope thoughtfully in her cold fingers a little.

It wasn't entirely Gusta's fault, what happened next. It was partly the fault of the weather: the glue had weakened, and the envelope was beginning to gape.

Her hands couldn't help themselves; they finished what the weather had begun. Gusta was staring at an open envelope, and inside, right there, was a letter.

Gusta had to hold it close to her eyes to see what that handwriting was saying.

Dear Mother, said the slightly frantic handwriting of Gusta's own mother. *We are all so grateful to you for taking in Augusta at this time. You will find her to be a faithful scholar, now in the fifth grade, and a good worker. My hours right now are long, to get us onto solid footing, but I have a promising job helping a professor with his books, and I have found a room in a good boardinghouse, very clean and economical, but alas they do not allow children. August will fill in the details, I am sure.*

Well, now, no, he wouldn't.

Oh, where was her papa now? In a cell? On a different bus? Closing in on the Canadian border? Sitting behind bars with his head in his hands?

The world swam in Gusta's eyes for a moment. She stared at the letter blindly and only a minute later realized she was actually staring at her mother's note at the bottom of the letter: *P.S. If need arises, the horn can serve as her room and board. I guess you might find a good price for it.*

It was like the letter had turned out to be some kind of poisonous insect and had stung her.

And then she did not think. She did not plan. She simply tore off the line at the bottom of the page (surprised by her boldness even as she did it) and wadded it into a paper pill.

She stood there for a shocked moment, with that little pill's worth of paper rolling back and forth between her thumb and her fingers.

It was a wicked thing she had just done, tearing

off that tiny strip of paper, but here's the thing: Gusta loved that horn.

August, her father, had gotten that horn from his father, also named August, who had played it in an orchestra in Germany.

The August who was her father hadn't brought much with him across the wide ocean apart from that horn. But he was so busy with his work that Gusta played it more than he did these days. At first he had been amused she could get any sound out of it, despite being so young and scrawny, and then he started showing her some of the horn's secrets: how your left hand pressed the keys that remade the maze your breath ran through, and how the way you shaped your lips could change the note that came out of the bell.

Gusta loved the golden sound of the horn, the way the notes could make you ring like a bell, from your hair bow to your toes. Its music was so large and grand. Every scrap of teaching her father gave her she hoarded in her mind and her heart and her breath and her hands.

She had practiced and practiced. She was quiet by nature, but the horn was the bravest part of her — her sweet, large, secret, brassy voice.

And besides, her heart was sore: her father had

disappeared. She couldn't let the horn disappear, too, no matter what.

The air was colder now than it had been, the sky a much darker gray, especially over there, ahead. She had better move along fast if she wanted to get to where she was going before the weather got worse.

And then the sun did that thing the sun sometimes does, before the storm actually arrives. It peeked through a low gap in the clouds and made Gusta's hands and the rest of the near world glitter, a sudden and unexpected brilliance against the black backdrop of the rest of the sky.

Oh, Papa, thought Gusta. Her father had a phrase for the way the sun catches things out against the darkness of a coming storm: *the clear light of trouble,* he called it. He always smiled when he said that, too, as if it were a good thing.

"What do we do, little thingling, when the storm is coming?" he said once, when Gusta had been much younger than she was today.

"Borrow umbrellas! Button up our coats! Run inside and close the door!"

But it turned out he was being serious, despite that smile.

"Ah, yes, coats!" he said. "But that's not all. When

the storm is coming, we must quickly find out who we are: who we are *in the light of trouble.*"

"We already know who we are," she said. "*You* are Papa, and *I* am Gusta."

"Yes, certainly, true. But can you be sure you will stay *yourself,* Gusta, once the wind is howling?"

He liked to talk that way.

Even in very strong wind, I will try very hard to still be Gusta, thought Gusta, standing taller in that last burst of sunlight before the storm.

And she set off, up what she hoped must be the last piece of road, with her little suitcase in one hand and, in the other, the awkward big horn case, bumping against the bruises it had already sprinkled over her shin.

❧ 5 ❧

The Girl at the Door

Gusta walked along a stretch of field that looked as cold and sullen as the sky above. From time to time, she had to stop and listen for a moment to how quiet everything was. In all her life she had never been somewhere so quiet. New York, for example, rumbled and crashed and beeped at you all the time, a cozy sort of din if that's what you were used to. And Boston had been plenty noisy, too.

The horn case's handle was firm in her hand, a narrow but well-sewn loop of leather. It had held itself together for thousands of miles and would hold itself together a little farther. This dirt road turning off to the right here was Hoopes Road. That's what the sign said, when you got close enough to read it. That meant that this big yellow house on the corner—once upon a time yellow, when the paint was younger—this house with the screened-in porch all down the left side and around the corner: this was it.

A snowflake settled on Gusta's mitten, just to remind her that the weather was on its way to worse.

Gusta took a deep breath and told herself to be brave and to keep her secrets secret, no matter what they asked her here.

All right, then! Gusta knew that if she stood there even four more seconds, she would lose her gumption and start being afraid, so she went up the steps quickly, racing to get ahead of her doubts, through the screen door and right up to the actual front door, which she knocked on several times.

The porch spreading around her was shadowy and filled with lumpy bits of furniture, some covered up against the winter weather. Wisps and scraps of sound came from inside the house. As usual, Gusta was listening more than looking. She could hear so many voices from inside—young voices shouting to each other, older voices telling younger people what to do—her grandmother's house sounded like a human beehive, an anthill, a — what did rabbits live in, out in the wild? There must be a word for that —

And then the front door flew open, and a girl was standing there, staring at her. She looked a few years older than Gusta. She was thin and wiry, had hints of red in her tidy brown hair, and her hands were blurry with what looked like flour.

"Hello! Who are you? And what in the name of biscuits are you carrying there?"

Gusta instantly felt the way anyone feels at a strange door: foolish and out of place and almost too dry-mouthed to speak.

"I'm looking for Mrs. Hoopes?" she said finally. She had wanted to sound brave, but it didn't work out that way. Her sentences kept adding question marks to themselves.

"Is this — Mrs. Hoopes's house?"

"Surely is," said the girl, and she turned to shout back down the dim hall: "A new one at the door!"

Then she whipped back around and asked, "And what's your name, new one?"

"I'm Augusta," said Gusta.

The older girl's eyes went wide. She craned her head around to look past Gusta, out toward the road.

"Augusta!" she said. "You mean, the Augusta we've been waiting for? The Augusta who's a Hoopes? But then, where's that foreign — *ohnevermind* —"

The girl bit her words back and slapped her floury hand right onto her mouth for a moment, as extra precaution.

Before Gusta could do so much as squeak, a voice from the hall — a very rapidly approaching voice, small and light on its feet — said sharply, "JOSIE!"

And the girl in the doorway clapped her hand back over her mouth again.

"So sorry," she said, through the muffling of her hand, though Gusta thought she heard a laugh hiding behind that hand, too.

"Mrs. Hoopes?" said Gusta to whoever it was who had just darted up to that door, correcting that right away to, "Grandmother?" But even as she said that, the quick-footed stranger said, "Oh, no, no, no!" in a voice that was too young to belong to any grandmother.

"You think Miss Marion is your *grandmother*?" said the girl in the doorway in disbelief. "Well, if that doesn't take the cake."

"Josie!" said the woman at the door, and she put a small hand (thin, but all muscle) on Gusta's arm. "You're Gladys's Augusta?"

Gusta nodded. Her brain was scrambling for the names of all the aunts. There had been three of them, before the one aunt died, plus the two uncles: Bill and Jay.

"But where's your father? We thought—they didn't send you all this way alone, did they?"

"No foreign bandits anywhere, that I can see," said Josie, from the side of the doorway.

"*Josie*," said the woman again. "Hark a moment, can't you? Come in, Augusta. Letting in all this cold air. Anyway, I'm your Aunt Marion. Is that thing yours?"

She was eyeing the French horn case as if it might sit up on its rear legs and growl at her.

And then through the hall's murkiness (which seemed to have faces in it; Gusta heard the shifting and rustling of small people) came a different sort of voice, quick and in charge.

"What's this bedlam?" it said, and by now the voice was becoming an actual person, the sort of person who knows what needs doing and can't understand why everyone isn't already doing it. "You, Josie, have you just left the biscuits to themselves in the kitchen? Here, now, let me investigate this child here."

Josie scooted off, through some passage down to the right. Aunt Marion was already shrinking back against the passage wall, making way for the person who must be Mrs. Hoopes, herself—*Gramma Hoopes*—to conduct her investigation.

Gusta felt the press of eyes on her, inspecting every inch of her dusty self. She had never liked being looked at. Other people's staring eyes felt like weapons trained on her. They made her want to squirm, but she remembered her papa just in time and did not actually twitch. Her papa wanted people to stand up straight and be counted. Gusta tried to stand up straight right now, and keep the squirming tucked away secretly inside.

"Where's your father?" said Mrs. Hoopes—*Gramma*—suspiciously. "Augusta! Speak up! Why's he hanging back outside?"

"It's just me," said Gusta. "Papa had to—he had to—"

She had a moment of not knowing what in the world she could say. She had to keep her father's secret, no matter what. Those horrible agents with their dark glasses, looking for August Neubronner: she couldn't let anyone know about that.

"Canadian Air Force," she said in a rush, because it was possibly true. Maybe it was true. Maybe he had managed to get away from those terrible men with their dark glasses. "He had to go north, for the war."

"What did he want to go and do that for?" said— *Gramma*. She did not sound like she approved at all of any of it, not of Canada, not of air forces, not of wars. "What are you telling us, child? They just dumped you onto some autobus all the way from New York City on your own?"

"Portland," said Gusta. "Papa came with me up as far as Portland. Then he—"

Then he had indeed put her on *some bus all on her own*. Gusta didn't know how to say that without making this frowning woman in front of her frown harder, so she stopped herself short again. She could feel her lips stretched tense across her teeth, which she tried so hard to never let show.

"He had to go on north," Gusta said feebly. "To Canada. He'll come back when he can."

"Well!" said the formidable Mrs. Hoopes.

"Think how nice it'll be for Josie to have another big girl around," said Aunt Marion in her smaller and much less formidable voice. "It'll be a help to her, I'm sure. How old are you now, Augusta? About ten or so, looks like?"

"Eleven," said Gusta. Even as she said it, she

remembered that letter from her mother, and fished it out of her pocket for Mrs.—*Gramma*—Hoopes. Of course, she felt a surge of guilt as she did so, but she tried to suppress it. Her father liked to say, *In war and struggle, we do what we must!* Now her "must" seemed already to have grown to include tearing bits off other people's letters.

"Well," said her grandmother again when she was done. (She made no mention of the letter's slightly ragged lower edge.) "Hard times all around."

Then she stood up.

"Your mother says you're a good student and willing to work, Augusta," she said. "I see you don't come with much, but believe me, we've had plenty of children show up here with less. And you're family. Family is family. Josie girl!"

Josie was there again in about a quarter of a second.

"Yes, Mrs. Hoopes?" she said. "Bread's set to rise."

"Good," said Gusta's grandmother. "You take Augusta up and settle her in with you. And then it's almost dinnertime."

"Gusta," whispered Gusta.

"What's that, girl?" said her grandmother.

"Nobody calls me Augusta, usually," she said. "Just plain Gusta."

"Gusty, Gusty!" echoed high-pitched voices from the shadows, and there was giggling and a crescendo of whispering rustle somewhere beyond the doorways.

It was like entering a forest, coming into that house, and sensing creatures lurking behind every tree. These creatures were whispering and giggling sorts, though. Probably not with very sharp teeth.

"That's right, Josie. You'd better introduce her to the current crop of shipwrecked sailors on your way upstairs," said Gusta's grandmother. "Who have no manners yet, though they're getting older every day. Come now, you lot!"

She said that not to Gusta, but over her shoulder to the rustling shadows.

And then it was like a human ocean spilled in through the door in a great boyish blur.

❧ 6 ❧

The Shipwrecked Sailors

They ranged in size from very small to just about Gusta's height. Josie took over as Gusta's grandmother marched out of the room, taking Aunt Marion with her as if they were on their way to a secret discussion of Gusta's arrival, which they probably were.

"The kids aren't really sailors," said Josie. "That's just Mrs. Hoopes's way of speaking. We all ran into hard times, or our families did, and here we are. I was the first. Sometimes they even call me First Girl, just to remind me. Left behind here as a tiny baby. Anyway. And then others came and went, came and went. This one is Donald. He's already big, twelve — does work for your uncle Bill on the farm when he's not in school.

He came here with this slew of his brothers, all in a crowd, more than a year ago now already. State kids. Stand up straight, Clarence! This is Augusta, named like the city, but who wants to be called Gusta. Here is Clarence, who can't be trusted with eggs—"

The moving blur that must be Clarence squawked out a laugh.

"They slip right out of his fingers. But he's strong and fast, so that's good, if he would just *think* sometimes. Then that's Laurence in the middle. Larry. How old are you, Larry, eight? There's one who *can* be trusted with eggs. This fellow's Thomas. He's six. He's small, but he likes bossing around the cows, so that's his specialty. Say hey to the new girl, boys!"

"Hey there!" said the other blurry faces all around her. How was she ever going to figure out who was who in that crowd?

She tried to smile, though, or at least made a weak effort. She was always so careful not to open her mouth when she smiled, so that her crooked teeth didn't show; her mother said Gusta's smiles always looked anxious, even when she wasn't anxious.

"And there's Ron," said Josie, pointing to a paler-headed kid in the back. "Also helps out with the farm chores. Here to rescue him from his weak lungs. Don't seem so weak now. And Delphine's over there hiding. She's too young to be much help, being only three and a half. Her cot's in with Miss Marion. All right, and that's the current crew of boarders. Rascals, all."

The blur of (mostly) boys grinned back at that. They seemed to like Josie pretty well.

"Where are you from?" they said, and also, "What's in that thing?"—pointing, of course, at the horn case.

"Now, I'm warning all of you," said Josie. "Give her no trouble, and you'll get no grief from me. She's not like all the rest of us. She's *family*—her mother's Miss Marion's own sister. So you all treat her right."

Discomfort prickled all through Gusta during this part of Josie's speech. All the faces around her seemed to soak it up, and back away a step. *Family.* Not like the likes of them.

"Wash up for dinner, now," said Josie, swatting the nearest boy to stand in for swatting them all. "We're having bean soup and biscuits. And someone please get that paint or paste or whatever it is off Delphine's face."

While the children dispersed, Josie led Gusta up the stairs.

"Mostly we all sleep up here," she said. "There's

the big room for the boys. Miss Marion and Delphine have the front room, that way. And I'm in here, and so will you be. In summertime we can sleep out on the porch when the heat gets awful."

The heat was certainly not awful in there at the moment. There was hardly any heat in there to speak of.

The room was not just cold; it was cold and small and fiercely neat, with a bed on one side and a lower cot on the other side. Through the window at the far end, there was a streak of what must be pasture across Hoopes Road and the blur of the woods beyond that.

The beds were made so tightly you could not spot even the ghost of a wrinkle on the coverlets. Under Josie's bed were two small boxes for clothes.

"I'll have to look out for another box for you," said Josie as an apology. "Though I see you've got a suitcase, and that's just about as good as a box, I guess. Does it fit under the cot over there? Cot's not that high above the ground."

It did fit, thank goodness, but Gusta didn't know where her underwear and socks (now choking the poor French horn) were supposed to go. Maybe another box would turn up at some point, and she could move them in there, but for the moment she just left the French horn standing, unopened and keeping all its secrets, at the end of the cot.

"Funny-looking thing," said Josie about the case. "Now we better scoot down to dinner, though, huh? You can show me whatever's inside there later."

"Just a French horn," said Gusta. Her lips were dry. She felt half-dazed, to tell the truth.

"All right," said Josie with good cheer. "Sure! Whatever that is."

They sat around a big table downstairs: so many people. The bean soup was plain but warming, like something Gusta's mother might make. There were bits of real meat in it, which was not always true about the soup at home. And there were mashed potatoes on the table in a large bowl. And biscuits, warm biscuits, on a plate. So much food! But the sense of all those eyes on her took the flavor out of it somehow.

"You really came from New York City all by yourself?" said the wriggly one, Clarence. (What did it mean to say a kid "can't be trusted with eggs"? Then he twitched a little and the brother next to him yelped, so that was a clue.)

"Not by myself," said Gusta, "until Portland." He was right across from her, so she didn't have to say it very loud, but Gramma Hoopes sniffed.

"Hard to fathom," she said. "What man in his right mind would put a girl on a bus and wander off like that? When he was supposed to come here himself, drop the poor child off properly. Well, there's no accounting for the things people do, is there? Especially foreigners. Seems downright cowardly."

"Mmm," said Aunt Marion.

Gusta felt a tingle of frustration run right down her tired arms. They were talking about her father. But there was so much they didn't know. They didn't know about the men with the glasses like pools of darkness hiding their eyes. They didn't—they couldn't—they mustn't know what those awful men had said they were doing: *looking for a fugitive.*

Of course, Gusta had to not say anything. That was her job.

But nevertheless, she put down her spoon.

Just because she couldn't say anything about what had really happened, that didn't mean she couldn't say *something* about *something.* Sometimes courage means speaking up. Even her father would agree that was true.

"My father—the thing is—he is actually a very brave person," she said, even though her voice betrayed her by wobbling. "He wanted to go fight the Nazis. I'd say that's brave."

And he had been so brave before that, too. Every time Gusta's papa went to get workers to vote for the union—that was brave, wasn't it? When he saw something unfair, he spoke up, even if it meant trouble. His eyes focused on a different distance than most people's eyes: on the glorious but faraway future, when justice would reign. That meant he didn't always see the things right around him the way most people did. And probably he hadn't meant to leave Gusta all alone on that bus—

She had to pull herself back from that brink. She was so alone in the world for a second, and the world was so blurry and quiet.

In fact, there was nearly utter silence around that table (with the noises of the youngest boys slurping up spoonfuls of soup, like they just couldn't help themselves).

Then one of the older boys—Clarence, was it?— said, "*We're* not fighting the Nazis. That's the war over there, far away, not our war."

"He's going up to Canada to join the air army," said Gusta. "Canada's in the war."

"Oh," said another boy. "Is your daddy *Canadian?*"

"Enough! Ron, start those potatoes around," said Gramma Hoopes briskly, breaking into that silence as if it were a block of ice and her voice a great ice-cleaving ax. "Augusta, I'll have you know that in this house we leave politics alone at Sunday dinner. Now, take a biscuit. I'm sure you are tired out from all the travel, but you still need to eat. And then you'd better write home to your mother, to let her know you're safely here."

Between the mashed potatoes and the biscuits and the letter home to Mama, though, came washing the dishes with Josie. It was more dirty dishes than Gusta had ever seen at one time, but Josie seemed to think nothing of it. She wiped dishes so fast that Gusta had to hurry to keep up with the dish towel.

"We all work to help out," she said in a matter-of-fact way. "The older boys help out on your uncle Bill's farm. Younger ones help out in the garden or with the chickens. Plus the state pays some money for the state kids. I'm too old for state money, but I'm useful so they keep me on. And you're family. Probably you don't even have to be useful, and they'd still keep you!"

Josie's laugh was quick and brisk, like the rest of her. She was looking at Gusta now with an expression that was all no-nonsense friendliness.

"My heavens, you are a serious sort of kid. You know what you need? You need to learn to '*whistle while you work. . . .*'"

From that barely one second's worth of singing, Gusta could hear that Josie had a very nice voice.

Gusta, personally, felt a little more like Snow White when she was sitting by her lonely well. Singing to those pigeons. She had seen the film more than a year ago, with her mother. It had been like walking into a fairy tale that had come alive. They had clung to each other during the frightening parts. And for months after that, Gusta had had nightmares of that witch's knobby fingers gripping something so round and so shiny and so very, very red, and that terrible voice saying, "This is no ordinary apple. It's a magic wishing apple! One bite, and all your dreams will come true. . . ."

"Hey, there!" said Josie. "You almost dropped that plate right onto the floor. Better wake up, now, sleepyhead. What are you thinking about, anyway?"

"*Snow White and the Seven Dwarfs,*" said Gusta.

"Good picture, isn't it?" said Josie. "Miss Marion took me, back ages ago, before all those Hansen brothers came crowding in here."

And then she started singing poor Snow White's

song, and her voice warbled right about as high as a bird's, and so sweet that Gusta couldn't help but stare.

"How do you do that?" she said. "If I try to sing, it's like frogs croaking. Yours sounds just like it does in the movies."

"Well," said Josie. "I don't know exactly how I do it. I just open up my mouth and sing, mostly. But can I tell you something? That you mustn't go blabbing around?"

Gusta nodded, though of course who was she going to go blabbing secrets to, anyway, even if she had been the type to blab secrets, which she wasn't?

"So," said Josie. "Miss Kendall in the Department of Music at the high school heard me singing and took me right into the senior girls' chorus. She says it's criminal to leave a gift *fallow*. That's a fifty-cent word, I'd say. Means a field that nobody bothers to plant, or a garden that's left to the weeds. I had to look it up in Mrs. Hoopes's dictionary."

"You don't sound so weedy to me," said Gusta.

Josie gave her a very friendly smile then.

"So Miss Kendall has me working on my singing," she said. "Before this year I didn't know singing was something you could *work* on, but I guess there's work in everything."

"That's so," said Gusta. She knew that well enough: she had worked very hard learning how to make the French horn sing out properly on her behalf; she had practiced and practiced, even though the people upstairs started pounding on the ceiling when she did.

"Wish the folks here thought it was *worth* working on. Trouble is, Mrs. Hoopes doesn't approve one whit, not of singing, not of the Kendalls, just because Miss Kendall's brother runs the mill, so . . ." Josie shrugged. "Guess I just wish it were a real thing, singing. Worth some trouble. You know, like jam."

"What?" said Gusta. She'd never heard anyone compare singing to jam before.

"They give out *ribbons* for jam," said Josie, as if she were explaining two plus two to a baby. "At the county fair. In August. Mrs. Hoopes and Miss Marion have about a hundred ribbons for their jams. Ribbons make things real, I guess."

Gusta blinked. Josie laughed and scalded the dish towel: the dishes were done.

❦ 7 ❧

That First Night Was Hard, Though

Gusta woke up at one point in the cold middle of the night and thought she was on her cot back home. Only the light was wrong, and the shape of the room was wrong, and the feel of the air was wrong—and then she remembered where she was and what had happened, remembered it all at once, which was a bit like slipping into a very cold sea. It was so hard to cry without making any noise.

It's all right to cry for a moment, she told herself. *It's okay to cry for a moment, a few moments, as long as you don't wake Josie up. I'm giving you five minutes for being sad, Gusta Neubronner, and that's all.*

When she had weathered the worst of those minutes, she remembered, of all things, the lost Wish. Maybe it was all the talk of Snow White earlier that had made her remember it: that magic wishing apple. But of course that apple had been poison, pretty as it was.

Gusta made herself think about the old sea captain's chest of Wishes instead. That last, lost Wish, *in a box on a shelf.*

She shifted onto her other side (the cot squeaked).

It was hard to believe in wishes in this not-so-comfortable cot, at this hour, in this strange old farmhouse. Indeed, this house seemed like the last place in the world that would have a Wish hiding somewhere in it. *I'll look anyway*, she said to herself. And that thought changed the feeling of that room somehow — it gave Gusta a little taste of hope.

Then she had another thought that was so sensible it almost made her proud. She thought, *Good thing I don't have that Wish in my pocket now!*

Because the crying part of herself would have used it right up right now, for sure. And Gusta was quite certain the part of you that cries in the middle of the night probably makes the sorts of careless wishes that you regret the next day.

And Gusta was determined, if she found that Wish, to be the very opposite of careless: to make that Wish work very, very hard for its supper.

❦ 8 ❧

Cousin Bess

How they got through that morning circus the next day, Gusta really didn't know. There was oatmeal to cook and dishes to wash and quite a number of mittens to find. Gusta basically just did what Josie told her, and the combination of Josie and Aunt Marion was a wonderful, efficient thing. Somehow the whole bunch of them were all walking along the road by seven, trudging through a new, discouraging layer of snow.

Delphine was too young for school, and Josie went to the high school already, so that meant Gusta would be heading into Jefferson Elementary with a pack of five boys. The thought was a little daunting, but a few seconds later Josie added an important detail.

"And we'll pick up Bess down the road a ways," said Josie. "She's your cousin, Bess. Lives on Elm Street, just closer to the main road than we do. You'll like Bess fine. She's another quiet one, but she's good with the jam."

"Oh!" said Gusta. An actual cousin! Why hadn't her mother mentioned cousins? That made her excited and nervous, and so for a moment she forgot about how excited and nervous she felt about school itself.

On the way down Elm Street to Bess's house, Josie kept up a streak of chatter, punctuated with instructions to the boys, who were spilling forward in an energy-filled clump in front of her.

"I'm a freshman now," said Josie. "I'm in the domestic science course. *Don't you wallop Larry! I just mended that shirt!* It's a fancy new place now, the high school, did your mother say anything about that? The school she and Miss Marion went to, it burned down to the ground a year ago, and they built it right up all new. *Stay off the road! You want some truck to flatten you?* You should see it inside. You know what we have? Glass chalkboards, the color of thick cream! Chalk's navy blue. Ever seen such a thing?"

Gusta had not. All the blackboards she had ever seen had been regular old-fashioned black and the chalk regular old-fashioned white. Anyway, how could a blackboard be made of glass?

"That street's Chestnut Street—we don't go down that street, because there's a bad dog. And here's Bess!" said Josie. "Bess, come see your cousin Augusta, up from New York City!"

Of course the house was too far away to be seen properly, but Gusta had the impression of a small building that leaned a little to the right.

A shadowy little figure came off the porch and sprinted down the path.

"Oh!" it said, but it seemed to be smiling.

"Kiss your cousin, Bess," said Josie. "Don't you be shy. I told her you'd show her where to go in the schoolhouse today. I don't want to be late."

"Hello!" said Bess in a whisper; now that she was closer, Gusta could see that she was definitely shy and definitely smiling. Gusta couldn't help smiling back— forgetting about her teeth for a moment.

"How's your father today, Bess?" said Josie.

The smile vanished from Bess's face, and she seemed to crumple up smaller again. "Same," she said.

"That's your Uncle Charlie by marriage, I guess," said Josie to Gusta. "Bess's father got hurt in the mills. Hand got mauled."

"Oh, no," said Gusta.

"Wasn't his fault," said Bess, almost in a whisper.

"No, I guess it wasn't," said Josie, whose role seemed to be to fill out Bess's words until they were large enough to be a whole story. "It was an awful accident. Something went wrong with a loom. Then he couldn't work for a while, which is hard. Hand's healing up now, Bess, though, isn't it?"

"Yes, but—" said Bess, and then she got stuck again.

"But what?" said Josie. "He'll be back at work soon, and things will be back to peachy. *Clarence, I see what you're up to! Let go of his collar!*"

"But now they won't give him his job back," said Bess. It was the longest sentence yet to come out of her mouth. Her eyes flashed fire as she said it, too. "Because his hand isn't perfect anymore. And the doctor still wants his money. And Papa's awful unhappy. So that's a lot of trouble, says Mama-Liz."

"Bess has a stepmother, too," said Josie.

"Not an evil one, like in the stories," said Bess in a hurry.

"Nope," said Josie. "Not evil at all. Tired out, though, I guess."

A thought snapped into place in Gusta's head.

"If your father got hurt at work, it's the factory that should pay the doctor," she said.

"There's a nice idea," said Josie.

"No," said Gusta. "It's not just an idea. I think it's the actual law. There are laws about that sort of thing."

Josie and Bess were staring at her now. Oh, well. In for a penny, in for a pound.

"That's why there are unions, you know," she added. "The union should help your father."

"What's that?" said Bess.

"Working people banding together, so they get treated right," said Gusta. She realized as she said it that she sounded just like one of Papa's pamphlets. And then she thought she had probably said too much already.

"I've heard talk of such things, but there's none of that union business yet in the Kendall Mills," said Josie. "And here's your school, Gusta!"

They had come out on the main road through town now, and right there on the left was what looked an awful lot like a school—at least, it was a blocky sort of large building, and around it floated the sorts of noises made by crowds of children.

"All right, off with you mob now!" said Josie, because the high school was farther down the road.

Gusta felt a brief burst of panic. It had been less than twenty-four hours since she'd arrived in town, but she had somehow already gotten accustomed to Josie being there to tell her what to do. Of course, she knew how ashamed her father would be of that kind of cowardly thinking, and she tried hard to pull herself together, to be a better, braver person, the sort of person who doesn't need anyone's help and never minds being left on her own. She could be that kind of girl; after all, she had marched into new schools before.

The Jefferson School turned out to be a two-story brick building, as old-fashioned as could be—there wouldn't be glass chalkboards in this place, that seemed certain.

"Good luck, Gusta," said Josie. "Bess and the boys will show you where the office is. Some of them know that better than they should—eh, Clarence?"

One of those all-alike brothers laughed and twisted away from Josie's jabbing elbow.

"I'm in the fourth grade," said Bess, waving a whisper's worth of a good-bye. "I go over this way to Miss Sampson's room."

The secretary in the office was very efficient, and looked at the note sent in by Gusta's grandmother and said, "A Hoopes girl!" and sent her upstairs to Miss

Hatch's 5A class. Miss Hatch put her in a desk on the side in the back, so at least she knew the wall wasn't staring at her from behind. And eventually, surely, the other children would have to turn back around to the front and look at the teacher, not at her. For a moment Gusta felt a pang of nostalgia for the dark classroom back in New York and the sharp voice of Miss Brownstein calling them all to account.

"This is our new classmate, Augusta Hoopes Neubronner," said the teacher. "Yes, she is Mrs. Hoopes's granddaughter, come back to stay a while. She has been living in New York City, where the skyscrapers are. The Empire State Building, one hundred and two stories high. Imagine that! We are glad to have her join us, aren't we, class?"

The class murmured obediently, but mostly they stared.

Gusta looked back in the direction of all those stares, trying to look friendly without smiling too much, so her teeth wouldn't show. That was pretty much second nature by now.

People apparently did not come and go — not so much — here in Springdale, Maine.

For the first hour or so, Gusta kept her head down and thought she was doing pretty well at being the ordinary girl sitting in the back, just doing whatever work the teacher described. There was the usual business in math, of having to listen extra hard to hear the problem, since the board was so far away, but for the most part, Gusta felt she was managing not to stick out, which was her usual goal in a classroom and pretty hard when you're the new girl.

And then disaster.

"Molly!" said the teacher. "Why don't you come up here and explain to our new friend, Augusta, why we have put these dear Scottie dogs on our wall?"

So that was what the speckles on the side of the room were! Now that the teacher had said that, Gusta could kind of make them out. Each dog-shaped splotch had a bunch of paper circles hovering about it; some had more than others.

"Yes, Miss Hatch," said Molly as she walked to the front. She must be one of the good students. The good students are always the ones invited to the front of the class to explain things to newcomers—that was as true in New York City or Boston as it seemed to be here in Maine.

"We are proud to be working toward our Seven-Point Health Certificates!" said Molly, with the enthusiastic singsong of someone reciting a poem for the class. "We hope all of our paper Scottie dogs will soon have all seven of their balloons colored in! When half of us have our Seven-Point Health Certificates, our classroom will get a special certificate, too. Being as healthy as we can is our best way to serve our country. We try to brush our teeth every day and drink every drop of our Sharp's Ridge milk, so that we can grow healthy and strong—"

"Springdale Dairy," said the boy with a mop of dark brown hair, who was sitting next to Gusta. It was almost as if he couldn't help himself. And maybe that Molly had meant to goad him into it, because she was standing with a somewhat triumphant air just now.

"Sharp's Ridge," she said again, prim and determined as can be. Gusta didn't know exactly what was going on here, but she couldn't help feeling her sympathy lay, just at this moment, with the Springdale Dairy boy.

A ripple of laughter was going through the room. The children seemed to have heard this debate before. The teacher tapped the desk with her pointer to settle them down.

"George, we do not interrupt," she said. "Molly was telling us what the Seven Points are for our health certificates. Molly?"

Molly did not seem at all daunted by the question. "Yes, Miss Hatch," she said. "Our Seven Points for the health certificates are (1) Hearing, (2) Vision, (3) Throat, (4) Teeth—"

(*Doc, Grumpy, Happy, Sneezy*—Gusta couldn't help it; any list of seven objects made her think of the *Snow White* movie: all those dwarfs!)

"(5) Teeth," said Molly again.

"You had teeth already, dear," said Miss Hatch.

"Yes, Miss Hatch," said Molly, and then rattled on triumphantly to the end of her list: "(4) Teeth, (5) Posture, (6) Birth Certificate, and (7) Healthy Growth!"

"Thank you, Molly," said Miss Hatch. "You may take your seat now. Children, do you know why we are talking about our health certificates today?"

"Because the new girl doesn't know about them?" suggested a girl, not Molly.

"In fact, no," said Miss Hatch. "The reason we are thinking about our health points today is because today we have a special visitor at the school who will be helping us get another balloon colored in for our Scottie dogs!"

There was a tiny amount of excitement in the class. Gusta, however, was not excited. She was on alert.

There was a knock at the classroom door.

"That will be a monitor calling us now," said Miss Hatch. "Class, please rise and form one quiet line. We are going downstairs now to meet with the oculist. An oculist, class, is a special doctor who will check us to see how our eyes are working."

"VISION!" said the boy sitting next to Gusta. He really did not seem to be very good at not speaking out of turn.

"Quite right, George," said Miss Hatch. "Although we must also remember never to interrupt. Come now!"

⊂⊃ 9 ⊂⊃

Betrayed by a Bunch of Letters

I n New York they had whole classrooms take vision tests, too, at least once every year. It wasn't as much of a problem as you might think, if you were clever about it. In the three years Gusta had spent in New York City, she had learned to hang back a little and listen to what the other kids had to say, and honestly, by this point, Gusta had that old eye chart pretty well down pat.

It will be all right, she said to herself sternly. *Listen up carefully, and then stand tall and look like you know what you're about!*

That was another of her papa's phrases. But then they got to the front hall, just as the previous classroom's worth of children started marching away in its own "quiet line," and Gusta's plan to hang back and listen was destroyed by a single sentence.

"Why don't we let our new friend go first?" said Miss Hatch. "We can give her a head start on her Vision balloon, since she is so far behind on her Seven Points!"

Sometimes even kind grown-ups do absolutely horrible things, more or less by accident or by not thinking through all the possibilities. Miss Hatch's hand on Gusta's shoulder, guiding her forward, felt like doom itself.

"This is Augusta Hoopes, Mr. Bertmann," said the teacher to the man standing there, the one who must be the "oculist." "She won't be on your list, because she is brand-new today. Here, I will write her name down for you."

"Neubronner," said Gusta, as Miss Hatch started writing down a name on the oculist's list. "N-E-U-B . . ."

Miss Hatch struck a line through *Hoopes* and wrote *Neubronner*, and the oculist made a curious, question-mark-size sound.

"Neubronner?" he said. He pronounced it differently than Miss Hatch said it. The "Neu" part sounded like "Noy," and the *r* in the middle was quite a bit like sandpaper. The way Gusta's papa said the name, when he wasn't being extra careful to make it sound "American."

"But that name is familiar," said the eye-examining man.

A pulse of worry went through her, but Gusta was careful not to say anything. She just shifted her weight from foot to foot, feeling the oculist's gaze on her.

And then he took his little light and his magnifying glass and had her open her eyes wide.

"Good, good," he said. His voice was friendly enough. "No evident disease. And now, young lady. Do hold this piece of cardboard over your left eye and read the letters on the chart for me."

She looked around a little wildly, trying to figure out which direction she was supposed to be looking. Going first! That was bad luck. But she had been through the chart-reading exercise so many times back in New York; that should surely help.

Stand tall and look like you know what you're about!

She did exactly that. She pulled herself tall and rattled through the letters that had been imprinted on her brain after the past three years of faking her way through school exams:

"E

F-P

T-O-Z

L-P-E-D

P-E-C-F-D

E-D-F-C-Z-P!"

There was a silence then. Perhaps she had gone too fast? Sounded too glib?

The line of students behind her had frozen in place, as if a fairy godmother had just waved her wand and muttered something powerful.

The oculist cleared his throat.

And Miss Hatch said, in a chillier voice than Gusta had yet heard her use, "Augusta, I'm surprised. Perhaps things are done differently in New York City, but we take our Seven-Point Certificate exams seriously here in Maine. We don't make jokes or interfere with the process. We are grateful to our examiners for participating in the work of the Maine Public Health Association."

"For your information, Augusta Neubronner," said the oculist quietly, so that only Gusta and no one else in that crowded hall could hear, "those letters you just so remarkably repeated—they are from a different chart entirely."

Oh! She hadn't known there were different charts! In New York it had always been the same chart, year after year. And she didn't remember any eye tests in the years before New York.

"Look over this way, young lady," said the oculist, louder now. He was gesturing toward that gray patch on the white wall that must be the dreadfully different chart. "Just tell me please, what is the largest letter you see there?"

"A?" she said, but the game was already up. The students were beginning to whisper — a whole line of whispers running all the way down the hall.

"Is that what you see?" said the oculist.

"What is there to see? I can't see anything," she said finally, and she was disgusted to feel tears of frustration welling up, uninvited, in her eyes. A fuzzy rectangle of gray against the white wall! Really, what magic did everyone else have that made them able to see things like that, letters and everything, from so very far away?

"Ah," said the oculist, and Miss Hatch shook a finger at the murmuring students. "Have you worn eyeglasses before, young lady, if you don't mind me asking?"

"No, no eyeglasses, never," Gusta said. Her father didn't believe in giving in to what he thought of as weaknesses. And they hadn't had any money, of course, for glasses. Glasses were expensive.

Miss Hatch leaned forward.

"I think, Augusta, that you should go see Nurse Renfield now. She can go over the other points we've been discussing in class. Don't be discouraged. Maybe there's some way you can earn a balloon after all!"

It was a most miserable moment. Gusta stumbled back down the hall, following the unlucky girl delegated to take her to the nurse's office, and as she walked past that endless line of students, some muttered those things people say about people who don't see so well: "New girl's blind as a bat! Couldn't hit a barn door with a rock, most likely!" Things like that. Gusta tried to hold her head high, but it was a chore. And it was bitter when she had to overhear that girl Molly say to the girl standing next to her, "How are we ever going to get our hundred percent class certificate now? It's just not fair. No Vision, obviously, and have you seen her teeth? Crooked old vampire teeth! Plus she looks scrawny, too."

It was like walking a gauntlet, parading down that hall. At the end of it was an ordinary school nurse's office, where the nurse tried to be comforting but kept missing the target slightly.

"Are you certain you've never had eyeglasses, dear?" said the nurse. "I don't know how you can possibly have come this far in school with eyes as bad as yours."

"I study hard," said Gusta, because she did have the tiniest little chip on her shoulder. "I've been promoted every year."

"Well," said the nurse, "hop onto this scale now, dear, and we'll see how your growth measures up."

It did not measure up. Gusta's heart sank when the nurse started shaking her head and clucking her tongue a little.

"And your poor teeth!" said the nurse. "I suppose you'll probably need some of those pulled eventually. No, no, don't look like that! No one's going to be pulling any of your teeth today. Oh, dear. Sit right there a moment."

Gusta could see that the nurse meant well. She did not mean to be making Gusta so unhappy that she just wanted to let her head sink down onto her arms and never look up at anyone again, never be asked to read their awful gray blobs of eye charts or have to open her mouth so they could laugh at her teeth.

The nurse had opened a door at the side of her cramped office—a closet, it seemed to be, full of junk in piles, as far as Gusta could tell. She had the vague impression of shoes, but maybe she wasn't seeing that quite right.

"Let's see what we have here," said the nurse, coming back with a battered box.

Inside were glasses, all sorts of old glasses. Some were held together with twine or sticky tape, and all of them were more or less ugly, and a few were made for people even smaller than Gusta and would never fit her in a million years.

"Don't tell the oculist," said the nurse. "He doesn't care for my slipshod half measures. But let's just see if maybe one of these might help you out. I know how expensive glasses can be."

In that box must have been all the glasses lost at Jefferson School over the last ten years. The nurse kept picking out pairs and making hopeful sounds, and then tucking them onto Gusta's face.

None of them came close to being right. Those glasses just took the usual blur and twisted it in various unpleasant ways. Or did nothing much at all.

"Too bad," said the nurse, scribbling something on a piece of paper. "Sometimes I'm lucky. Well, now, don't worry too much—I'm sending a note home with you for your grandmother, asking for her to send in your birth certificate, and explaining that our screening has determined you need a follow-up appointment with the oculist, and probably a prescription for glasses."

Gusta just stared at her. Where was her grandmother supposed to come up with the money for eyeglasses? (And that triggered a twist of guilt in her belly, of course. But she tried the thought out in her head, and she still could not stand the idea of giving up the horn.)

It was easy enough to tell that the school nurse had had dozens of students stare at her in just that way before, while she told them they needed glasses, or expensive dental care, or shoes that fit better, or just Pick Your Impossible Option Here. She looked at Gusta and sighed.

"I know it won't be easy, but I'm going to have a nice talk with the oculist as soon as I can manage, and I hope we may be able to work something out for you. And of course I will talk with your teacher, too, so that things aren't so hard for you in class while we're all still figuring out what to do about the glasses. And meanwhile you just keep eating your vegetables and drinking your milk, Augusta, so we can get you healthy and hearty."

"Springdale Dairy," said Gusta, without even

realizing she was speaking aloud. Then as soon as she did realize, her hand flew to her mouth, she was so embarrassed. But to her surprise, the nurse was laughing.

"Oh, my stars!" she said. "I forgot! You're in Miss Hatch's class, aren't you? Right in the middle of the Dairy Wars!"

Gusta couldn't help staring. What did the nurse mean by that?

"You've got George Thibodeau and little Molly Gowen in that one room of yours, don't you?"

Gusta nodded: she remembered the names George and Molly, yes.

"They are always going on about their dairies," said the nurse. "You know the Thibodeaus run the Springdale Dairy—and the Gowens have Sharp's Ridge Farm. I've seen those children glare at each other like they were on two sides of a battlefield. Most ridiculous thing, isn't it? But your grandmother will feed you well. Plenty of children come through here, starting skinny and wild-eyed as fawns and then plumping up nicely under Mrs. Hoopes's care. So don't worry too much, Augusta. You may not be able to qualify for that Seven-Point Certificate, but I hope we will be able to send you back home, when the time comes, haler and healthier than you are today."

The first place she sent Gusta, however, was back upstairs to Miss Hatch's 5A classroom with another little folded note, and that was not easy.

All the heads in the classroom turned to look at her as she came in, defeated, to take her seat below the reproachful army of balloon-wielding Scottie dogs.

She was never going to have many balloons to offer any of those eager paper dogs, that was clear. In one efficient day, she had already managed to bar herself from three of those seven possible points: Vision, Teeth, and Growth. (What were the other ones again?)

And then things got a notch worse: there was someone sitting in Gusta's desk, and Miss Hatch was already gesturing to another seat, way up in the front.

"I hope you'll be able to see better from up here, Augusta," said Miss Hatch, and everyone in that room watched as Gusta gathered up the things in her desk and walked, fighting to keep her head up the whole time, to the dreadful, exposed front of the room.

❧ 10 ❧

Uncle Charlie in the Gloom

Bess was waiting patiently on the front steps of the school building at the end of that disastrous day. What with a little extra lecture (meant to be encouraging) from her teacher after the bell rang, Gusta was just about the last person out of the doors.

"Thought Miss Hatch might keep you for a while after," said Bess. "Since you're new. So I sent all the boys on ahead. And Josie came by while I was waiting, and she said she'd better scoot home for chores. Are you really blind?"

"No!" said Gusta, somewhat taken aback. "I'm walking along beside you just fine, aren't I?"

"I guess you could be blind and still have feet that work, couldn't you?" said Bess in her matter-of-fact way. "I mean, I've never met anyone who was blind before, that's all. So when they all started saying in class did I know my new cousin is blind, I did wonder."

"They said I need glasses, that's all."

"Oh," said Bess. "Well, that's not as exciting."

Then she thought another moment. "I bet they cost a lot of money, glasses. What's Gramma Hoopes going to say about that?"

"It doesn't matter," said Gusta. She felt a little prickly about the whole thing, to tell the truth. "I've been doing fine without them. They were just fussing about nothing back at that school."

"Mm-hm," said Bess. It was a sympathetic sort of sound, and then they squished along together through the already ugly-looking snow, their footsteps slippery on the icy patches.

"Well, here's my house now," said Bess, giving Gusta's hand a good-bye squeeze. "See you tomorrow morning, I guess!"

And she darted up the porch steps and through the slightly squeaky screen door.

For a moment, Gusta stood there, just savoring the feeling of having someone in the world who was already glad today about seeing her tomorrow.

It was good to have a cousin. It made this long, slushy stretch of Elm Street a better place, now that she knew Bess was living here. And just as Gusta turned to face the rest of the slog home, the porch door squeaked open again.

"Gusta!" Bess was pelting back down the walkway toward her. "Come in for a moment, can you? Mama-Liz says you should come on in."

The blurry shadow standing by the door turned out to be a woman, with dark hair pulled back sharply from her tired-looking face.

"You're Gladys's girl?" said the woman. "Up from New York, says Bess?"

"Yes, ma'am," said Gusta. (She wasn't quite sure what you called the woman married to the man who had been married to your mother's deceased sister.) "I'm Augusta."

"Seems like it might do Charlie some good, seeing you," said the woman. "He always spoke highly of your mother. Quite the scholar, wasn't she? And now she's living in the big city. Going places. Might get him out of his mood, seeing you. He hasn't been the same since his accident. He's been right down in the dumps. Well, come on in, then."

She held the door open for Gusta, and Bess leaned close so Gusta could see her encouraging smile. "He'll be *glad* you're here, Gusta. You'll see."

Tha-bump! That was Gusta's heart saying hadn't she met enough new people for one single day? But of course an uncle was something different. And in particular, an uncle who had been hurt in the mills. She obediently picked her way up the steps to the door.

"Right in here," said Bess.

Inside that door was a room full of gloom and clutter. The shadows were blue. There were blurry objects all higgledy-piggledy on the shelves, and when Gusta put a hand on the couch for a moment, to steady herself in that sad space, she could feel how all the softness of the fabric had been worn away long ago.

The darker shadow in a great lump of a chair ahead moved its head: it wasn't a shadow at all, but a person.

"Look who's here, Papa," said Bess. "It's my cousin Augusta, up from New York."

The shadowy person nodded, maybe—it was hard to tell.

"Well, hello, then, Augusta. Come over here so I can see you better," said the shadowy one.

The atmosphere in the room had that peculiar

smell rooms have when someone has been sick in bed for a while in the winter, like the room itself was crying out for all the windows in the world to be flung open, and for spring finally, finally to come.

But spring felt very far away in that place. Gusta made herself step closer, and then a little closer still.

"Well, you look like her, that's for sure," said Uncle Charlie. "Spitting image of Gladdy when she was just a girl. You a force of nature, girl? She sure was."

Was it a good thing or a bad thing, to be a force of nature? Up close, Gusta could see the extra shadows pooling on Uncle Charlie's face. He must not be eating right, she thought. He would certainly not earn many health certificate balloons for his Scottie dog, if he were in the fifth grade at the Jefferson School. One of his arms was in some kind of wrapping, too, she noticed. Bandaged up.

He must have noticed her noticing, because he raised that hand a little in the air and turned it this way and that.

"See that? They shoulda shut down the line so I could fix that loom properly, but guess what—they didn't," he said. "Now it's healed up all wrong, and I'm useless. Can't do anything with it because the skin's knotted up so tight. Doctor says it's scar tissue. Maybe some fancy surgeon could fix it for a pile of money. But a pile of money is what we just haven't got, isn't it? Anyhow, done is done."

That made Gusta indignant. *Done is done!*

What would her papa surely say, about what they had done to Uncle Charlie? Her father wasn't here to say it, so Gusta figured it was up to her.

"You know, Uncle Charlie," she said, "it's not right for them to leave you this way. It's the *mill* that's supposed to pay to fix your hand."

Uncle Charlie barked out a bitter little laugh into that gloomy air.

"Sweet of you, Gladdy's little Augusta, but it's not the mill that got its arm hurt—it's just me," said Uncle Charlie. "And the mill doesn't care a nickel's worth about me. They don't pay anything for anybody except for themselves."

"Some places there are laws, though," said Gusta. "That would make them pay. And that's what the union does, too—fights for the rights of the Working Man."

Uncle Charlie laughed, but the laugh faded into a cough. Even Uncle Charlie's cough was ragged and worn out, like the furniture in this shadowed, gloomy room.

"You got a lot of big, shiny ideas in your head

there, Augusta," he said, "like your mother used to. I remember the way she went on and on about all sort of things. Anyway, no union yet in the Kendall Mills. And that's that. How's your mother been getting on, anyway, down there in the big city?"

"Fine, thank you," said Gusta. Then she pressed her lips together for a moment so that her doubts wouldn't show. If a mother were really "getting on fine," her daughter probably wouldn't have been shipped away to live with the folks in Maine.

"We'll let Augusta get home now, won't we?" said Mama-Liz, and she ushered Gusta back out the porch door.

Gusta was so glad to get outside again that she took a few deep, desperate gulps of cold air, just to get the sickbed smell out of her nostrils.

But as Mama-Liz held the door open with one hand, she used the other to reach out and grab onto Gusta's wrist — not in a mean way, but like someone grasping at straws.

"You'll put in a word with your mother, won't you?" she said. "Now that she's in the big city and all. You'll let your mother know, how he is? You heard your uncle. We don't have any union in the mills."

It wasn't until half the way to Gramma Hoopes's

house that Gusta realized Mama-Liz was hoping Gusta's own mama might have *money*. That made her heart sink, right there.

That evening she gathered her curiosity and her courage together, and she said to Gramma Hoopes that she didn't think it was fair, all that had happened to Uncle Charlie's poor hand.

"Fair?" said Gramma Hoopes. "What's fair got to do with anything, child, I'd like to know?"

"He said the doctors looked at his hand and thought it could be fixed."

"Mm, well," said Gramma Hoopes. "Guess it'd be a hundred dollars if it's a nickel, to get a surgeon to fix up that hand. Too bad money doesn't grow in cornfields or on berry bushes, isn't it? But no use crying over spilt milk."

And that's injustice, thought Gusta. *A person's actual life should not be treated like spilt milk.*

Sometimes even a small and unimportant person can find herself facing injustice—Gusta knew that was so. Then you have to do what you have to do, or the world just will never get any better. *(Right, Papa?)*

Aloud, she said, as politely as she could possibly

manage, "Gramma Hoopes, may I please have paper and a stamp? I was hoping to write a letter."

She did not even have to tell a lie. Gramma Hoopes assumed Gusta must be wanting to write to her mother and handed over a piece of notepaper, an envelope, and a stamp, just like that.

Gusta wrote out the letter very carefully. She described what she knew about the injustice done to Mr. Charles Goodman, currently residing on Elm Street in Springdale. And she said she thought the Kendall Mills were about over-ready by now for a union, so could New York please send someone up to help with some organizing? She hoped the union would make things right for Charles Goodman and for all the other folks working at the Kendall Mills.

She signed it with a scrawled version of her name that didn't give anything away, like for instance what her name actually *was*.

And she addressed that letter to Mr. Elmer Smith of the big textile union, all the way down in New York City. She was able to put the correct street address on the envelope, because she happened to have met Elmer Smith personally, not that he would remember her. She had been to that union building many a time with her parents. She knew what street it was on, and even what number the building had on that street.

And she sealed up that letter and went to the post office, the next day, to see it sent along to New York City.

People are not spilt milk, she said to herself as she handed the letter over. People deserve justice.

"Your papa's from away, now, isn't he?" said the woman in the post office, looking right over the tops of her glasses at Gusta, who jumped in surprise and nodded.

"We'll see that gets there safely, then, dear," said the woman, patting the letter kindly as she whisked it into the basket behind her. It took about three full seconds before Gusta understood that the post office woman assumed Mr. Elmer Smith must be Gusta's own absent papa.

Which just went to show two things:

1. Everyone knew everything about everybody in a town as small as Springdale, Maine.

2. Nobody knew anything much about anybody, all the same.

⊗ 11 ⊙

Boxes on Shelves

Not every injustice and sorrow in this world can be tackled by posting a letter, however. There was, for instance, the case of her missing papa. He believed in taking action to make the world better, but what action could Gusta possibly take that could bring her papa home?

It made her think about that Wish again, even though she knew her papa would not possibly approve.

But still: What if there *were* such a thing as a real Wish? What if there just happened to be one real Wish left in all the world, and it was the one her sea-captain great-grandfather had misplaced in this very house? Wouldn't it be logical—whatever her papa might say—for Gusta to keep her eyes peeled for it, just in case?

Gusta made a plan: she would try her best to scout out all the various rooms of the house, starting with the places she could look through without seeming terribly sneaky. It didn't take long to determine there was no "box on a shelf" in the bedroom she shared with Josie, nor in the parlor downstairs, nor even in the open parts of the kitchen, which she was coming to know pretty well, thanks to all the dishes she and Josie washed and dried. There was nothing that looked like a Wish anywhere.

There *was* one space that had shelves and boxes in abundant quantity, though, and that was the pantry next to the kitchen. So one quiet evening, when by some rare chance everyone seemed busy elsewhere, Gusta took a great deep breath and tackled the pantry shelves.

She tried to be practical about it: the big flour bins couldn't have kept a Wish secret for decades, not at the rate the Hoopes Home went through flour. In fact, none of the boxes on the lower shelves seemed very likely, and of course pickle relish jars weren't boxes at all. But up there on the high shelves, closer to the ceiling, was a line of smaller, older boxes that must have supplies used much more rarely. Gusta quietly hauled in the step stool from the kitchen. If she stretched her arm up very high and was careful not to wobble or fall, she found she could snag a box by its corner and tease it forward until it was half off the shelf and graspable —

"Augusta!"

The box hit the pantry floor and split right open, spilling entirely Wish-less tea leaves every which where.

Gramma Hoopes wasn't all that tall, especially compared to Gusta on a step stool, but Gusta had never felt as small as she did now, shakily descending from her perch and trying not to step on the spilled tea.

"What in *heaven's* name, Augusta?" Speaking of tea, Gramma Hoopes looked pretty much exactly like a tea kettle boiling over, just at that moment. "What are you even *thinking* of? I thought it must be one of the boys again. But *you* —"

Then she stopped short, as if she had just had an idea. "Not getting enough dinner, even now, are you?" she said. Her eyes were as pointy as needles.

"So sorry, Gramma Hoopes," said Gusta under her breath, looking away so she wouldn't have to face those needles. "I didn't mean to make a mess."

She knelt down and tried to brush the loose tea into a tidier heap.

"Oh, leave that now," said Gramma Hoopes. "You'll sweep up properly when I'm done talking to you. Shouldn't have assumed you'd be different than the others, should I? But I guess I figured Gladdy must be doing all right for herself, down in that big city."

It was the shift in her gramma's voice that caught Gusta off guard: it had suddenly gone from angry to something else, almost regretful.

Even though she knew her father would be ashamed of her for such cowardice, Gusta couldn't quite find it in herself to lift her eyes from the floor.

"Well," said Gramma Hoopes. "Seems I forgot about what cities can be like. Gladdy trying to make do down there without a garden, nothing to can, and surely not an extra dime for beefsteak. What did she feed you on, anyway?"

Gusta looked up. "We had food," she said. She didn't mean to be contradictory, but she really was a little confused. Of course, there hadn't been a *lot* of food, but that just meant stretching the soup another day. And late that autumn her school had been one of the ones to get those new penny bottles of milk in, and her mother had always been able to find a penny somewhere. She wasn't as badly off as some kids in her class, that was for sure.

"They're all hungry when they come here, Lord knows," said her grandmother. She seemed almost to be talking to herself now, more than to Gusta. "Those Hansen boys! It was like having a pack of rats in the house, the whole first year, the way they'd sneak things out of the pantry, no matter how many potatoes you'd fry up for dinner. Well, now they've settled down some, since they see I won't let them starve. Why did I think things would be different with Gladdy's girl, just because she's Gladdy's, and Gladdy was mine? *Augusta!*"

That was directed right at Gusta, so she had to look up.

"Yes, ma'am," she said. "I'm sorry."

"Pshaw," said her grandmother. "Important thing is, you don't need to sneak food here. We're going to build you up and put some flesh on your bones. If your mother weren't so prideful, she would have sent you up here earlier, I guess. But she's a Hoopes, and so she's stubborn, and so am I, and so are you, and so that's a matched set of us right there."

She laughed right out loud then, so it seemed like Gusta wasn't in terrible trouble after all, thank goodness.

"I'm really sorry about spilling the tea leaves," said Gusta.

"Sweep it up now, and I'll boil you an egg instead," said her grandmother. "But no more sneaking food. I don't like sneaking around. Oh, don't look like that; I'm not going to wallop you. I believe in punishments that fit the crime."

Gusta blinked. Of course, Gramma Hoopes didn't even really know what the crime was, did she? Gramma Hoopes thought Gusta was pilfering food when really she was scouting around for lost Wishes. But that wasn't something Gusta could very well explain.

"Here's what you'll do now, Gusta," said Gramma Hoopes. "It happens to be egg-cleaning day in this house. So you'll go down cellar with that boy Laurence and help him clean those eggs. He's got thirty dozen to pack up by tomorrow, and that brother Clarence of his who's supposed to do it with him is a slippery rascal — always manages to disappear instead of helping. Thinks I don't notice, but I most certainly do."

Gramma Hoopes turned and hollered out into the hall: *"Laurence! You're wanted in here!"*

And that was how Gusta ended up getting her introduction to the Kingdom of the Hens.

⁌ 12 ⁍

The Kingdom of the Hens

S hould be Queendom, I guess, really," confided Larry, while he held open the door so Gusta could slip into the warm dusk of the henhouse. "But around here it's always been called the Kingdom of the Hens. Anyway, pretty fancy for a henhouse, see? Look how clever the nest boxes are."

While the chickens murmured and rustled in that space of theirs, moving around and commenting quietly to each other, Larry showed her the nest boxes: the opening in front the chicken could use, and the sneaky way you could swing up a little door from the other side of the rows of nest boxes to grab the eggs that were in there.

Boxes! Gusta stopped in her tracks.

"Hey, Larry, have you ever found, well, something that wasn't an egg in one of these nest boxes?"

Larry thought it over.

"Like a mouse?" he said. "That what you mean?"

"No, no, not mice," said Gusta. "More like a funny old coin."

Larry threw back his head and laughed. He had a very nice, friendly sort of laugh.

"Money under one of our hens? I wish!" he said. "That would be easier than cleaning and packing the eggs up to sell them, wouldn't it? Just skip right to finding money! Gosh! Though I guess money doesn't fry or scramble as well as a real egg."

Then he led Gusta down the cellar steps at the rear of the big farmhouse. It turned out that the cellar had quite a few different corners and sections. One whole part was for the storing of everything canned. Gusta couldn't see much of it but had the dim impressions of different colors glinting on shelves, like a treasury for jar-size jewels. (Jars but no boxes, Gusta noted.)

The part of the cellar where Larry was taking her now was not exactly a treasure cave, however. It was a protected, cool-temperatured place to store up eggs until you had enough to fill one of the "30 dozen" cases and take them into town to sell.

The smell down there was not good.

The thing was, every one of those eggs had to be cleaned, and then tucked into a cardboard tray, and the tray in turn stacked in the big cardboard carton.

"Here you go," said Larry. He tossed her a scrap of fine sandpaper. "Now we get the poop off these eggs, fast as we can."

Once the cleaning was under way, the smell was not just not good. It was terrible. You picked an egg up out of a pail, and you polished it with that piece of sandpaper, getting the dirt off. And then the egg went into its carton. And you did that over and over and over, being careful not to clutch too hard, because of course then you had raw egg on your hand as well as chicken poop.

Laurence didn't seem as bothered by it all, but oh, Gusta could see why everyone else in the house was willing to do just about anything not to end up down here on egg-cleaning duty. Larry moved quickly through his eggs, chattering as he went. He had been a lot quieter upstairs with all the other kids. Maybe he was a little like his chickens and needed an enclosed space to feel safe enough to cackle a little.

"Hey, Gusta, do you remember your mother?" he asked Gusta out of the blue.

"Of course, I do," said Gusta. "She put me on the bus to come up here."

"Oh, right. That's right. Well, you know, I remember mine, too. That's what's different between me and Tommy, even though he's just a year and a bit younger. He doesn't remember, but sometimes he'll say he remembers, and then he gets something wrong, so you know he's just making things up. But I really do."

"What's your mother like?" asked Gusta.

"She liked the color blue," said Larry. Gusta noticed the past tense; a tiny little shiver went through her. "Sometimes she said, 'Laurence, your hair is not combed one whit.' And she had very nice, thin fingers, too. I remember all of that very well, from back before she even got sick."

"Oh," said Gusta. "I'm sorry. She got sick?"

"She was *overwhelmed*, I guess," said Larry. "I heard someone say that to our daddy. I guess that's pretty bad. She died from overwhelming, when Tommy was still little. And our father couldn't handle the lot of us, so we ended up here. It's all right here. I like the chickens, and Tommy likes the cows. And someday our daddy will come back to get us, I think, once we're all trained up to be more useful. We're getting more useful as we go. I'm already pretty useful with the chickens, I guess, and Mr. Bill says Donald is almost as helpful as Jay, but I think that's mostly to poke at Jay."

"Oh," said Gusta again. Mr. Bill and Jay were her uncles. It was all a lot to absorb. And she was beginning to feel like chicken poop dust was coating the inside of her nose, so that she hardly knew anymore whether it was better to breathe in or to breathe out.

"Well, that's that, just about," said Larry. "Thirty dozen! And you only broke two; that's pretty good. Clarence always makes sure to break at least half a dozen, so he won't have to help with the cleaning the next time. That's not right, is it? When egg money is so good?"

"Not right at all," said Gusta, feeling the words beginning to trip up and gag in her throat a little. "Not at all."

But she also thought, very secretly, as she scrambled up the cellar stairs to fresh air again, that even though she disapproved of shirkers and wasters and really of anyone who went to lengths to avoid the work they should be doing, she did, very privately, and in this particular case, understand why Clarence would rather do almost anything than clean those end-less stinky eggs.

ℭℜ 13 ℘

As Real As Jam

So, really now, what's in there?" said Bess. It was a Saturday, and Bess was poking at the funny, curving sides of the old horn case, which was an indescribable hue after all its many decades of existence, a leathery yellow-green-gray. It would have been a hideous color if you saw it on anything else, but for the horn case it was perfect—the old, sturdy, worn color of secrets.

According to Josie, Bess might spend more time at her grandmother's than at her own house, if you added up all the hours. But that was fine, according to Josie, because Bess was a help with anything that needed another hand.

"She's a quiet little thing, but a good worker," Josie liked to say. She had respect for good workers.

At this particular moment, however, all three girls weren't working at all, because Aunt Marion had said the rest of supper was under control, and they could skedaddle. They had skedaddled upstairs, and now Bess and Josie and Gusta were perched on Gusta's cot and Josie's bed, talking.

"That's my French horn," said Gusta, and she opened up the case to show them. It was safe to do this because she had moved all the underwear and socks into a tidy box under her cot. Only the beautiful horn was in that case now; her chest expanded with pride as it always did when she looked at it. She took some quick peeks over at Bess and Josie as she opened it to see whether they were appreciating that amazing instrument properly.

"Ohhhh!" said Bess. It was an entirely satisfying reaction. "It looks like—like a car engine almost!"

Gusta blinked in surprise.

"Car engine!" she said.

"I mean, a beautiful car engine." Bess was whispering and blushing at the same time. It made Gusta's heart soften right up all over again, to see how much Bess didn't want to be saying the wrong thing, or any unkind thing. "And not just only an engine, you know, but like it's combined with one of those big seashells. The kind that's all twisty and turny."

"Oh, for the sake of oranges, Bess!" said Josie. "Forget the seashell engine stuff, Gusta. Just play us something. I assume it makes sounds, your—what did you call it again?"

"French horn," said Bess. "Right, Gusta? Why is it French?"

"It's not actually French. That's just its name," she said. "But the people who made this one didn't call it a French horn—they called it *Waldhorn*. That might be a better name. It means 'forest horn.' I guess they used to play them in the woods, back in the old days."

All the while Bess was smiling, and Josie was looking pretty interested, too. Bess stretched out a finger to the bell of the horn, just to feel the cold brassiness of it, and whispered while she did so, "Play a song?"

"You better!" laughed Josie.

Gusta wanted them both to understand how wonderful her horn was. She wanted that so much that her hands were on the verge of actually shaking. But she tried hard to settle down.

She took the horn out, fitted the mouthpiece into

the lead pipe, and tucked the little finger of her left hand into the hooked metal tab there, just like a pro. Then she settled her right hand, bent just slightly, into the bell.

It did look something like a machine, a beautiful machine, but in fact to make a French horn sing, you had to work a bit of muscle magic. There were only three metal levers to push on Gusta's horn, which was probably older than the century and had traveled so far in its life, all the way from Germany to New York (and all up and down the mill towns of New England) and now to Springdale, Maine. Push a lever, and the air went through a different set of winding tubes — but there were all sorts of different notes that each of those pathways could produce, and it was up to you, up to the tension in your lips, to determine which of those notes would emerge.

You had to have a picture in your mind of the note you were aiming for. Your mind had to be singing out that note, for your mouth and lips to know what shapes to take to make it. It was a kind of paradox, her father liked to say: to find a true note, you already had to have found it.

Gusta licked her lips, murmured the "mmmmpit" that got her mouth into shape, and then blew air into the mouthpiece, and the horn sang out a sad, enormous note. She let that note blossom into a hunting call, a call that was way too large for this narrow room.

Bess and Josie applauded.

"Do it again!"

So Gusta did it again. She turned the hunting call into an old German folk song her father had taught her years ago, when she was still pretty little. It felt good to be finding the proper notes, to be shaping the air of the world into music, which is really what you do when you play the horn. Then Gusta started playing the glorious scraps of things it had amused her father to teach her—bits and pieces of what he said was famous music, nothing you'd expect a scrawny kid to be able to play, but only a few measures of anything in particular—and the room began to resonate with the sound, as if it were itself an enormous instrument, a square-cornered bell. Not just the room, but Gusta herself, who was for that wonderful long moment not awkward or out of place or scrawny or extraneous or foolish, but as large and sonorous and deep as the music itself, a glorious brass-voiced version of Gusta.

And then the door flew open, and there on the other side of it, looking highly annoyed, was Gusta's grandmother, wiping her hands on her apron, and behind Gramma Hoopes, a crowd of blurry faces, all curious.

"What in heaven's name?" said her grandmother. "What is this racket? Downstairs these boys keep making more noise than a flock of crows, and now there's going to be foghorns in my bedrooms?"

"It's just my horn," said Gusta, holding it out.

"No," said her grandmother, with a sharp-edged shake of the head. "*That* is no sound for the inside of a house. You'll wake up Delphine and frighten the cows. Or wake up the cows and frighten Delphine, and I don't know which is worse."

The cows were all the way across the road in the barn that belonged to Uncle Bill and Aunt Verla, so this all seemed a very unfair line of argument.

"Not in this house," said her grandmother firmly, and she turned around and went back downstairs, while Gusta and Bess and Josie sat very still, each of them for that first moment simply trying not to giggle.

"We can take it outdoors when it gets a bit warmer around here," said Bess. "Out into the woods on Holly Hill, since you said it's a forest horn."

"Golly, it's like my singing, isn't it?" said Josie.

"Mrs. Hoopes just doesn't see the point of it, music. Not horns, not singing. Too bad it's not jam—then they'd appreciate it. Hey!"

The other two looked at her.

"It's an idea I just had. Just now, this very minute! Singing and jam!"

"What?" said Bess and Gusta together.

"Miss Marion's jams take the blue ribbon at the fair, don't they?"

Bess nodded. "Sure they do!"

"And that makes that jam really truly worth something, doesn't it? Even for Mrs. Hoopes! Well, listen: we can do that, too! I flat out forgot about the Blue-Ribbon Band! That's it, girls: we need to start a band."

"What?" said Bess and Gusta again.

"We need to enter the county fair contest for Blue-Ribbon Band this summer," said Josie, as if explaining something very simple to a child about the age of Delphine.

"Oh!" said Bess. "But, Josie, that always goes to the Kendall Mills men. You should see them, Gusta—uniforms and big drums and everything. Now that's a *band*. That's got nothing to do with us."

"Think, Bess! Why can't we be a band, too? Not

the same as the Kendall Mills Band, sure. Not as fancy. Not as tall. But our own kind of band. And I'll sing, and Gusta will play her twisty horn, and you'll do . . . something band-ish, and we'll be so good they'll just plain have to give us a ribbon. Don't you see? A ribbon doesn't have to be blue to be a genuine, real ribbon. Any color ribbon will make people sit up and take notice. But think: everybody *assumes* the Blue-Ribbon Band is always the one from the mills. So who even enters against them? Almost nobody!"

"Ohh!" said Bess, as if she were understanding Josie's argument all at once. Gusta was still a few feet behind, scrambling to catch up: something about a band, and the Kendalls again, and a fair.

"And if they give us a ribbon, a red ribbon, say, then even Mrs. Hoopes will have to admit singing is real. *As real as jam.*"

The girls sat in silence for a moment.

"Golly," said Bess. "That's so clever, Josie. Except I still don't know what I could possibly do in a band."

Josie flicked her hand through the air, a gesture that meant finding a role for Bess in their band would be easy as pie.

"You're saying we'll enter a contest against grown men with uniforms and everything? So we can win a second-place red ribbon?" said Gusta. She was finally beginning to catch up.

"Exactly," said Josie. "I mean, we'll take the blue ribbon, if they hand it to us—don't get me wrong. But, hey! Red'll do."

ᝡ 14 ᝠ

Aviation

A s you know, children," said Miss Hatch one morning, "the new airport is nearing completion, down in South Springdale. This is an important milestone for the economy of southern Maine, and in these times of trouble . . ." and so on.

Miss Hatch was a very principled and well-meaning teacher, but sometimes she became overly enthusiastic about certain topics, like, apparently, the construction of new airports. Now that Gusta was sitting right up front, she could do nothing to amuse herself at moments like this but stare in the direction of her teacher's voice and tell herself stories secretly, inside, trusting that her face looked like the face of a girl who was paying very careful, close attention to everything her teacher had to say.

And then she heard a few magical words, *twenty dollars* and *contest*, and she started paying close attention for real. Twenty whole dollars! That was real money—one-fifth of that operation Uncle Charlie needed—and unlike lost Wishes, these twenty dollars got extra possibility points from being mentioned by a teacher in class.

What Miss Hatch had just said was, "The Springdale Aviation Committee and the *Springdale Tribune* are sponsoring a contest for the best patriotic essay on the theme of 'A Vision of America from On High.' And, children, the winner will win twenty dollars and see his or her essay printed in the newspaper!"

There was a lively rustle of interest in that classroom. From the box of old glasses and rows of old shoes in the nurse's office, from everything Bess had said about her father, off work and struggling, Gusta knew perfectly well she wasn't the only person in town who really needed some extra money.

"What an honor it would be if the writer of the winning essay came from our classroom!" said Miss Hatch, while the students all imagined what they would do with twenty dollars. "I have decided, class, that we will all write essays this spring on this subject. The best will be presented by their authors as recitations at an all-school assembly in spring, and the very best sent on to the contest. Children, we all must try our hardest to write a fine essay! What a wonderful opportunity to improve our writing!"

A hand had zoomed into the air somewhere to Gusta's right.

"Yes, Molly?" said Miss Hatch.

"The theme of vision works so well with our Seven-Point Health Certificates, too, doesn't it, Miss Hatch? The patriotic duty of having good health and good vision? Isn't that right?"

Oh, heavens. The worst thing about that Molly Gowen, Gusta thought fiercely, was simply . . . *everything*. And then in particular, on top of *everything*, the way she was so earnest about it all. It was like she coated all her meanness with a hard-sugar layer of wholehearted sincerity. *The patriotic duty of having good vision!* Who was that aimed at, if not at her, Gusta? But Molly wasn't finished, of course.

"And, Miss Hatch! Good vision is all about nutrition, keeping our eyes healthy, right? Every morning and every evening, a glass of healthy, nutritious—"

Just as the knot forming in Gusta's stomach was

about to pull itself as tight as a noose, she was rescued by the rumble of a voice from the far back of the room: "SPRINGDALE DAIRY!"

Even though they all knew it was terrible—awful—unforgivable—to interrupt, the sound of most of the class trying to swallow back outright laughter all at once filled the room, as if the air had changed to something lighter and brighter.

"—Sharp's Ridge milk!" finished Molly nevertheless, shooting the sharpest possible arrows from her eyes to the back row of the room.

"George Thibodeau!" said Miss Hatch, and from the complicated layers of irritation and affection in her voice, Gusta somehow knew that Miss Hatch was truly fond of—and at the same time truly aggravated by—the representatives of both sides in the Dairy Wars. "I'm sure you don't mean to be so thoughtlessly rude to your classmate, but this is really too much."

And off he went to the principal's office, poor George Thibodeau, but at least they weren't talking about vision anymore.

"Molly," said Miss Hatch, once George had left the room. "I'm glad you are enthusiastic about this project, and I'm sure we will each one of us be able to come up with our own interesting approach to this theme. Now come see me up front while the rest of the class works on the morning math problems."

Since Gusta now sat as close to the teacher's desk as anyone in that room could sit, she had the advantage or disadvantage of having to overhear a lot of conversations between Miss Hatch and her fellow pupils. She couldn't really help it. Her ears worked fine, and the thing about ears is that you can't turn them tactfully in a different direction.

What she heard now was Miss Hatch saying very kindly, "Molly, dear, I'm sure you will write an excellent theme! But do remember that your contributions to our classroom discussion do not always have to be advertisements."

Oh, but it would take more than a mild hint like that to shut down Molly Gowen. Molly paused only for a millisecond—Gusta's pencil hovered above the long-division problem, waiting in some suspense—and then Molly said, "Miss Hatch, advertising is patriotic—they just said so in the newspaper. My father read it aloud to us: 'Especially now when the world is so full of'—What did they say? 'Misery,' I think—'Especially now when the world is so full of *misery*, it's good to get the pleasant news that comes in the ads!' They said that *in the paper*, Miss Hatch!"

"How interesting, I'm sure," said Miss Hatch patiently. "Nevertheless, Molly, I'm certain there's a difference between what's appropriate in a newspaper and what belongs in our classroom discussions. But quick now, back you go to your desk: I don't want to keep you from your mathematics."

That very afternoon, Molly and a couple of the other girls stood up to say that they were going to be starting a Real Americans Club, sponsored by the Women's Patriotic Society of Springdale, and that they would be happy for anyone who was or wanted to be a Real American to join. They were intending to undertake fun and educational activities, like preparing a theatrical entertainment on the history of the flag.

"And in a world at war, we can't be too careful about the people around us. Why, there are more than one thousand four hundred aliens hiding in Springdale right now! They did a count, and that's what they found. So my father says it pays to be cautious. We should be proud to be Real Americans, and we should give our business to Real Americans, and maybe ask some questions about people running businesses that sound American but when you think about it are run by people with names like Thibodeau, and what kind of name is that—"

"Thank you, Molly," said Miss Hatch hastily. "Let's not wander off the rails here: Thibodeau is a fine old French-Canadian name. And no one has said anything about aliens *hiding*. Noncitizens have been registered, that is all. That's really the opposite of *hiding*."

"Plus, I'm American!" said George Thibodeau from the back of the room. "And my dad's American. Thibodeau is an American name now."

"Yes, it is," said Miss Hatch. "It certainly is. In our class we are proud to have American names that come from different places in the world. But raise your hand when you want to comment, *please*, George."

Miss Hatch seemed quite put-upon by the Dairy Wars today. She sighed and started over again.

"If there's going to be a point in having a Real Americans Club, children, it has got to be to help all of us, wherever we may come from, become better citizens of this country, to become better Americans, no matter who we are or what our names are. I'm glad that Molly and Sally and Jane are inviting everyone in the class to be part of their club, because we *know* that everyone here—no matter where he or she was born or who his or her parents may be — aspires with all his or her heart to be a Real American."

Gusta's own heart fluttered a little during the second half of Miss Hatch's second sentence. What did it really mean, to be "real"?

There was so much Miss Hatch could not know about her students — so much she didn't know even about Augusta Hoopes Neubronner, sitting right there in the front row and carrying all those secrets buried in her heart. Did Miss Hatch guess? Did she know what she was saying?

Because it was another one of the Seven-Point Certificate items looming over Gusta now. The school nurse had called her into her office two days ago to ask again about Gusta's birth certificate.

"Your parents must have it," said the nurse. "I can't understand why they wouldn't send you up with it, since they knew full well you would be enrolling in school."

"Everything was in a hurry," Gusta had said. "I'm sure my mother didn't even think of it, since I was just coming to stay with family."

"We will write to her and ask," said the nurse, so the problem was delayed.

But here's the thing: there was no birth certificate.

Here's the other thing: if there had been, it would have spilled one of Gusta's secrets.

Her parents had traveled up and down New England before they settled in New York City, where the labor union movement was so vigorous and strong.

When Gusta was born, they were living in Calais, Maine, which is so far north it's on the border with Canada. Her mother had wanted to give birth at home, which was how it was done in the corner of Maine where she had been raised, but Gusta's father thought his new son, the future "young August," who might even hope to live long enough to see the twenty-*first* century, should be born in a hospital, because that was clearly the modern and sensible thing to do. So when the time came, they went across the river, because that's where the closest hospital was, and everything went as well as they could have hoped (except of course that "August" turned out disappointingly to be "Augusta")—only *that* meant that Gusta had been born in Saint Stephen, technically, and Saint Stephen wasn't in the United States at all. It was in Canada.

Nobody had seemed to care at the time. People traveled back and forth across that river every day. But

Gusta's father had worried about it enough that he didn't want any pieces of official paper saying Canada was where Augusta had been born.

Gusta's mother joked that Gusta would never become the president of the United States, that's all. Apparently presidents had to be born on this side of the river. But who ever heard of a girl becoming president, anyway?

That was why Gusta's stomach was tying itself up in knots now, the second time in a single school day. And the second time caused by something said by that Molly Gowen!

Was Gusta a Real American?

Gusta wasn't even sure she knew, and Molly certainly seemed to have her doubts.

During afternoon recess, for instance, Molly Gowen made a point of walking by Gusta a few times, staring at her from so close by that Gusta could see the wild, worried sparks in her eyes.

"Neubronner," said Molly, as if something troubling had just occurred to her. "You, *Augusta Neubronner*. What kind of a name is that?"

ᥭ 15 ᥫ

The Need for a Horn

So it wasn't the very best of days, but after school Josie was waiting out front, bubbling over with news.

"Gusta!" she said. "They want your horn over at the high school—how about that?"

Gusta must have looked as surprised as she felt, because Josie laughed.

"Listen, silly. No need to look all worried. I was telling Miss Kendall about your horn—"

"You were?" said Gusta.

"Well, yes," said Josie. "It just happened to come up. We were talking before the chorus rehearsal. Anyway, I said Mrs. Hoopes's own granddaughter just came to our door with a great big old horn in a case, and Miss Kendall's eyes lit up—you should have seen them! She said what kind of horn? And I said I didn't remember exactly what it was called, but the twisty kind, sort of seashell-looking, not skinny like a trumpet. And she said, 'Oh! A French horn! That's just what I've been looking for!' And then she said, 'Do you think there's any chance Mrs. Hoopes's granddaughter would be interested in selling her instrument? A horn like that, if it's in good shape, might be worth a whole lot of money.' And I said—"

"But why does the chorus want a horn?" said Gusta. She had the very beginning of a sick sort of feeling growing in her, as if a seed of ice had planted itself in her belly and was beginning to grow. It was the words *whole lot of money* that had done that to her. They surely did need money, didn't they, with Uncle Charlie sitting hopeless in the gloom that way, and her father gone, and her mother working to make ends meet—

"You haven't been listening to anything I've been telling you all this time, then, have you? Miss Kendall runs most of the music program at the high school— all the choruses and the orchestra, too. And they're short on instruments because of the fire last year, when the school burned down and everything in it. But don't worry, I said you wouldn't sell your horn in a million years. I didn't tell her exactly why, but there's our band to think of, after all."

Gusta felt an icy wave of guilt run through her. She remembered that pill's worth of paper, and her mother's anxious footnote: *in case of need . . . that horn . . . her room and board.*

"I wonder what it means, 'a lot of money,'" said Gusta sadly.

Because now they were passing by Bess's house, where Uncle Charlie languished in his shadows for want of a surgeon's care.

Gusta's uncle Jay, her mother's youngest brother, came over for supper that night, which he did now and then, though he boarded down the lane at the farmhouse his older brother Bill had built when he got married to Verla. Uncle Jay had a happy-go-lucky grin that made Gusta like him right away, and not just Gusta: Jay was popular with all of Gramma Hoopes's boarders. The younger boys spent the early part of supper telling him all about the big school essay contest on the topic of "America from On High." Everyone around that table had a lot of respect for the meaning of twenty dollars, and of course appearing in the newspaper wasn't anything to sneeze at, either. But what Donald and Ron and Clarence were actually most excited about wasn't even the money or the newspaper—they didn't really think they had a chance of winning—it was the *airplanes.*

"Wouldn't I just like to ride in one of those things!" said Donald. "Wouldn't I just like to look out of those windows and see the clouds like pillows all beneath me!"

"Well, and that's just what I mean to do, kids," said Jay. "I saw a notice in the newspaper that they're looking for Aviation Cadets to train up, and I mean to volunteer."

"Jay!" said Gramma Hoopes.

"Oh!" said just about everybody else around that long table.

"It said in the paper, if you qualify to be an Aviation Cadet, you get paid money to study in that program! They're building up the army, they say, but all the planes are no good unless there are pilots to fly them!"

A sigh from some of the other boarders.

"Then I'll join up, too!" said Donald.

"Sorry, kid," said Gusta's uncle Jay. "Got to be

twenty-one years of age and a high-school graduate. You fellows have a long wait ahead—too bad. Glad I scraped through and got my diploma! Not going to spend the whole of my life mucking out barns!"

"This is *nonsense*," said Gramma Hoopes, and it was as if thunder had suddenly clapped its enormous hands. Everyone froze. "That's what this is. Nonsense! Nobody on my watch is going up in the air in a tin can. Not when there's real work to be done here on the ground."

"But, Mother," said Aunt Marion, and already those two words came closer to actually contradicting Gramma Hoopes than any in that house since Gusta had arrived. "That's a real good career, isn't it? With the airport here? And a salary even while they train him up? Wouldn't that be a great opportunity for our Jay?"

"Not a bit of it," said Gramma Hoopes, slapping the saltshaker down onto the table. "I won't have a child of mine going up in the air! This is absurd on your part, Jay, and I won't hear another word about it. Augusta!"

Gusta jumped in her seat.

"We had a surprise visit today while you were off at school."

Gusta's heart pounded out a quick, hopeful

rhythm, even though her head knew better. Her papa was far, far away from here, and always getting farther. He was not going to show up in something as simple as a surprise visit—no, sorry, no.

"It was that eye doctor man, Mr. Bertmann," said Gramma Hoopes. "In the company of Miss What's-her-name, the Jefferson School nurse. Imagine that! He told me quite an interesting story about your eyes, Gusta."

All up and down that long table, faces were turned toward Gusta. All up and down that long table, breaths were being held.

"Oh," said Gusta.

"Indeed. He and that nurse came all the way out to the house here today, because they were wondering when we were going to act on the glasses the school says you urgently need. Apparently I should already know about this business? A letter was sent home with you?"

Gusta gulped.

"I didn't think—" she started. "I mean, I've been getting along fine. . . ."

"Well!" said Gramma Hoopes. "Gladys seems to have let things slide on this score, down in the city. The nurse says you really can't see well enough for school. I'm tempted to take that nice old Mr. Bertmann up on his offer."

"What offer?" said Gusta.

"It seems that Mr. Bertmann is willing to give you a job," said Gramma Hoopes. "As a way of your earning yourself a pair of these glasses they are saying you need so much."

"But Gramma Hoopes, what kind of job?" said Gusta.

"Well, as far as that goes, tidying up his workshop, I imagine," said Gramma Hoopes, and Gusta could tell from the way she said it, that this decision had already been made. "Making yourself generally useful. That sort of thing."

The boys made a lot of clamor around the table. Apparently they all knew Mr. Bertmann, at least by sight. And (Gusta noticed) they didn't seem to find him too terribly frightening. That was a relief.

Larry even went out of his way, after supper, to whisper into Gusta's ear, "Wish I was you!"

"You do? Why, Larry?"

Because, to be scrupulously honest, even Gusta sometimes found it hard to be herself.

Larry gave her a smile that was just as gentle as you'd expect from a boy who could be trusted with eggs. "That Mr. Bertmann—he keeps *pigeons*!"

❦ 16 ❧

Oculist, with Pigeons

After school the next day, the rowdy band of kids heading back up Elm Street dropped Gusta off at the front stairs of the building on Main Street where Mr. Bertmann, the oculist, kept his shop (and, apparently, pigeons). "Good luck!" said Josie with an encouraging wave, and the boys echoed with their usual motley assortment of good wishes and waving hands.

The sign on the front of the building said OCULIST and FINE LENSES, PHOTOGRAPHY, CAMERAS, EYEGLASSES. Gusta peered at that long list carefully, and sure enough, it didn't mention any pigeons. Could the boys have been pulling her leg?

She pulled herself together and knocked on the door. To her surprise an older lady with the red face of someone who has just been arguing opened the door and looked at Gusta. Or rather, *over*looked her.

"I'm quite serious, Mr. Bertmann," the woman was saying. "I've been checking the rolls, as part of my patriotic duty, you understand, and because my Molly is starting a Real Americans Club at school, and she came home asking how safe we really are, here in Springdale, in these days of doubt and uncertainty on the global stage. So I went and looked through the county records, and it really does seem to be the case that you, a person who has regular contact with schoolchildren around the issue of their eyesight and suchlike, are not just unregistered, but a foreigner and an alien."

A man's voice said something, but nothing that Gusta could hear properly.

"Now really, Mr. Bertmann," said the angry woman. "It's very serious business, to be an unregistered alien in York County in 1941 — Oh, now then, who are *you?*" she added, having almost run right over Gusta on the threshold. That lady must not have heard Gusta's knock at all.

"Oh, sorry," said Gusta. "I'm just Gusta. I'm here for Mr. Bertmann. My grandmother sent me—"

"Well, *I* was just *leaving*, little girl," said the woman icily. "And I recommend you do the same, unless doing business with aliens doesn't trouble your conscience. You mark my words, Mr. Bertmann!"

She flung the last phrase behind her the way you might fling an apple core over your shoulder, and then stalked out the front door and down the walk. Gusta stood well to the side, so as not to be accidentally bowled over.

"Hmph!" said another voice from inside. "Oh, and look at this: it's the little girl with that most intriguing name, the little Neubronner! Come in, little Neubronner! Come in, so we can get acquainted and get to work."

Gusta went in. It was a very interesting space to be entering—everywhere she looked she saw complicated blurry objects and mechanisms that looked like they would be quite fascinating to look at, closer up, or to explore with your hands. Gusta had very perceptive hands. But she kept them strictly plastered to her sides now, trying to be polite.

"My grandmother tells me you might, um, have something I can do. . . ." she said, and then those words turned out to be a dead end. "Because of the eyeglasses, I mean," she added. And then she remembered the main thing: "I mean, thank you."

"Well, now, child, you are most welcome, and I'm

very happy to say that I have some equipment here —
courtesy of the United States Army, young lady — that
will make getting you the proper eyeglasses much less
of a chore. Just look at this wonderful mechanism!"

Now that she had been officially invited, she
went very close to look. It was an extraordinary thing
that he was tapping with such enthusiasm just now: a
super-complicated mechanical mask of some kind, sus-
pended by metal arms in the air, with what looked like
a dozen moving pieces, round bits of glass and dials of
various kinds.

"What kind of a machine is that?" she said. She
couldn't help feeling somewhat suspicious. "What does
it do?"

"It will help us diagnose what's going on with your
eyes. They are recruiting Aviation Cadets, and to fly a
plane, young lady, you need the sharpest possible eyes."

"I'm not sure, but I don't think I ever want to fly
a plane," said Gusta. She was trying to be polite about
all of this. "And I'm too young to join the army, so why
do they care about my eyes?"

The oculist laughed.

"They do *not* care! You are entirely right about
that. They are just borrowing my space here and my
various tools and tables; they will house this machine

with me for a while, run the local recruits through their paces, find their new crop of Aviation Cadets, and then move on somewhere else. But meanwhile, we can use this astonishing mechanism to see what kind of lenses your eyes require. Step over here now, Augusta Neubronner. I will have to adjust the height of our machine, but as you can see, it's designed to be flexible."

The crazy-looking mechanical mask hung at the end of a metal boom that could be raised or lowered to match the heights of all sorts of people.

Gusta stepped forward, but not without trepidation. It was such a strange device to put one's face up into the middle of. She tried to match her eyes to the glass holes, and Mr. Bertmann fiddled with the dials and the joints between the halves of the mask until finally she had one eye looking through one tiny glass window and the other eye looking through the other. It was a little like putting glass bandages on, though, because she could actually see nothing.

"So, child, now the fun begins," said Mr. Bertmann, and he turned a knob of some kind so that the lens in front of Gusta's right eye went completely black.

He twisted more knobs.

"This is an amazing machine," he said. "We will start by examining your left eye. Look at the eye chart over there now, and tell me, Augusta, which of these images is clearer, number one . . . or number two?"

"What chart?" said Gusta.

"Ah!" said Mr. Bertmann, fiddling with the dials. "Now this. Try this: number one . . . or number two?"

This time there was a smear of darker gray just visible against that blurred background of nothing in the second version of the little window, so she said, "Number two?"

And it went on that way for a very long time indeed, with Mr. Bertmann fussing with lenses and mechanisms and then making little notes in his notebook, while blurry letters, then not-so-blurry letters, then sometimes letters that looked so definitely themselves that it was like Mr. Bertmann had added a microscope to his machine appeared first in the left-hand eyepiece, and then in the right-hand lens.

"Good job, Miss Augusta Neubronner," he said finally, moving the machine away.

"It's quite some machine, Mr. Bertmann," she said, just to be polite. "What did it tell you about my eyes?"

Mr. Bertmann laughed.

"That they are complicated eyes indeed! But we live in modern times, and so we can order very complicated eyeglasses now, to match them. It is my hope that those complicated eyes of yours will see more clearly then."

"Oh," she said. *Complicated* eyeglasses sounded like *expensive* eyeglasses. "And Mr. Bertmann, can you tell me something? How much will they cost, the eyeglasses?"

She was determined not to skitter away from the topic of money. Her papa was so scornful of people who skittered away. It was his passion, making everyone see how it all worked, the mechanisms that turned actual human effort into stuff and into money. Sometimes he gave whole speeches at the dinner table about the price of things, the prices you *saw*, in dollars and cents, and the prices you *did not see*, the sweat and labor of the people who had worked in the factory that made the plates you ate off, the farmers who had raised the chicken whose drumstick you were maybe about to sink your teeth into, who had sold that chicken for almost nothing to someone else, who eventually brought it to the city and sold it to Gladys Neubronner or to her daughter, Augusta, sent to the butcher with a dollar and a basket. "The shoes on your feet, Augusta! What did you think, that they appear in the world by magic? No! Somewhere someone cut out that leather, stamped that pattern into the sole—and how much do you think *he* was paid for that work?"

There was no shame in talking about the price of things. And yet now here Gusta was, writhing a little on the inside and trying with all her might not to let the writhing show.

"You see, Mr. Bertmann, the thing about these eyeglasses," she said, "is that I've done pretty much perfectly fine without them so far. It does seem an awful waste of money, buying glasses for someone who has been getting along all right without them, all this time."

"Well, now, no," said Mr. Bertmann. "Really, no. I'm afraid there is no question about the spectacles. In your case they are a necessity, an absolute necessity. And I do not speak lightly of necessity. Of course it's a shame that your prescription is so complex—I will have to order the lenses especially, and that is what makes the eyeglasses in your case more expensive. But you are not to worry: we have a business arrangement, don't we? See, I am taking this page in my ledger book, and I am making a little document for our records."

He turned the page in his book and drew a line

neatly across the top, using a very sharp pencil and a ruler. Then on the line, he wrote her name: *Augusta Hoopes Neubronner.* Gusta leaned closer to look. Mr. Bertmann's handwriting struck her as very strange: more zigzaggy than ordinary writing, somehow. If Gusta had not known those words he was writing must be her own name, she would never have recognized it there.

"Six seventy-five," said Mr. Bertmann, "which from experience I'm afraid will be the cost of eyeglasses such as these. That comes to twenty-seven hours of labor at twenty-five cents an hour. Is my math correct?"

Gusta moved the numbers around in her head, checking them.

"Yes," she said. "But—"

And here it was her father's voice she suddenly found herself channeling, all the stories he had told in all the places they had lived. She tried to stand up straight and look like she knew what she was about.

"It's just that—shouldn't that be thirty cents an hour, Mr. Bertmann?"

"However so?" said the oculist. He seemed more than a little taken aback.

"Because there is a minimum wage now in this country," said Gusta. "I know there is, and I know it used to be twenty-five cents, but they raised it to thirty cents more than a year ago." Then she thought twice and added, to give him the benefit of the doubt, "But maybe you hadn't heard yet. About the change."

She could not read Mr. Bertmann's face, of course. He wasn't quite close enough for that. For a moment she was afraid he was about to shout at her, and she planted her feet very firmly on the plank floor of his office, ready to withstand whatever needed to be withstood—because Gusta's father was adamant about this: that if a worker did not stand up for his rights, he brought down not just himself, but everyone else who had to work to earn his bread—and then Mr. Bertmann surprised her by breaking into a laugh. He laughed so long and so heartily, in fact, that he had to wipe tears from his eyes with his handkerchief.

"What a strange child you are!" he said. "Strange, strange child! A—what did you call it?—minimum wage? For a child who does a few errands for an old oculist! You are spinning stories, *but*—"

Fortunately he got to the *but* before Gusta even had time to get properly mad.

"But I have also been a rouser of the rabble in my time, and so I take off my hat to you, Miss Neubronner." (He did not actually take off his hat, because he wasn't wearing one.) "I take my hat off to you, and I am willing to raise your salary to this absurdly high amount that a full-grown man doing full-grown work might expect, even though you are an untrained child on behalf of whom I am trying to do a kindness. *Thirty cents* I will account to you for every hour. In which case, you owe me . . . how many hours? Please do the math."

Gusta noticed her hands were shaking a little, but she ignored the tremor and moved more numbers around in her head. "Twenty-three hours," she said, and to show she was reasonable, she added: "I rounded up."

"From what strange place has this child come?" Mr. Bertmann asked of the room in general, and he shook his head.

He started making a list on the ledger paper.

"So. For this princely sum, you will have the following duties: dusting—that is easy and dull, to start with, but you'll find I don't care for dust and will see very instantly if you are shirking this task; note-taking, if you have a neat hand; perhaps some help with accounts, if I find your mathematical skills sufficient; and caring for my pigeons."

"Oh!" said Gusta, because he had mentioned the pigeons!

"Yes, indeed," he said. "It is my cherished hobby, raising pigeons. Come now, and I'll introduce you to your charges."

CR 17 DO

Pigeons

The pigeons had their own private room upstairs, where they lived in relative luxury, for pigeons. One of the windows had been fitted with a clever swinging board that let them in, but not out.

Their names were Mabel, Bella, Nelly, and Ruth. Mabel and Bella had interesting mottled patterns to their feathers (Bella with splotches of darker brown here and there); Nelly was almost entirely white, like a dove in a church picture; and Ruth had ash-colored feathers and a spark of independence burning in her eye.

"My beauties. My talented ones," said Mr. Bertmann. "They are very special pigeons."

"Yes," said Gusta, who could see right away that they were different from the pigeons she had met before, fluttering raggedly in the streets of, for instance, New York.

"Not merely because they are *beautiful*," he added. "They are special because they are highly trained adventurers. Partners in scientific inquiry!"

He showed her how they could carry little metal tubes attached to their legs, bringing messages home from the woods. That was the proper term for them, he said: *carrier pigeons*.

"Who are the messages from?" asked Gusta.

"Well, in fact," said Mr. Bertmann, "as of now, they are just messages from me to myself. Disappointing, no? Mostly I don't even bother to write out the words, because I know them so well in my mind. But it is all a part of their long-term training."

"Oh," said Gusta, petting the regal backs of Mabel and Bella. Ruth was still wary of her and kept herself just out of reach.

"You perhaps have experience with pigeons, Augusta?" asked Mr. Bertmann.

Experience with pigeons? Apart from seeing them fly blurrily by in every city she had ever lived in with her parents, none. She shook her head and felt a whiff of disappointment emanating from Mr. Bertmann.

"*Ach*, too bad!" he said. "But still: perhaps not

personal experience with pigeons? Perhaps a family connection?"

Now Gusta really was perplexed.

"What do you mean, Mr. Bertmann?"

She did not see how a human person could be related, as family, to pigeons.

"Ah, well," said Mr. Bertmann. "If you don't mind, I will explain. But to explain, I will need to ask you some questions. About your heritage, Miss Neubronner, and about our pigeons."

He cleared his throat as if he were about to enter into very important, serious topics of conversation, but of course Gusta simply wondered what he could possibly mean by any of that.

"When I was first told your name, child, I thought I recognized it: Neubronner! There are not so many little Neubronners running around the villages of the state of Maine. Agree?"

Gusta agreed, but only very quietly, on the inside. She still wasn't sure where the oculist was heading.

"And then I kept thinking, and my thought was, your father, little Augusta Neubronner, might very likely be a fellow exile from the Old World. I mean: from Germany. Is that the case, child?"

Now Gusta felt just the faintest tinge of alarm.

She pulled on the fingers of her right hand, trying to figure out where all these questions were leading, and what it was right or safe to say.

"Yes?" she said. "He was born in Germany."

Surely that was vague enough?

But Mr. Bertmann's eyes lit up. "Indeed! Now let us see how far the Goddess of Coincidence is willing to take us! Gusta, was *his* father, your German grandfather, by any chance, an apothecary?"

Gusta looked at him in confusion. Now she really was flummoxed. "What's an apothecary, Mr. Bertmann?"

"Someone who crushes up powders and mixes tinctures and in general dispenses medicines to keep the ailing as hearty as possible."

Someone who sold medicines!

"I don't know, Mr. Bertmann," said Gusta. "I don't think so. I never met my grandfather, but I know he played the French horn. The *Waldhorn*. I never heard about medicines."

"Or about experiments with pigeons?"

"Pigeons?" said Gusta. What could pigeons possibly have to do with medicines or horns?

"Ah, well," said the oculist, that spark of wild hope in his eyes somewhat subsiding. "Of course, it was foolish of me to assume. But sometimes, you know, the coincidence does bump into you, like a door you forgot was open. There was an apothecary, in Germany, when I was a younger man, who made wonderful experiments with pigeons. He was, in fact, a kind of inspiration to me—and his name was Julius Neubronner. So you see why I hoped. Foolish of me. But there it is."

"I never heard of my grandfather experimenting in any way with pigeons," said Gusta. But she felt a little sorry for the oculist now. "What kind of experiments? Feeding them pills?" (And *that* thought made her feel rather sorry for the pigeons.)

"Oh, no!" said the oculist. "No, not at all, at all, at all! I haven't explained properly. His experiments— his famous, tremendous experiments—were not medicinal, but photographic."

"Photographic," echoed Gusta.

"Photographic!" said Mr. Bertmann with great emphasis and definition. "Precisely so! He trained his pigeons to take quite wonderful *photographs*."

"Excuse me, Mr. Bertmann," said Gusta. "But I'm not sure—I don't think pigeons could possibly take photographs. They don't even have hands."

The oculist nodded, enthusiasm for these remarkable pigeons and this remarkable long-ago apothecary lighting up every corner of his face.

"That is the beauty of his project, Augusta," he said. "He built the tiniest little cameras and set them up with a mechanism to take a photograph like that"—he snapped his fingers lightly in the air—"Au-to-ma-ti-cally! While the pigeon flew through the air!"

"Is that really true?" said Gusta.

"It is really true," said the oculist. "It is actually really, truly true. Julius Neubronner is the father of the great and underappreciated art of pigeon photography. Look at this, young Augusta: it is one of my most cherished possessions. I brought it all the way across the ocean with me."

And he fished a small envelope out of his coat pocket, and in that envelope was a little square of cardboard that he held out now to Gusta so carefully that you might think it had been made of pounded silver and flattened gold.

It was a photograph, but at first Gusta couldn't see what it was a picture *of*—there was a lot of rough scrubbly stuff, and what looked a little like a castle, but from a very odd angle, and there, where Mr. Bertmann was pointing, an astonishing pale feather's worth of pigeon wing, in the upper corner of the image.

"Self-portrait with landscape," said Mr. Bertmann.

"Oh, that clever, clever bird! She managed to get a bit of herself into the picture. So everyone can know it was really a pigeon who took the picture."

And then he added, as if it were a secret he was spilling, "It seems almost impossible, does it not? But I share with you now, Augusta Neubronner, that that is my most cherished dream. To build a tiny camera for my talented, intelligent pigeons! Well, we must all have dreams—dreams with wings, dreams with quickly clicking little shutters. Why don't you bring Mabel downstairs now, like a helpful assistant, and I will show you where I've gotten to with my new secret project. Come along, come along!"

Mr. Bertmann gave her some seeds to help with the luring of Mabel, and then went downstairs ahead of Gusta, to give her practice in gathering up pigeons. Fortunately it turned out Mabel was perfectly willing to be lured.

"You're wanted downstairs!" Gusta simply said to Mabel, gathering her into her hands.

Mabel didn't protest in the slightest.

In the main room Mr. Bertmann was already beaming with pride at one of his worktables.

"Good, good!" he said to Gusta and Mabel, and then he showed them the astonishing thing that he had been working on, he said, for a very long while already, his secret project: the tiniest of little cameras, still all in bits and pieces. Eventually, he said, it would have a spring he could set to trip the shutter way up high in the air.

"Can you believe that?" he said.

"I don't know," said Gusta honestly.

The oculist laughed.

"First things first," he said. "First we must make you comfortable with each other, the person and the pigeons."

He slipped Mabel into a little travel cage and said, "Now, Gusta, this will be part of your work for me, yes? Why don't you run off homeward with our Mabel, and send her flying back to me before you step inside your grandmother's house. Then I will know you are safely home, and Mabel and you will both have had some practice."

"Yes, Mr. Bertmann," said Gusta.

So she did just that: she carried the pigeon cage back up Elm Street, and ever so gently tossed Mabel into the air at the corner of Hoopes Road. And mottled Mabel vanished as quickly as a dream, rose blurrily into the blurry air, and flew away home.

❧ 18 ❧

Accounts

I don't understand why a grown man needs to play games with pigeons," said Gramma Hoopes, "but as far as the note-taking and accounts-keeping and so on, that sounds like good training. In fact, I think Marion might as well get some use of that kind out of you, too. Marion?"

Marion looked up from the desk in Gramma Hoopes's room where she was working over a large ledger book, dull red in color.

"Yes, Mother?" she said.

"I'm saying we might apprentice Augusta here to you, so she can get extra practice with accounts. Mr. Bertmann's interested in her as a recordkeeper."

"Oh, are you nimble with numbers, dear?" asked Aunt Marion.

"I don't know," said Gusta. "I guess perhaps so. I hope so."

It seemed like something a person would want to be, "nimble with numbers."

"Come over here, then, and I'll show you a thing or two about keeping accounts."

Gusta pulled the stool over to Aunt Marion and looked dutifully at the ledger book, which looked as incomprehensible as account books usually look, with lists of things written down the left-hand side of the page, and then lines of numbers running in columns.

"Good, then," said Gramma Hoopes with a satisfied nod, and she turned to leave the room. Marion and Gusta watched her leave, and as the door of the room swung shut behind her, both of them let out identical little sighs. And those matching sighs broke some thin, lingering layer of ice Gusta hadn't even known had still been there, keeping her and Aunt Marion at arm's length from each other. Now Gusta and her Aunt Marion glanced at each other, and very similar giggles bubbled up from deep within them. Suddenly Gusta could see that Aunt Marion was secretly much younger on the inside than she let people know.

"Look here. It's not so difficult, really, if you are friendly with numbers," said Aunt Marion. "I just keep all the expenses listed, like so, down the side of the page here—all the boys' clothing, flour and so on, whatever the garden doesn't grow, coal for the furnace, boots for me this year because my old ones fell apart, the new chicks in the spring—and income listed over here."

There weren't a lot of line items on the "income" part of the page—*Board (State); Board (R. S.); eggs*— but then one line had a pretty substantial sum by it and only a check mark for a label.

"What's that?" said Gusta. She had to get her face pretty close to the paper to see the words and numbers there.

"Oh," said Aunt Marion hurriedly. "That's just the fund for improvements. That's quarterly. You know, we got plumbing in the downstairs a couple of years ago, earlier than almost anyone else down this far on Elm Street. Though your grandmother still prefers to use the backhouse, I do believe."

And she giggled again.

She went through a little pile of receipts and scraps of paper and transferred the numbers there into the various lines of her ledger book. She added numbers up so quickly, it was almost as if she were copying the totals down from some invisible piece of paper.

"You're so fast!" said Gusta.

Aunt Marion was clearly very friendly with numbers. She tapped with her pencil against the table: *tap-tap!* It was a smiling sort of sound.

"I like keeping accounts," said Aunt Marion. "I had a bookkeeping class at the high school, you know. I even worked in accounts at the mill for a while!"

"You did?" said Gusta. "For a salary?"

"Yes, well," said Aunt Marion. "That was long ago and much bigger numbers!"

Gusta knew better than to ask why she wasn't working with bigger numbers at the mills these days. The Depression had cost so many people their jobs.

But then, to Gusta's surprise, Aunt Marion added, "Then, of course, Mother needed help with the Home. Mostly the work's very simple here, keeping the children fed and dressed. But the account book makes me happy in a different way. I hear you like school, so maybe you understand."

Gusta nodded. A smile, quick-blossoming and shy, made Aunt Marion look very young for a moment, but then she went back to business. "Well, now,

Mother says you may be helping Mr. Bertmann with his accounts. Of course, I don't know how he keeps his books, but I'll show you what I do. Can you see all right? Watch how I work them . . ."

And she went over those numbers again. It made more sense this time. Gusta did the math in her head as they went, and Aunt Marion was pleased when she came up with all the right answers.

"You'll have the knack of this in no time," said Aunt Marion. "It's a good skill to have, and it will be good to be useful for Mr. Bertmann. Maybe he'll keep you on after the spectacles have been earned out! That would be a fine thing, wouldn't it?"

Something in Aunt Marion's voice wrapped around Gusta's heart like warm arms. Maybe it was the way it sounded just a little bit like her own mother, but with something younger in it.

It was only later that Gusta realized not everything about Aunt Marion's logical ledger book made logical sense. Of course, it made sense that money for special projects, like plumbing a toilet indoors, would show up in the family accounts. But why would that money show up on the income side of the page? Why would it show up quarterly? That made no sense. There was something strange about that line in Aunt

Marion's accounts, thought Gusta. Her mind poked at that thought for a while, and then it got distracted by thoughts of pigeons.

Pigeons and *need*.

Because Gusta had done some other bits of math recently, and the numbers weren't very encouraging: What if Mr. Bertmann were willing to keep her on, helping with the pigeons in exchange for the official minimum wage of thirty cents an hour, after she had worked through the cost of her eyeglasses? It would still take approximately forever to make enough to pay some room-and-board money to Gramma Hoopes, and longer than that if she wanted to do something really helpful in this world, like pay for doctors to undo some of the damage done to Uncle Charlie. If Gramma Hoopes was right about surgeons wanting a hundred dollars to work on Uncle Charlie's scarred-up hand, she figured she would have to work another — (math, math, math) — 333 hours. *Three hundred and thirty-three!* And that was only if Mr. Bertmann kept wanting that much help with his pigeons and was willing to pay actual money out, which was different from allowing Gusta to work off a debt, and Gusta knew that was not a sure thing.

Even with Mr. Bertmann being willing and able

to pay her, if you figured about five hours a week of pigeon care after school, that meant more than a year of Uncle Charlie waiting in the gloom.

In other words, it couldn't be done that way. Not through pigeons alone.

Nor could pigeons bring her papa home.

And meanwhile, the probably nonexistent Wish stayed stubbornly hidden, too. She had searched the parlor while dusting, and the front hall, too, and nothing there looked the slightest bit like an unused Wish.

But if pigeons and Wishes would not help her, and if Mr. Elmer Smith turned out to be the sort of labor organizer who never answered letters, what was left for Gusta to do?

Gusta's heart felt sore as she sat on the edge of her cot and looked at her horn, all comfortable and unsuspecting in its case.

It was her heart and her voice, that horn.

But in hard times, what was a heart and a voice compared to a *need*?

↜ 19 ↝

The Horn Goes to School

And that was why, the next morning, a some-what trembly Gusta came downstairs with her horn case in her hand.

"Augusta Hoopes! What on earth are you doing with that thing?" said Gramma Hoopes as Gusta swung her books over her shoulder with her other hand. It was going to be a long, bruising walk to school today, and her poor shins were already cowering.

"For my class," said Gusta. "For show-and-tell . . ."

She hadn't adequately thought through this moment ahead of time, she realized—this moment when Gramma Hoopes would be pointing at the horn and wondering why Gusta was hauling it off to school, of all places. For that matter, Josie was staring at her, too.

The truth was complicated: the gist of it was that her conscience had been aching for days.

The truth had Uncle Charlie in it, who needed that hundred-dollar operation on his hand, and all the secrets piling up in her, and the missing bit of her mother's letter, and the Wish that, if it had ever existed, seemed determined never to let itself be found.

As happens sometimes, she was going to have to break a bunch of rules, trying to do the right thing: she was going to sneak over to the high school that afternoon, instead of coming right home. She had thought about it and thought about it, and she saw no way around the moral difficulty: she had to talk to Miss Kendall about the value of horns.

It was indeed an actual show-and-tell day in Miss Hatch's class. That much was true. Miss Hatch had Gusta take the horn out and play a few notes for the class, and then when she asked for comments, up went Molly Gowen's hand, quick as fireworks.

"I would like to point out, however, Miss Hatch," said Molly Gowen, "that this metal horn thing of Augusta's is not the biggest object ever brought in for show-and-tell, because I'm pretty sure my new Schwinn bicycle, which I brought in last month, is much bigger. Maybe you forgot about my bicycle, though, Miss Hatch? It's bright green. And for another thing, that funny-looking case is not in very good shape. It looks like its owners may have been rather careless with it. I'd think probably we're supposed to take better care of musical instruments than to—"

"Thank you, Molly," said Miss Hatch in some haste. "And Augusta, I know your French horn must mean a lot to you, for you to have brought it with you all the way up here to Maine."

It was like Miss Hatch had just whacked a knife through an enormous onion, not four feet from Gusta's face.

A pang in her eyes and her heart made Gusta blink. She could not speak right away, because so many feelings were racing to the surface all at once, and they were all feelings that Gusta did not much want to have to share with everyone in that class.

"Yes, Miss Hatch," she said, finally. How puny her voice was, apart from her horn! "It's . . . It's . . ."

"It's PRETTY GREAT!" said George Thibodeau from the back of the room. Gusta was so grateful to him for interrupting that way—right when an interruption could not have been more needed—that she looked right out into that blur of faces and smiled instead of crying.

The sneaky, secret part of the plan came after school. To Josie and Bess, Gusta had said she would be staying late at school. That was true; what she didn't say was that she was staying late *so that Josie and Bess would go on home without her, not suspecting a thing.*

At the end of the day, Gusta waited in the classroom until Miss Hatch started asking whether she felt all right, and then she walked out of the building and turned right instead of left, the French horn bumping in its usual way against her leg. The high school wasn't too much farther down the main road.

It was a bold, new building, that high school, and Gusta tried very hard to stand tall and look bold herself, even though there's something about a French horn bobbing against your aching legs that makes it rather hard to feel tall or bold. Nevertheless, step by step she got up to the front door of the high school, and right into its new, still-shiny halls. There were a lot of very confident, very grown-up high-school students flowing past her and out the front door; she could feel them turning to wonder who she was, this little kid with the weird-shaped case swinging from her hands.

One older girl stopped and asked what she was looking for, and then actually led her the rest of the way to the door of the music room, which was a kindness. Gusta hadn't realized how *big* the high school would be!

The music room itself was enormous, with risers stacked at the sides and what must be music stands punctuating the general blur.

"Yes?" said a voice, coming closer through the blur. "Are you looking for me, perhaps? Oh, look at that instrument! I think perhaps you are!"

The woman who appeared was not very old — perhaps a little older than Aunt Marion — and wore a very practical but tidy-looking suit. Her hair was a lovely dark-red color, pinned up on her head. And her voice was — the only accurate word for it — melodious. Miss Kendall was an entirely melodious sort of person.

"Who are you, dear? Perhaps the new boarder that Josie was telling me about? Surely you must be! Mrs. Hoopes's grandchild from New York?"

"Augusta, yes, that's me," said Gusta, feeling her lips drying out from nervousness already. "Josie said Miss Kendall — I guess that's you —"

"It is, it is! Come over here, child, and sit right down so we can talk. Josie told me you showed up on their doorstep with a French horn in hand! It's such incredible good luck. It's like a miracle, almost—just the very thing we need for our orchestra. Did Josie tell you I was wanting perhaps to buy it from you? She thought you wouldn't want to sell it. I wasn't entirely clear as to why. Perhaps because you would need your parents' permission? Well, whatever the reasons are, of course I respect your feelings, if you don't want to sell it."

Gusta could see why Josie was so smitten with Miss Kendall. Her voice was very sweet, that was one thing. But still something twinged in horror in her at the word *sell*—sell? *Sell?*

In order to be brave, in order to forge ahead, Gusta had to make herself think about Uncle Charlie, sitting in his awful gloom.

"I was wondering what a horn might be worth, Miss Kendall," she said. "What this horn might be worth, I mean. If a person were to sell it. Were to think about selling it."

Miss Kendall gave her something of a quizzical look.

"Well, now, it depends on the horn itself, you know. May I take a look, Augusta?"

Gusta nodded. She made her hands undo the

latches on the case, so she could pull the trusting, unsuspecting horn out into the bright light of the music room. It looked shiny and beautiful in this light, but Gusta could also see the collection of little scars, here and there, that it had gathered over its long life.

"How lovely," said Miss Kendall, turning it this way and that in the light. Gusta wasn't entirely certain Miss Kendall wasn't just being polite, so she jumped in to defend the little dents and scratches.

"It's old, of course," she said.

"It belonged to your father, I believe Josie said? He was a horn player?"

"First his father was," said Gusta. "And then my father, too, yes, but you see, he didn't have time anymore."

"Ah," said Miss Kendall. "Well, too bad we don't have one of them here to play something for us! I'd like to hear what it sounds like. Does it have all its pieces and parts? A good old European horn like this would probably cost more than a hundred dollars these days. With the war, Germany isn't sending instruments this way anymore."

A hundred dollars! Gusta's heart took off like a rabbit. A hundred dollars! But that was exactly what Gramma Hoopes had said it might cost to fix up Uncle

Charlie's hand! For a moment she could hardly even breathe under the pressure of that coincidence, but Miss Kendall was still talking.

"Yes, yes, it looks fine. It does. But I'd like to hear it played. I could bring in one of our trumpet players, maybe, just to get an idea . . ."

"Or I could play something, Miss Kendall," said Gusta, almost taking her own self by surprise. "I— well, I could show you, if you want. So you could hear it. It's a good horn, really it is."

"Oh!" said Miss Kendall. "Do you play a little yourself? It's a very difficult instrument, I know. But let's hear what you can do. It would be nice to hear a note or two, certainly."

She did hand the horn back with grace and kindness, which was the only way Miss Kendall did anything, seemed like.

Oh, Gusta really did want her to understand about the horn. How lovely it truly was. She took a breath or two to settle her nerves.

And here's how it went: when Gusta produced that first, unquestionably pure tone, a note that seemed to set her rib cage and the bell of her horn vibrating together in harmony, she saw Miss Kendall straighten up a little in her chair. When Gusta played several notes up and down in a row, just warming up, Miss Kendall clasped her hands together, as if she wanted to say something. And when Gusta then started running through all the little bits and pieces of things that she had learned from her father, Miss Kendall broke into an outright smile, wide and broad. The last piece of music Gusta remembered was the one closest to her heart—it made her feel so much larger than she ever was, outside of a song. It made her feel sadder and deeper and gladder, all at once. She forgot about everything else, all the dings and scratches and dents in her horn, in herself, in the world, when she was in the middle of music like that.

"Augusta!" said Miss Kendall a moment later, when Gusta paused to come up for air. "But that's remarkable! That's truly remarkable! Do you know what you just played, that lovely bit of music just now?"

It was embarrassing to have to shake her head, but Gusta did shake her head. "I think it's by a Russian?" she said. "My father said—"

Then she found her merely human voice getting stuck.

Her father had actually said, as the horn balanced

lightly in his strong hands, "Even a clever parrot like you, thingling, will have trouble with this one. Most famous horn solo ever."

There had been another man, an organizer who worked with Gusta's father, there in their room at the time, sitting over at their table and having a cup of coffee. He had a bruise on a cheek because a strike had gone badly a few days before, but he was one of those people who shrugs off bruises. He had leaned forward and said, "Bet the girl could learn it, August. She played 'Yankee Doodle' last month, didn't she? Here, I'll wager two whole silver dollars she can do it."

And he had flung those coins onto the table. They made quite a heavy ringing sound as they hit the top of the table. Two dollars was a lot of money.

Gusta's father and the bruised man had shaken hands on their bet, right then and there, before Gusta's mother came back into the apartment, because Gusta's mother would never have stood for it, putting Gusta at the center of a wager, one way or another.

It wasn't just because her father had bet money she *couldn't* do it that Gusta had had to learn that melody and show she *could*. The thing went deeper than that. It was to show her father she could do more than any ordinary *clever parrot*. To show that she could amount to something—though of course she hadn't wanted to cost her papa money.

Anyway, she had done it. She had learned that lovely scrap of music her father had played for her, and he had lost his bet because of that, because of her, and had frowned when he had to pay up, even though he must surely also have been proud. And she couldn't explain any of this now to the kind and melodious woman who had just clapped her hands together and bounced to her feet.

"Augusta! It's by Tchaikovsky. It's a beautiful thing. But *that's not all*. Have you heard this?"

Miss Kendall went over to something sitting in honor on a little cart by the wall, and Gusta followed her over so she could see. But she hardly believed her eyes when she got close enough to recognize what it was: an actual gramophone. In a school! But of course this was a fancy, new-built school. Perhaps anything was possible in a school like this.

There was a closet with records in it. Miss Kendall looked through it and came back to pop the disk in her hands onto the spinning part of the gramophone.

"Listen up, dear," said Miss Kendall. "This is the Glenn Miller Orchestra, playing one of their biggest hits of 1939, 'Moon Love.'"

What that had to do with Gusta's horn or Tchaikovsky, Gusta had no idea. She knew who Glenn Miller was, of course. He led one of the most famous jazz bands in the world.

But as far as she knew, there was no French horn in that outfit. It wasn't that sort of band. She listened closely now, and no — no French horn.

Miss Kendall was bouncing slightly on the balls of her feet. Even without looking very closely at her face, Gusta could tell she was smiling, smiling, smiling at her, as if Gusta were unwrapping a present Miss Kendall had just thoughtfully handed over.

"I don't —" said Gusta.

And then it was a few seconds further into that song, and she *did:* the melody of the song was familiar! More than familiar! It wasn't being played by a French horn, but it was Gusta's own French horn solo, the one that had lost that bet for her father.

"Are you telling me Mr. Glenn Miller stole that tune?" said Gusta. "From the Russian guy, from Tchaikovsky?"

"When it's musicians doing the stealing, we call it borrowing, and we admire it," said Miss Kendall with a laugh. "And look at this, anyway: Glenn Miller's perfectly honest about it. Tchaikovsky gets his name on the label."

She showed Gusta the bright-blue Bluebird label on the record. If you squinted close, you could see the explanation: *MOON LOVE — Fox Trot (Adapted from Tschaikowsky's 5th Symphony, 2nd Movement) Glenn Miller and his Orchestra.*

"How about that, Augusta? You've been playing a number-one hit! Pretty wonderful, yes? And you play so well already. How old are you, anyway? You simply can't be as young as you look."

"I'm eleven," said Gusta, pulling herself up as tall as possible. "I'm in the fifth grade."

Miss Kendall laughed again. "Oh, my!" she said. "Now, what are we going to do with you?"

And she paced about the room for a minute — her pacing was as melodious as her voice. It was almost more a dance than it was pacing.

This was clearly when Gusta should ask about that hundred dollars.

"Miss Kendall . . ." she said, and as soon as she spoke, she could feel herself wobbling, her love for the way her horn filled the world with a voice that was so grand and lovely, that sang out truths while Gusta's own voice just tripped over secrets—oh, her selfish love was making her wobble, yes, it was. So she pulled herself up straight and made herself think of all those scars constraining Uncle Charlie's poor bandaged hand. And her mother, working so hard, back in New York City. And her father, doing what he thought was right, even when that meant something as hard and scary as organizing a strike, or leaving your daughter behind so you could fight in a war.

"*Miss Kendall,*" said Gusta for the second time, a bit stronger already. "Is the horn really worth what you said, do you think? A hundred dollars? If I—sold it to you?"

"Oh, but Gusta!" said Miss Kendall, laughing and shaking her head. "We mustn't take your horn away from you, now that I've heard what you can do! You must keep it and play it. In fact, I have a grand idea! At least, I think it could certainly be terrific. We have the spring concert coming up, and—oh! I see it now. A way to use my string players and give the band something to do as well. Tchaikovsky meets Glenn Miller. It'll be great. You'll have to learn the whole of that solo, but you played me almost half of it already. I'll send music home with Josie. And can you come over for a practice session sometime, after school, do you think?"

"You want me to play with the high-school students?"

Gusta could hardly believe it. This whole conversation had gone in a direction she had not expected—like her great-grandfather's boat, finding itself suddenly shipwrecked off the coast of Madagascar.

"Yes, isn't that a fine idea? Think how surprised everyone will be! Won't you say yes and play with us?"

Well, yes, of course, Gusta wanted to play—she wanted that with all her heart. It was like saying she wanted to "still be Gusta," despite the price for remaining Gusta being so awfully high. But that was not necessarily the Gusta her father might have wanted her to be, when the storm arrived.

She tried to say something else, to get Miss Kendall back to the subject of prices and dollars and horns for sale, but Miss Kendall was too full of enthusiasm for her new plan, and Gusta's voice, without the horn, wasn't forceful enough to make a dent in that enthusiasm. Miss Kendall just waved Gusta's attempts aside.

"Not a word, not another word, Augusta," said Miss Kendall. "You'll see—it will be wonderful! I'm so glad you came to Springdale. What a lucky chance for all of us. It will make such a lovely show!"

So Gusta found herself walking home with her horn still comfortably bumping against her shins — and no money in her pocket.

"Maybe afterward," Gusta said to her ship-wrecked self, so torn between disappointment and thrill. "Maybe after this concert Miss Kendall is so excited about, maybe then I'll finally be able to get her to buy the horn."

❧ 20 ❧

Treasures in the Attic

U p here," said Josie, with the almost smug satisfaction of someone about to unveil a great
surprise—or in this case, about to use a
hook-ended pole to catch hold of a coordinating metal
loop in the hall ceiling (that Gusta, with her bad eyes,
had of course never noticed) and pull down, out of
nowhere, a kind of magically folding ladder. "Up you
get—there's everything up there, you'll see."

It was a Saturday morning, and Aunt Marion was
looking for another set of bedclothes she remembered
there being in the house somewhere, so Josie had
jumped at the chance to volunteer to search the attic;
looking for something tucked away up under the roof

was preferable—no doubt about that—to any of the other chores Gramma Hoopes and Aunt Marion had planned for this Saturday. Gusta caught the feeling from Josie's quick grin: it was practically getting away with something, coming up to look for Aunt Marion's sheets and pillowcases.

Gusta had read about attics in children's books, and one year when she was much younger, she seemed vaguely to remember having lived with her parents in a house with an attic—which town had that been?—but this was the first time she had climbed into an actual attic by means of a magical ladder. Her first impression was of shadows, and of rows of objects waiting patiently in those shadows. Then Josie flipped some switch, and a lightbulb blared into life, making them both blink. It dangled from the ceiling—no lampshade nonsense, just a concentrated circle of bright light, casting funny shadows all around.

It was cold up in the attic this time of year, but it smelled secretly of summer, of many, many summers, of old wood cured over many long years and through all kinds of weather. Everywhere all around was the usual stuff that finds its way to attics: a slightly broken ironing board, forlorn little figures that must be abandoned dolls, and lamps that almost certainly no longer worked. There was also the tiniest edge of mildew in the air up there, and that made sense because along the whole length of that attic on one side were low bookshelves, just two shelves high, and on those shelves were old books with the spines out, and some newer ones more higgledy-piggledy, and a number of boxes containing who knew what.

"Oh!" said Gusta. All these BOXES on SHELVES! The hunt downstairs for the Wish had become discouraging; she had even taken half-hearted peeks into the sugar box and bean boxes in the pantry, but no Wish could have lasted undisturbed in boxes people used every day—it was as silly as thinking a Wish could have waited quietly in a nest box for years, while hens, eggs, and straw came and went. Not very likely.

And then she said, "Oh!" again, because whether or not there was an actual Wish hidden up here somewhere, the shelves in this attic looked to Gusta like a wish come true.

So many books! There weren't a lot of books downstairs. She had had no idea the Hoopes Home had a secret library under its roof.

"Those are the old captain's books," said Josie. "That's what they told me, anyway. Go ahead and paw through them if you want. I'm looking for something that will make a nice noise for our band—seems to me I saw something like that up here once."

Gusta sat on the floor by the bookshelf and started paging through the books. Some of them were ancient and uninteresting, but there were also children's books with old-fashioned pictures, and dictionaries, and *The Arabian Nights*, and then she started opening up some of the big boxes, just to check.

No Wish rattling around anywhere—instead, notebooks. Not cheap notebooks that you might use at school. Nothing like that. Leather-bound tomes, very heavy, and when you opened them, sketch after sketch of wonderful, strange, beautiful creatures, and here and there, a landscape. It was hard at first to read the writing that explained and surrounded all those incredible pictures, but Gusta quickly became more used to it. It wasn't the illegible zigzag scrawl of Mr. Bertmann's ledger book.

It was the precise writing of an old sea captain, in love with all the strange and lovely things of the world.

"The old sea captain was an artist!" said Gusta to Josie, and she held up a picture of a strange-looking monkey-like creature, clinging to a tree branch with long, knobbly fingers and eyeing the world with suspicion. "Look how he drew all the little fluffy hairs along his back!"

"Pretty good," admitted Josie.

Relative of the Lemur, called locally the "aye-aye," the Island of Madagascar, June 1896, it said at the bottom of the picture.

Madagascar! Then maybe — maybe — there would be some mention of the most important thing, right? The Wish that had survived sea and shipwrecks in the sea captain's pocket, and that had eventually come along home to Springdale.

Gusta paged through the notebook carefully, looking for clues as if she had turned right into Sherlock Holmes. In any case, these books didn't feel like things that should be packed away and forgotten in the attic of a farmhouse in Maine. If she hadn't been sitting on the cold planks of the attic floor, she might have been able to imagine herself in an ancient library. Or in a museum.

She turned the page and saw a parrot, absolutely perfect in all of its feathers, and quite understandably proud of that, too, to judge from the glint in its eyes.

He had sketched some maps in his notebook, too. Gusta had no idea what they were of. But islands somewhere, she assumed? And stretches of coastline?

No Wish anywhere, though.

She set that notebook very carefully back in its box, and opened up the next one.

"There, now!" called out Josie from the other end of the attic, where the lumpier objects had clustered. "Not what I remembered seeing, but what do you think of this?" And she raised her hand and waggled some object in Gusta's direction.

"What is it?" asked Gusta, balancing the big notebook on her knees.

Josie came over closer to Gusta to show her what she had found. "A sailor's squeezebox," she said.

What Josie called a "squeezebox" was a smallish, six-sided thing, with rows of little round buttons on either side and the folds of a bellows in the middle.

"That's got to be some kind of accordion," said Gusta. "Right? But where'd it come from, and how'd it ever get up here? Looks kind of complicated to play, though, doesn't it?"

All those little buttons! How were you supposed to know which one to press at any particular time?

Josie shrugged. Maybe she wasn't the type to be so easily discouraged by little buttons. Gusta had to admire her nerve. She watched Josie pull the little accordion open and shut a few times, just messing around to see what might happen. And what actually happened was that a tremendously loud wheezing *blat* of a note rolled out into the attic.

"Oh, no, don't!" said Gusta, suddenly full of alarm. "You know Gramma Hoopes will just hate that if she hears you!"

"Maybe that's not the one for me, then!" said Josie as she set the squeezebox down on a box by the stairs. "Who knows how it even works? I'll go rummage some more. But hey, now, Gusta—what's that picture there?"

The second heavy notebook had fallen open on Gusta's knees to a picture that seemed very far removed from lemurs and parrots: a funny sort of tower rising up, with woods behind it, and a woman sitting on a low step with a baby in her arms. It was drawn from a peculiar sort of perspective, so that the woman and her baby looked close and large, and the tower oddly shrimpy behind them.

"I don't know," said Gusta. "People in front of a lighthouse? Who do you think they are? *Where* do you think they are?"

Josie leaned in for a closer look. "That must be your own Gramma Hoopes right there," she said, pointing at the baby in the woman's arms. "Which would make the woman there your great-grandmother, I guess. Her name was Prudence. I remember about her because she was the one so beautiful and charming that the old captain left all the seven seas behind, to come live in the Maine woods. Even I've heard that story a hundred times by now, believe me."

"What about the lighthouse? Did they live by a lighthouse?"

"Well, as far as *that* goes," said Josie, "that's just one of the old captain's follies, up on the side of Holly Hill. I've seen it with my own eyes. There's a nice view out the direction of Portland from there. He built it himself. Mrs. Hoopes says her father could never not be building or whittling or carving—I guess that's the usual thing, for sea captains."

"A lighthouse in these woods?" said Gusta. That didn't make sense. Lighthouses stood on the edge of the ocean. On rocky cliffs. Where there were barnacles clinging and huge waves all the time. But here they were so far from the sea!

Josie shrugged. "I don't know *why* he wanted it out in the woods, but I guess a lighthouse is what he wanted to build, so he built it. Turn another page, Gusta. What else is there?"

Gusta turned the page, and another page, and

there were birds from the Maine woods there, and a squirrel, and then—

"Ew!" said Josie. "Bats!"

Not just one single bat. Pages and pages of bats took over that whole notebook. An infestation of bats! Bats peering out from their own wings. Bats hanging upside down from some strange surface, bats stretching out their wings, bats in such close-up detail that you could see every nuance of their mixed-up little faces: point-like eyes, sharpest miniature needles for teeth, squidgy little noses, all dwarfed by those extraordinary ears. Arrows pointing to the details, especially, again and again, to a stripe of gold running down the backs of their furry heads.

Josie had been driven back to the other end of the attic by that horde of two-dimensional bats, but Gusta found herself turning the pages slower and slower, sinking into the details of the pictures. They were hideous and beautiful, those bats, both at once. Adorable and horrible. And the artist, the sea captain—her own great-grandfather—must have spent hundreds of hours sketching those adorable/horrible bats. You could tell, looking at those pictures, that he had not just been interested in them: *he had loved them.*

And that sent an odd pang through Gusta's own

heart: to think of someone actually *loving bats* — ugly-toothed, ugly-faced, blind little bats. Monkeys and parrots — those are lovable, it's easy enough to understand. But bats!

"*My-o-tis lu-ci-fu-gus cle-men-ti,*" she read aloud. That was the name of these bats, apparently. She turned the pages ever more carefully, not wanting to damage the pictures. She was so careful not to put a finger on the pictures, to see if the furry heads felt the way they looked, but she imagined doing so.

One page was unlike the others: all gray shadows, so much so that at first glance you might think he had had an accident with his inks. And then on second and third glance you saw that there were rocky sides to that shadowy space, and little creatures dangling from the top of the picture. A place inhabited by the sea captain's bats. It must be the names of the place and of those bats written in neat ink beneath that picture: *Hibernaculum, Holly Hill. Myotis lucifugus clementi.* And then a phrase that made all the little hairs up and down her arms tingle and clamor a little: *Here I have found treasure!*

Gusta took a closer look, trying to spy out any signs of chests or jewels or pieces of eight or Wishes. Any traces of treasure.

She couldn't see any of that, no matter how much she squinted.

Nevertheless, it was an amazing image, once you knew what it was showing you. Everything in that cave was sleeping. Everything was quiet. It was like the bats themselves: ugly and beautiful, scary and somehow peaceful. She stared at that picture for the longest time, letting herself slip right into it, almost as if she were there.

"Aha!" said Josie, emerging again from the far corner, where the biggest trunks and boxes were. "*This* is what I remembered! This banged-up little guitar!"

She was so happy to have found it that Gusta didn't have the heart to speak her doubts aloud. It didn't look like any guitar she'd ever seen — it was so small. Half the strings were busted, and one was missing. But it had a pretty striped pattern ringing its sound hole, and a faded sticker up on the end where the tuners were.

"'1915 Panama' something or other," said Josie. "Where's Panama? This must be a Panama guitar."

"It won't play," said Gusta. "Not without strings."

Josie laughed.

"Not to worry about that!" she said. "I'll take it in to show Miss Kendall. She'll help me out. She knows every instrument there ever was, and I just bet she can help me figure out how to string it up again."

"Girls!" called Gramma Hoopes from the hall below. "Are you lost up there? I need you right this minute, Augusta. Mr. Bertmann has come by and wants you."

Mr. Bertmann! Why would he just show up out of the blue like that? Gusta hurried to put the notebooks back in their box, while Josie scrambled for Aunt Marion's pile of pillowcases. She would have to come back, Gusta decided, to read more of those beautiful pages, even if they neglected to mention the most important thing, the Wish. She was curious now, about a person who would build a lighthouse so far from the sea, and who could see the beauty even in snaggletoothed bats.

Once back downstairs, Gusta found Mr. Bertmann waiting very patiently in the front hall, with a dark pigeony blob in a little cage in his right hand.

"The parcel has come, Augusta Neubronner!" he announced. "Of course, they will need adjustments and so on, so come along now, do. Your grandmother says you may."

"Mr. Bertmann assures me it won't take so very

long. Hurry along now, and hurry back," said Gramma Hoopes.

Oh, it was the *glasses* they must be talking about! The glasses must have come. Had it already been two weeks since Mr. Bertmann had placed the order?

Gusta grabbed her coat and hat.

Once they were outside, Mr. Bertmann paused to take the pigeon out of her cage. It was ash-feathered Ruth.

"Fly along home, you adventurer!" Mr. Bertmann said to his pigeon, and she fluttered up and vanished into the sunny blur of the air above Elm Street.

"She will arrive before us," said Mr. Bertmann. "We will have a pigeon and your own new spectacles waiting for us when we arrive. So you see there is much to look forward to."

Gusta's stomach felt a little tossed and turned, like a ship on an unknown ocean far away.

And by the time she entered the already rather familiar space of Mr. Bertmann's workshop and office, her heart was pattering along at almost a pigeon pace.

What if these fancy eyeglasses, whose value had been set at twenty-three hours of her labor—what if these eyeglasses worked no better than the cheap things the school nurse kept in the box in her office? She suspected that would be the case. Nothing had ever made much difference in how she saw.

And that was fine! She reminded herself to *stand up straight and look like she knew what she was about.* It was fine to see exactly as she already saw. She had come this far in life without the help of eyeglasses, and if she had to travel the rest of her life the same way, well, that was just what she would do.

It was exciting, though. Gusta's hands were beginning to feel just the slightest bit clammy.

"Take a seat here, Augusta," said Mr. Bertmann, and he went over to his desk in the corner to fetch something. There was a small, rather fancy mirror on the table, a mirror that could tilt up and down. She tested its movements with the tip of a finger, wondering why anyone needed such a mirror. Her face, slightly blurry and more than slightly worried, looked back at her from the glass. She looked so serious and so gloomy! She made herself smile into the mirror, but without letting any of her snaggled teeth show. Although she couldn't be sure, she didn't think the smile did all that much to erase the worry.

The oculist had returned to the little table. He sat across from Gusta, pushed the fancy mirror to one side, and reached forward to place something on her nose—actual spectacles!—and to tuck the sides of those eyeglasses safely around her ears.

The world changed. Gusta blinked. In that moment everything became suddenly harder and brighter and *louder*! And then Mr. Bertmann made a dissatisfied harumphing sort of sound and took the glasses off her nose and back to his workbench, while Gusta's heart beat very fast and her hands refused to stop trembling.

"Is there—is there something wrong?" she asked in a faint voice.

"No, no! Everything is fine so far," said the oculist. "I am adjusting the frames so they fit your young face."

He leaned over what must be the eyeglasses on his workbench, and he poked and prodded and pried at them, using little tools that were really too thin to be seen.

Gusta waited and tried to think calm thoughts.

"One little moment!" said Mr. Bertmann. "And there!"

He came puttering back, leaned forward again, and placed with such great, extraordinary care those eyeglasses on the bridge of her nose, with the frames over her ears—more comfortably, she had to admit, than they had fit at first.

Instantly he looked like a different sort of person, someone with a face carved out by an obsessive artist whose aim had been great precision in every line. It did not necessarily improve him, beauty-wise, but it certainly changed him.

"How is that, Augusta?" said that face to her now.

The strange thing was the way the voice and the face no longer fit together in the usual way. The face was so insistently moving its lips to speak every one of those sounds, in a way that Gusta found just slightly grotesque—but the voice was the crispy-consonanted but familiar and gentle voice of Mr. Bertmann, a voice she already knew well. She could not combine in her mind the familiar voice and this brand-new face. For a moment she put her hands over her eyes, shutting out the world.

"Now, now, now," said Mr. Bertmann soothingly. "Are they painful in some way? Tell me how they feel, and what you see. Let's try our old friend over there, the eye chart."

And Gusta turned to look at the eye chart, and it was as if the wall had zoomed forward magically and was right before her nose, almost.

"Oh, it's right there!" she said, pointing.

"Can you read it?" said Mr. Bertmann.

She could. She could read it as if it were in a book just inches from her nose.

The wall had given up being a blur. Next to the eye chart, there was a hook in the wall, and on the hook there hung a bunch of keys. Above the eye chart, there was a knot hole in the wood paneling, a sworl of thin dark lines against the slightly less dark panel.

"Is that fourth line still difficult for you?" said Mr. Bertmann to her, while his face made those distractingly precise little movements with its lips and its teeth and all. She had stopped reading the eye chart by accident; she had simply shifted to reading the wall. Now she rattled through the fourth line for him—the fifth—the teeny-tiny sixth. Only at the very bottom of the chart did the letters hide themselves from her, and even then it didn't feel like they were blurry, it just felt like they were being shy.

"P," she said. "Or F. I'm not sure. Is it changing its mind?"

"Excellent, excellent, excellent!"

The oculist was really delighted.

He clapped his hands together, and Gusta realized she could see every little line in his fingernails, which was disconcerting. She kept looking away from his face, because it felt too close, seen through those amazing eyeglasses.

She turned her head, and it kept happening: the world kept being entirely different in appearance than it had ever been. She pulled the eyeglasses off and looked again: everything was comfortingly blurry again. Soft. Unthreatening. But, now she saw, at the same time: absent.

She put the glasses back on and blinked.

"You may feel a little dizzy at first," said Mr. Bertmann. "But I think you will adjust with rapidity. Young people have such excellent skills in adjusting! And now—it is almost your dinnertime, and I promised your grandmother I would not keep you long. Here's a case for those new glasses of yours, and here's a little cloth to clean them with. Don't rub them on your clothing like a wild animal! They will scratch!"

For one moment the funny image of a leopard rubbing its glasses on its necktie sprinted through Gusta's head—the new spectacles must be making her giddy. She took the case for the glasses and tucked the cloth inside it. Then she started to unhook the eyeglasses from behind her ears, but Mr. Bertmann stopped her.

"Why?" he said. "What are you doing?"

"Putting them away safe," said Gusta.

The oculist laughed, but kindly.

"They are not things to be kept hidden away safe, dear girl. They are to be worn, every minute of every day if need be. They are companions to your eyes. You must practice moving through the world with your eyeglasses on. Like our friends, you know, *the pigeons*."

Gusta blinked. "The pigeons, Mr. Bertmann?"

She didn't see what pigeons had to do with eyeglasses, but she was trying to be perfectly polite.

"But yes!" said Mr. Bertmann. "The pigeons! You know my great ambition: to follow in the steps of the apothecary Neubronner, who is not, after all, your relative. To turn my pigeons into photographers."

"Um, yes," said Gusta. (But it still seemed to her like the least likely project anyone had ever thought up in the history of unlikely projects.)

"Well! Inch by inch, dear child, is progress. And the next inch, while I work on my little lenses and little shutters and you work on getting used to your eyeglasses, is, it seems to me, to accustom our winged friends to carrying something heavier than feathers. See, I have made a harness . . ."

And suddenly he was bringing out a little leather contraption with a cardboard box, where he said the camera would eventually go. He fetched Nelly down from the pigeon room in her travel cage, and showed Gusta how you put a harness on a pigeon, which turned out to be a fiddly sort of thing to accomplish.

And then he said, as he led Gusta to the front door of the workshop and popped the pigeon cage into her hand, "It is an assignment for you, dear girl, to help you practice being out in the world with your new eyes. Take our Nelly on a walk this afternoon. Go up the road a ways past your grandmother's house, so that it's a bit of a challenge for her. And we shall see how she does. And now, off you go!"

It was almost as if Gusta were one of those pigeons, being tossed into the air.

Gusta waved good-bye and turned to face Elm Street—and all of a sudden, of course, she was facing a brand-new world.

❧ 21 ❧

The Budding Trees

Even those first few steps down from the oculist's door required great caution. Everything felt nearer than it had a few minutes ago, and that made her feet just slightly uncertain about where the ground actually was.

She didn't want to stumble and fall, because there was Nelly in her fragile little cage, depending on Gusta to carry her safely through this suddenly so complicated-looking world.

To tell the truth, Gusta hardly knew which way to look first. There were little earthy bubbles and clods everywhere that wasn't paved. She hadn't thought about how rough and grainy the ground mostly is, except where human beings have covered it over with stone or slabs of wood.

And the bark of the trees! She crossed the street to start down the road leading to the Hoopes Home. There was a sign on a pole over there—*on the other side of the street*—and she knew as soon as she looked at it exactly what it said ("Elm Street"), almost as if her eyes now had seven-league boots and could bound far distances whenever they wanted.

That was a silly way to put it, Gusta told herself sternly. Honestly! Seven-league boots?

But when she raised her head and looked at something, no matter what it was and no matter how far away it seemed to be, that thing was suddenly present in her immediate world, in a way it had never been before. She kept looking down and then looking up again, at one thing and then at another.

She could see the paint fading on the walls of all the houses. This was not a town where anyone had extra money for painting the outside of their houses, that seemed clear. But she hadn't really *known* that before. It was a brand-new piece of knowledge for her now.

On top of the nearest house was a black shape, pointed at one end. It looked at Gusta, spread its wings, and flew away with a great, thunderous *CAW!*, and the funny thing was, she could see it fly. It didn't just disappear. It was in the air—hard to focus on, true; her eyes weren't very quick about catching it— but it was there. Not suddenly invisible. *In the air, and still there.*

She repeated her rhyme a few times, under her breath, and then stopped walking so she could catch her balance again.

She had stopped right next to the trunk of a tree. It was comforting to stretch out her hand and *feel* all those lines of rough-edged ridges that her eyes insisted, suddenly, were there. She still believed her hands more than her eyes. She looked up that trunk—but it wasn't anything like an ordinary tree anymore! Where there was usually a soft woven texture of dark and light, this time of year, there was now an incredibly specific tangle of branches, large ones and tiny twigs, each one as if an astonishingly gifted artist had spent hours drawing it with the most fine-nibbed of pens. The branches weren't smoothly gray anymore, either. They were, each one, quite knobbly. They would be rough under your fingers if your fingers could reach them. It was almost as if her eyes were suddenly reaching out and *touching* things!

And some of those knobbly branches had bits of green leaking out of them.

Little oval bits of green.

Oh!

Gusta actually clasped her hands together in awe as she tilted her head back.

For the first time — the first time! — in her whole entire life, Gusta Neubronner was seeing LEAVES — not the ones underfoot, that you pick up and think about one by one, but the thousands of tiny, living, green-as-green, just-beginning-to-be-growing *leaves on trees*.

And it was wonderful!

❧ 22 ☙

Into the Woods

Gusta arrived in time for the last bit of dinner, so Mr. Bertmann had kept his promise after all. She parked Nelly in her cage in a dark corner of the front hall, knowing that pigeons are not fond of light and noise. To be honest, the darkness of the hall was actually quite soothing for Gusta, too, after the strain of seeing so much, all that way home from Mr. Bertmann's. She took off her new glasses and rubbed her eyes, and then made her way to the long table surrounded by the familiar general blur of all those boys and Gramma Hoopes presiding at the head. Aunt Marion came in at that moment with more food from the kitchen—dinners kept her busy.

"Oh, hello there, Gusta!" she said. "Just in time. Sit down and have some chipped beef, child."

Gramma Hoopes tapped her plate twice with her fork, just to get Gusta's attention. "Well?" she said. "Aren't you supposed to have eyeglasses now, Augusta?"

Gusta jumped a little. Her glasses were still clenched in her right hand. She held them up now.

"Well, that's not how they work, as far as I know," said her grandmother. "Put them on, for goodness' sake."

"Yes, go ahead, show us, Gusta!" said Josie.

Even before she had tucked the frames behind her ears, she knew that every face around that table was staring at her — but when she looked up with the glasses on, the vividness of those stares made her gasp and look away.

"Heavens, what's that about, Augusta?" said her grandmother sternly. "I hope you're not vain. Nothing wrong in wearing spectacles, since it seems you need them."

Gusta couldn't find the words to explain. It was so shocking to see all those eyes and noses and mouths everywhere all around her. Her own eyes hardly knew what to do with them all. She looked down at her plate instead.

Larry had the next place at that table; he leaned closer so he could murmur, "I think you look fine."

Even though Gusta hadn't actually been thinking at all about how she looked, she felt comforted. Larry was as gentle with people as he was with eggs.

"Do those things make the world look funny?" said Thomas, the youngest of the brothers. Being six apparently gave him the courage to ask the question everyone was wanting to ask.

"Well, I have to get used to them, that's all," said Gusta.

"Quite true," said Gramma Hoopes. "Now, after dinner I'll ask you to help Josie and me with some cleaning."

"Oh!" said Gusta, looking up from her chipped beef over mashed potatoes (with a pretty tasty garnish of canned corn and peas). "I forgot to tell you about Nelly!"

"Nelly? Whoever is Nelly?" said Gramma Hoopes, setting down her fork. Gusta had never properly noticed before how interesting Gramma Hoopes's hair was. The crown of her head was silver-gray, but a long braid ran around that head, and the braid was a lovely dark color, so that the head of Gusta's grandmother was a kind of snow-capped peak.

"Nelly's one of Mr. Bertmann's pigeons. I'm supposed to take her up the road into the woods this afternoon and let her go. It's part of this experiment he's been undertaking. He thinks specially trained pigeons could eventually be used as, well, actually, photographers."

"*Photographers!*" said Gramma Hoopes. She said it as if certain suspicions she had secretly been harboring about Mr. Bertmann were suddenly being proven true.

"It's an experiment," said Gusta. "But he's paying me to release the pigeon."

"You brought home a *pigeon?*" said Thomas, popping up like a jack-in-the-box from his chair. "Where's the pigeon?"

"Sit down and stay put, silly!" said Josie. "You can't all barrel off looking for the poor pigeon. She'll keel right over and die of fright."

Gusta had a flicker of fear that might be exactly what Nelly would do. All these wild people! With all of their fiery, vivid eyes. She felt like she herself might be just about to keel over.

She took the glasses off, just to have some peace for a moment. Four or five voices chimed in immediately to ask her what she was doing and to tell her to put them back on. It was quite flustering. She put them back on, and all the faces around her became louder-looking again.

Then Clarence started saying in his jokey voice, "How many fingers am I holding up, Gusta?" and there was an unseemly din until Gramma Hoopes actually had to rise up from her chair to quiet them all down.

"Since you're so *powerfully clever,* Clarence," she said, with a voice that could have quarried blocks of marble from a mountainside. "You can go along with Augusta on her errand for Mr. Bertmann."

So that was that. Clarence made a face, but under the glaring eyes of Gramma Hoopes, he followed Gusta into the front hall.

"That's the pigeon? You just carry the pigeon somewhere, and then let her go?"

"More or less," said Gusta. She didn't feel very confident about Clarence and pigeons. He was the one who "couldn't be trusted with eggs," and wasn't a pigeon at least as fragile and valuable as an egg?

They set off up the road that went past Gramma Hoopes's home and then on up Holly Hill into the woods. Gusta had been up the road this far before, of course, but it turned out the road went farther than that.

This was the north-going road. It made Gusta

think: If you walked and you walked and you walked, where would you eventually get to?

And she couldn't help it: she imagined for a moment her father looking up from some oh-so-Canadian table, turning his head her way in happy surprise. *Gusta, my little thingling, are those new glasses you're wearing?*

"Hey, Gusta, be a pal?"

Canada vanished.

Gusta looked over at Clarence, who was kicking at the dirt road and fiddling with a strange-shaped object that her eyes and brain figured out, slowly, must be a slingshot.

"You're just gonna walk a little on this road into the woods, let the silly pigeon go, and walk home, right? You're not gonna wander off and get lost or anything."

Gusta shook her head.

"So you don't need me tagging along, do you? I wanna go knock down some cans we've got stashed over in that field there. When you get home you can say you sent me on to Mr. Bill's or something. All right, then!"

And he skedaddled.

To be honest, Gusta was relieved. Clarence was

such a twitchy sort of boy. Maybe it was just making up stories in her head, but she felt like Nelly gave a pigeon-size sigh of relief when Clarence went loping off with his slingshot.

Pigeons must not like the look of a slingshot one bit, thought Gusta. It must be in their blood not to like slingshots, like fear of snakes and the desire to fly away home.

Now it was just Gusta standing there, and Nelly in the little cage in her hand, and the north-going road, climbing Holly Hill into the deeper, wilder woods.

Papa, thought Gusta.

And she let her feet follow the tug of that road.

⟨ 23 ⟩

The Far Side of the Hill

I t was an exaggeration, honestly, to call the Holly
Hill road a road, if by "road" you meant the usual
thing—a smoothish, widish track that a motorcar
could roll along on, or a bicycle. As the woods thickened around her, rocks seemed to bubble right up to
the surface of the dirt road, so that it was no longer
even slightly smoothish. In fact, in some places it was
really more like scrambling up a dry creek bed than
walking down a road.

The trees came together high above Gusta's
head; they stretched out their bare branches like long,
scratchy-skinned arms as they whispered secrets to
one another.

There was something else out here on Holly Hill: a whole lot of hush.

Gusta wasn't very used to hush, having grown up in noisy places, in cities and (now) in a house absolutely jam-packed with rowdy kids, but she found she liked it. Nelly was quiet in her little cage. The trees kept murmuring in the breeze. Gusta's feet quietly avoided the pointiest rocks and deepest potholes.

Her eyes kept noticing things: the details of the trees, their first buds, their twigs, the white papery trunks of the birches. And then the places where a path would climb off to the left, up the hill, or a mossy old stone wall would loom up in the middle of nowhere.

"Why are there walls in the middle of the woods?" she asked Nelly, and her voice sounded funny out here in such a quiet place.

A little farther down the road, the rocky bits began to wink at her, as if they had streaks of glass or diamond in them. She stopped to take a closer look, and as she did, the quiet of the woods, down past a little bend in the road, was interrupted by the sound of twigs breaking and the rustle of—*wait, what kinds of animals lived in the Maine woods?*

Gusta stood up quickly, thinking alarming, incoherent thoughts about enormous squirrels, deer, *bears*!

But her eyes with their new glasses looked again and saw only a human being—which could have been a little alarming in its own right, of course, but this person wasn't some kind of rugged backwoods hermit with a long beard and two rifles.

This person coming up the woods road was an ordinary, medium-size boy.

A boy who had just seen her and was now waving his hand in her direction.

"Hey, there!" he was calling up the road. "NEW GIRL, Augusta Neubronner, is that really you?"

She recognized the voice right away, though the face the voice was coming from looked rather different than it used to, now that those eyeglass lenses were busy working their detail-etching magic.

It was pretty much the last person you might expect to meet on an empty dirt road over Holly Hill: George Thibodeau, of the Dairy Wars.

He wasn't wearing his schoolgoing clothes. He was dressed in boots and a rough jacket, and he had an old knapsack on his back, and (it was amazing how much information eyes wearing glasses could reach out and grab) a notebook in his hand, as if he were out here to be taking notes on something.

"George Thibodeau," she said, just to state

the obvious and because she was so surprised to see him here.

Had they ever talked to each other at school? Not much, anyway, beyond whatever you say to someone waiting in line behind you at the pencil sharpener.

"Are you out here trapping birds?" asked George as he sped up the last part of the road.

"This is Nelly," said Gusta. "I didn't *trap* her. She's one of Mr. Bertmann's pigeons."

"Mr. Bertmann? The eye doctor man? Why does he need pigeons?"

"They're very clever," said Gusta. "They know how to fly home. He says they are even going to learn how to take photographs, eventually."

She felt embarrassed as soon as she said that, of course. It sounded so much like boasting, and anyway, it didn't explain why Mr. Bertmann *needed* his pigeons.

"He really loves them," she added.

"WHAT did you just say?" said George. Now he was really interested. "Photographs? What? And I didn't know you had glasses. You don't wear them at school, do you?"

"They're completely brand-new," said Gusta. "I'm working for Mr. Bertmann now some to help pay for them. That's why I've got Nelly with me. I'm to carry her into the woods and release her. So she can get used to the new harness. It's part of practicing for his pigeon photography experiment."

"Do you really mean the pigeons are going to take PICTURES?" said George. "Are you kidding? How could that possibly work in a million years?"

Gusta was used to reading people's emotions in a general way, from their voices, from the overall gist of their movements, so the overly specific details in George's face right now—the way his eyes lit up with interest and the way a dent appeared in his left cheek when he grinned—actually overwhelmed her so much that without really meaning to, she pulled her glasses off with her left hand, the one not holding Nelly's cage. And the world calmed down into blurriness all around her.

"Does it all look very different with the glasses on?" said George, somehow more recognizable when blurry.

"I'm in the process of getting used to them," said Gusta, and with as much dignity as she could pretend to possess, she slid the glasses back onto her nose and hooked them back behind her ears. "Because of them being so new. Mr. Bertmann told me to go out walking to get used to the glasses, and to send Nelly back in her harness."

"With the CAMERA!" said George.

"Not yet," said Gusta. "Mr. Bertmann hasn't finished putting the camera together yet. I'm sure it must be a very tricky sort of thing to do, making a camera for a pigeon."

There was a silent moment, and then all of a sudden Gusta found herself asking, "Anyway, I was wondering where this road would go, if you kept walking and walking and walking."

She let her mind's eye imagine the north-going road for a moment, pushing ever deeper into the woods and the wilderness, maybe—who knew?—all the way through the hundreds and hundreds of miles of deep Maine forest to the border of—

But George was already shrugging his shoulders. "Nowhere much. Just up over Holly Hill and down, through the woods. Then it swings back around into town, eventually."

"Oh," said Gusta, disappointed. No Canada, after all. "But it looks so wild up here."

George laughed.

"Hate to break it to you, then, but our own farm's

only about five minutes along the road, when it folds back toward town, over this side of the hill. We're just about neighbors, I guess, the Hoopeses and the Thibodeaus. Though nobody's been keeping up these woods for years and years and years. The Hoopeses, and I mean no offense to you personally, have pretty much let most of the hill go back to scrub. Anyway, follow me. I'll show you where I live."

It was a tiny bruise of a disappointment, to so soon be heading in the opposite direction entirely from Canada. But of course she couldn't explain that to George Thibodeau.

She followed him down the road, which, sure enough, soon turned away from the north and became a little less rocky and then suddenly was much less rugged, and finally spilled them out into a lane running between fenced pastures, with what looked like a very large farm sprawled over the shoulder of the next hill.

There was probably some weather on its way: the farm buildings gleamed very white against the dark sky. *The clear light of trouble*—

"Oh!" said Gusta aloud. She had never seen how specific that *clear light* could be—how it wasn't merely brightness, but etched out all the edges of things. She glanced at George, and of course at that moment he was, like his farm, an extra-crisp, super-definite version of himself.

"You like it?" said George Thibodeau. "Springdale Dairy, the one and only! Best milk in town."

"You forgetting Sharp's Ridge?" said Gusta.

George snorted. "Ha, ha!" he said. "So. Guess you could let the pigeon go from here, couldn't you? Unless you think it'd be too far."

"Nelly's a very good flier," said Gusta. "I guess she'll be fine, even with the harness."

She showed him how it strapped like a funny backward backpack onto Nelly's chest. Nelly didn't fuss about it at all. She seemed proud to be one of the pioneering pigeon photographers of Springdale.

"That's so great!" said George. "All she needs now is a little tiny aviator's cap! She's like the Amelia Earhart of pigeons! You know who Amelia Earhart is, right?"

"Sure," said Gusta. "She got lost in a plane."

"In a Lockheed Model Ten Electra," said George. "She was flying around the world and just disappeared. Over the Pacific Ocean somewhere."

"Okay," said Gusta. "But Nelly isn't going to get lost. Are you, Nelly? You fly home safe, now, before the clouds get here!"

And she tossed Nelly gently into the air.

Gusta and George tipped their heads back, watching the pigeon fly away over the tops of the trees. It felt like a dozen tiny little muscles in Gusta's eyes were being asked to do things they'd never done before. And maybe that was just plain fact, because she had never been able to see birds flying through the air before, and if you think about it, it takes a lot of focusing and refocusing to track something as small as a bird moving through something as vast as the air.

She had to take her glasses off again for a moment and rub her eyes after all that hard work.

"I'll tell you the truth—I'd like to fly," said George. "I hope I will someday. You know they've been building an airport on the other side of town."

"Of course I know that," said Gusta. "We're all writing those essays about it."

"Oh, right," said George. "So are you walking back over the hill now, Augusta?"

"Why won't you call me Gusta?" said Gusta. "Only teachers and my grandmother and Mr. Bertmann call me AU-gusta."

"Only person I know named after a state capital," said George. "Funny sort of name, Augusta."

"Thanks a lot for your opinion," said Gusta. "I didn't give it to myself."

"My name's funny, too. Bet you can't spell it."

"Thibodeau? Maybe I can't."

"Not even Thibodeau. *George*."

"G-E-O-R-G-E," said Gusta right away. "I'm really not sure about Thibodeau, though."

"You messed up even on George," said George. "It's really G-E-O-R-G-E-S, with a silent *S*. That's the French way. But nobody at school knows about the *S*. I bet maybe it's not even on the folder they keep all my teachers' complaints in."

"Oh," said Gusta. "Well, does the silent *S* matter to you?"

He thought it over a while.

"I guess it does a little bit. Is that foolish?"

"So what if it's foolish? If it matters to you, I'll be careful to think it every time I say your name," said Gusta. Seemed like a matter-of-fact sort of thing to her.

That was about the first time Gusta had ever seen Georges Thibodeau run out of words. He stared over at her and said nothing for several seconds, until he gave a little twitch as his inner motor started running again. "You have to get home now, didn't you say?"

"Right. Guess I'd better," said Gusta. "Gramma Hoopes is going to worry if I'm out here too long. Oh, but here's a question: Why is there all this gold in the road here? Or is it diamonds?"

They had reached that part of the road where the rocks sparkled.

"Ha!" said Georges, being very good-natured about the interruption. "Don't you have fool's gold where you come from? You know, mica? When I was little, I thought it really *was* gold. I brought a whole pail of it home once, proud as could be. Did they ever laugh!"

"So it's not actually treasure," said Gusta. "Too bad."

"It's just pretty. If it had been worth anything, people would have dug it out of the road fifty years ago, I bet. Anyway, it's downhill for you from this point. Guess I'll see you Monday. Let me know if you need some more pigeons carried anywhere."

"Sure will," said Gusta. "Thanks."

"And if they really get little CAMERAS, you really HAVE to show me!"

"All right," said Gusta.

And Georges (now forever accompanied by that silent S) waved good-bye and started back the other direction, down toward the pastures and barns of the Springdale Dairy.

❦ 24 ❧

Liberty with Glasses

I t is never too early," said Miss Hatch, "to begin our preparations for the end of the year."

She had a stack of just-collected papers in her hands, which were the class's inky-fresh, hopeful compositions on the theme of "A Vision of America from On High." Miss Hatch squared the corners of the papers and set the pile gently down on her desk.

"Of course, we all hope that the winner of the honor certificate and the cash prize will come from our classroom," she said. "But I want you to know that the writers of the best essays *in this room* will have a reward of their own: they will recite their compositions for an audience as part of our all-school celebration in June."

Polite murmur from the class. All-school glory, though lovely, had a hard time competing with *twenty dollars*, the prize for the best essay in town.

"I am still working out our classroom's contribution to the school performance, which this year is to be a Patriotic Pageant, but I can assure you there will be tableaux celebrating our flag, and several of our greatest heroes portrayed in their moments of glory — we practiced some of these in the fall; do you remember "Washington Crossing the Delaware"? And all the while on a pedestal in the back of the stage, our own Statue of Liberty will stand, holding her torch high, sending her light blazing forth to all the world."

While Miss Hatch assigned historical roles to various members of the class and reminded others of the parts they had played in the fall, Gusta amused herself by reading all the notices and posters on the walls of the room. The classroom seemed a much smaller space, now that she had her glasses. All of those words and pictures and Scottie dogs right there at her figurative fingertips!

". . . And I can think of nothing more suitable than having our new school friend, Augusta Neubronner, playing the important role of Liberty."

There was a sudden silence in the room. Gusta

tore her eyes away from the walls, and looked right up at Miss Hatch with what must have seemed like alarm, because Miss Hatch said soothingly, "It won't be a hard role, Augusta, and I think you'll do beautifully. It will mean standing up high and holding the torch with pride. What, Molly?"

Molly Gowen must have been waving her hand. But now, when Gusta turned around to look, she could see even the littlest of the angry lines at the corners of Molly's mouth. It was overwhelming sometimes, how much a face wanted to tell you.

"Miss Hatch," said Molly. "I think there may be a *small* problem here. *She* can't be our Statue of Liberty. The Statue of Liberty doesn't wear eyeglasses. The Statue of Liberty's supposed to be a symbol of *perfection*, and perfection doesn't mean eyeglasses. Or bad teeth. And anyway, Augusta's probably not even all American, that's what my father says. My father says Neubronner is probably a *German* name. The Statue of Liberty should be a pure American, isn't that so?"

Now, by turning her head Gusta could see both Molly's face and Miss Hatch's face at almost the same time, and both of them contained much more information than she really wanted to have. Molly had those angry, self-righteous edges everywhere, and

Miss Hatch—Miss Hatch was also angry or upset or something, but trying in vain not to let any of it spill into view.

"Molly Gowen," she started. "We have to think—"

That's when Georges Thibodeau not only interrupted, he stood right up from his seat in order to interrupt with fullest effect: "WE ARE GETTING A NEW ELECTRO-PURE PASTEURIZING MACHINE AT THE SPRINGDALE DAIRY!" he said, with his half bellow of a voice.

"Georges!" said Miss Hatch. (Gusta, listening, loyally added the silent S.) "You really must not—"

"WHAT I MEAN IS," said Georges, as stubbornly as a calf making its way up a muddy, muddy field. "I guess being PURE is a fine thing for MILK. But that has nothing to do with PEOPLE."

And then he blinked, almost as if he was surprised to find himself standing up in class and bellowing like that.

"Sorry, Miss Hatch!" he said, and he plopped right down.

ᑖ 25 ᑗ

Not Panama, but Hawaii

S o!" said Josie, whipping another shirt onto her board. "About *Miss Kendall*!"

She was calling them to order. Bess and Gusta grinned at each other. This was why Bess had come home with them, despite it being wash day: to hear the latest high-school news from Josie.

They had the three old ironing boards set up, like a factory line almost, and Gusta soldiered away at her sheets and pillowcases and handkerchiefs— all the simplest things—while Bess and Josie turned the shirts this way and that with their clever, super-competent hands.

They, unlike hapless Gusta, could iron anything, even shirts, without scorching the sleeves or sizzling their own fingers or causing any other sort of damage.

Aunt Marion seemed perplexed, sometimes, by all the things Gusta didn't know.

"I *know* your Mama can iron a shirt!" she said. "I can't imagine why she hasn't trained you up a little better. Never mind; Josie and Bess will teach you, and there's always the sheets."

Even sheets can be scorched if you forget to clip on the iron's jacket, though. Fortunately, Josie's eyes were not only naturally sharp, but seemed to be able to look in about fifteen directions at once. And she could talk a mile a minute at the very same time.

"She told me that thing I found up in the attic isn't a guitar at all. It's called a u-ku-le-le, and it comes from Hawaii," she announced, all grandly. "And Miss Kendall's going to find it some strings."

"So how'd it end up all the way here?" said Bess.

"The old captain, I figure," said Josie. "Well, look. You know how ships are. Ships go absolutely any-wheres. And now we're going to get ourselves ready for the fair! It's perfect—I'll sing and strum the ukulele thing, and you'll play your horn, and Bess will play the—well, Bess, I guess you'll whistle and maybe shake a jar of dried beans around, and we'll have our At-Least-Red-Ribbon Band all ready to go!"

"Oh!" said Bess. "Do you really think we could?"

"Why not?" said Josie. "Ever heard of a band like this? Forest horn, ukulele, and dried beans? No, you have not! So that gives us an edge right there. In big-time show business in New York City, it's always the strange acts that bring in the audience."

Gusta wasn't sure about that, but Josie's confidence was a powerful force. You could probably build actual bridges out of that confidence and walk on them over deadly fire pits and deep ravines.

"I guess we'll have to be actually able to *play* something, if we want to win ribbons," Gusta said.

"Oh, now, of course!" said Josie. "I won't hear any of your worrywart nonsense. Here, fold up these shirts for me, now your sheets are done. We have *ages* to learn how to play. I figure that's the easiest part of the whole thing."

And Gusta couldn't help herself—she put a foot out onto that bridge made of pure confidence, and then she put another foot out, and when she stole a glance over at Bess's face (which also turned out to make all sorts of expressions Gusta hadn't been used to seeing so clearly, before her eyeglasses), she saw that Bess was clambering out onto that bridge, too.

"We'll need a name," said Bess, who seemed ready to leap right the way over to wholehearted adoption of Josie's crazy schemes. "Don't all the good bands have names? There's the Kendall Mills Band here, you know. The ones who always win. And the Glenn Miller Orchestra—I've heard that on the radio."

(At Bess's house they had a radio, but maybe not for much longer, said Mama-Liz, because it had been bought on what they called installment, and who had money for any payments, with Bess's papa so unfairly out of work?)

"We need something catchier," said Josie. "So they aren't expecting the usual whatever, clarinets and stuff."

"The Horn and Ukulele and Bean Jar Orchestra?" suggested Bess.

"Naw," said Josie. "That's too specific. That'll ruin the surprise."

Gusta folded up her pile of shirts and bit her tongue. It seemed to her to be a backward sort of thinking, to worry about a band's name first and only then consider learning to play some actual songs.

"Three Girls Band," said Bess.

Josie groaned.

"Elm Street Band," said Bess.

Josie groaned again.

"Well, that's what we have in common," said Bess

practically. "We all live on Elm Street, and we're all girls. Two of us are cousins. One of us wears eyeglasses. Some of us are more or less orphans."

"Orphans!" said Josie. "That's catchy!"

"Hey," said Bess, pointing with her head over at Gusta. "Not Gusta. Gusta's not an orphan at all, and I'm only half."

Josie raised her eyebrows at Bess—a question mark of an expression. Then she turned to Gusta.

"Now you know I don't mean this in a bad way," said Josie. "But I haven't so much as seen your mama in years and years, and I sure have never seen your papa, and he's gone from the country anyway, and here you are without either one of them. I vote we make you an honorary orphan. Then we're one of us all orphan— that's me; one of us half honorary—that's Bess; and you all honorary. It's perfect! We'll be the Springdale Honorary Orphan Band."

She looked sideways at Gusta and grinned until Gusta had to smile back.

"And I know where we can practice our songs in peace and freedom, too. A nice, quiet place. We'll go out there soon as Miss Kendall fixes up those strings. . . ."

Music and Stone Lambs

So that was how the three girls found themselves walking up the Holly Hill road a few days later, Delphine perched on Josie's shoulders and the bruise-making horn case banging out its usual comments on Gusta's poor legs. Miss Kendall's promise of strings for the ukulele had come true, so Josie said they'd better up and rehearse.

Bess and Josie led the way up another track that angled off from the Holly Hill road.

Another path that probably never gets as far as Canada, thought Gusta, with the secret, sad part of her brain that was always wondering how her papa was doing, and wishing so much that he could find his way home.

Gusta's secret sadness was interrupted by the sounds of a three-year-old whining: Josie had put Delphine down on the ground, but Delphine generally preferred being carried.

"No need to fuss, Delphine. Here we are," said Bess.

Gusta was trying to follow Bess, which meant she almost walked right into the rusted iron fence. It was only knee-high anyway, not the sort of fence you build to keep people out. Just a way of marking out some part of the woods as special. And then she realized that the stones here were not the same wild rocks they saw everywhere in the woods. These had been tamed and shaped by human beings.

In fact, they were gravestones.

Gusta's heart galloped for a second. She hadn't ever been in a cemetery before. She'd just heard about them. But she certainly hadn't expected to find herself tripping over gravestones out in the Maine woods.

"Should we be in here?" she asked. Her knees were feeling rather uncertain about everything, while the horn case weighed down her arm and hand.

"Why not?" said Josie, but from the other side of the fence.

"Of course we should," said Bess. "This is ours."

"What do you mean, ours?"

"Look there," she said. "That stone lamb there? That's for our Uncle Hammett, who died when he was little. Of course I didn't know him when he was alive, but I like his lamb. I'm glad the pretty lamb is right next to Mama. We didn't have the money for another lamb for the baby. Her name was going to be Harriet, but of course she didn't get to use her name very long at all."

"Oh, Bess!" said Gusta. A mama and sister in a cemetery in the woods were farther away even than a papa in the Canadian air army, when you thought of it properly.

Gusta had never noticed this graveyard was even there, walking by on the main dirt road.

"Your mama brought you up to visit then," said Josie. "When Bess's mother passed away. It's coming back to me now. You were very little, and Bess, you were an outright baby. They argued about something, all of them, your mother and Miss Marion and even Mrs. Hoopes. Ha! Hadn't remembered any of that until right just now!"

"Arguing?" said Gusta. "Why would they be arguing?"

Josie shrugged.

"How would I know? I was pretty little myself. Maybe your grandmother didn't so much approve of your father or something—that's usually what makes for arguments. Anyway, I was so young and stupid I got the feeling somehow I had done something to make them all mad, and I went and hid in the attic most of an afternoon, and that's all I recall, which is a lot more than I would have said I remembered about any of it."

There were stumps for sitting on, right out there among the graves. Josie and Bess took two stumps for themselves and pointed to another for Gusta while Delphine floated around them all like a noisy butter-fly. Josie and Bess were cool as cucumbers about being out here among all the dead people, but Gusta wasn't quite so sure.

"You think it's all right?" she said. "Playing music in a graveyard?"

"They're our people!" said Bess. "They'd be glad about the visit!"

So Gusta shrugged and got her French horn out.

They played the songs they all knew, and Bess sometimes whistled and sometimes rattled those dried beans in their jar, and it was quite the joyful racket indeed.

Josie had a voice so sweet that it could make any

old song sound pretty good. She had the gift. And it is never wise to underestimate either a French horn or a jar of dried beans.

Gusta's horn sounded different out here in the woods than it had ever sounded indoors. It sounded like it might be able to send its music a very long distance—like messages carried by the most powerful of pigeons.

If she played a truly beautiful note, she liked to think—an absolutely most perfect note—it might travel very far indeed. Maybe as far as Canada. Maybe as far as the war. Maybe it would never stop traveling, until, as powerful as a wish, it bumped into the one it had been sent after.

❧ 27 ❧

The Airfield

The next pigeon expedition went in an entirely different direction from Holly Hill, and that was thanks to Georges Thibodeau.

It was his obsession with airplanes that caused all the trouble.

Apparently he had spent the days since that Saturday when Gusta walked over Holly Hill thinking and thinking about pigeons and airplanes, and those two thoughts had twined into one larger plan that he pitched to Gusta during the noon recess.

"Hey, Gusta," said Georges. "How's Mr. Bertmann's pigeon camera coming along?"

Gusta thought about that one particular workbench in the corner of Mr. Bertmann's room, the surface covered with tiny little lenses and screwdrivers and ends of wire.

"It's not quite ready, not yet," she said. She felt a certain loyalty toward Mr. Bertmann and his experiments, so she didn't want to say that it was hard to imagine that camera would *ever* be ready.

"Oh," said Georges. His disappointment silenced him for a few seconds, but not longer than that.

"I was thinking of things it would be interesting to see," he said. "I mean, to see from a pigeon camera's point of view. Like airplanes. But we could go anyway. Want to take a look at the new airfield on the other side of town? We could carry a pigeon over that way, right? The pigeons need to practice wearing their camera harness, don't they, even if the camera isn't ready yet? That's what you said before."

In the end his sheer stubborn enthusiasm wore Gusta down, and she found herself walking on past the high school, with Georges carrying the pigeon cage on her right side. Inside the travel cage today was Mabel, who kept standing up and turning a couple of steps to the left or right as they went, as if she were just slightly unsettled in some way.

"It's all right, Mabel," said Gusta. "We're going somewhere new. A labyrinth in the air for you!"

They had to walk to the airfield and then all the way to the other side of it, too, so that Mabel would cross over the airplanes on her way home. And then after all that walk, in fact there were only three planes. They climbed a little hill on the far side and looked at the landing strip there, the way this field had been carved out of the woods on one side and tucked up next to someone's pasture on the other side.

"Pretty wonderful, isn't it?" said Georges happily. "An airport out here?"

Airplanes were probably incapable of disappointing Georges, even when there were only three of them.

"I guess so," said Gusta. She was lying: what she saw was a raw stretch of clearing, a newly paved landing strip, a tractor busily grading more land on the far side, and those three small airplanes. It didn't strike her as "wonderful," exactly. And the breeze was kicking up and getting chilly again. She was worried about Mabel becoming confused in the wind.

"Shall we let her go?" said Gusta. "Here, I'll tuck her into her harness."

When all the tiny buckles had been buckled, Gusta had a generous inspiration.

"Here," she said, holding Mabel out to Georges. "Why don't you let her go? You just say 'Mabel, fly on home!' and give her a little toss into the air—there, like that! Yes!"

Georges made the happy sound of someone who has just become a part of the great unfolding history of pigeon photography.

"Wow!" he said, watching Mabel head out over the airfield and homeward. "Wow! Look at her go! I can't wait until she's carrying an actual, real camera."

Gusta clapped her hands, too. She was extremely proud of those pigeons. It was downright exhilarating to watch them fly.

Then an awful, awful sound interrupted their happy celebration: a voice, scandalous and displeased and (oh, no!) familiar.

"Georges? *Gusta?* What in heaven's name are you two *doing?*"

It was Molly Gowen, breathless from some combination of surprise, suspicion, and having just clambered up the slope to the top of this hillock.

"What are *you* doing here?" said Georges, who seemed to find it hard to maintain a baseline level of calm politeness around Molly Gowen. *"We're* on a walk, and admiring the new airfield. That's a Curtiss-Wright trainer down there, a CW-12."

"It is?" said Molly, furrowing her brow. "How do you know that, anyway?"

"Can't I just be someone who likes planes?" said Georges.

Gusta thought she'd better intervene before these two slipped right into another round of the Dairy Wars, Airfield Edition.

"Hello there, Molly," she said. "Do you like airplanes, too?"

"Not particularly," said Molly. "I'm here because my brother's on the grading crew over there, and we're giving him a ride home in the truck. You know this is potentially a sensitive military site, right? I don't think they want foreigner types hanging out watching them work or anything."

"Oh, for Pete's sake," said Georges. "I AM NOT A FOREIGNER, Molly Gowen!"

"Well, that's what you say. *Thibodeau* sounds pretty foreign to me. And what about her?" said Molly, rudely gesturing at Gusta with her pointed chin. "I keep saying, what kind of name is Neubronner? I hear rumors—"

"RUMORS!" said Georges. "What kind of RUMORS?"

"Never mind," said Gusta, but she could tell it was too late now. Molly and Georges were glaring at each other.

"I've heard Augusta Neubronner spends a lot of time hanging around with that Mr. Bertmann person," said Molly. "Don't you, Gusta? And he's German, for sure. Plenty suspicious, the way he walks around town pretending to be an innocent old loon, but actually carting his stupid, dirty birds everywhere—and what's that there, anyway?"

She was pointing at Mabel's empty cage, and she looked genuinely taken aback.

"That's Mabel's travel cage," said Gusta. "Mabel's a pigeon. She is a very clean pigeon, by the way."

"That cage is empty," said Molly.

"That's because Mabel's flying home," said Gusta. "She'll get there faster than we will."

"She's not stupid, either," said Georges, and Gusta felt two things at once: warm gratitude for his defense of Mabel, who was so truly such a fine pigeon—and also the dread one feels when watching someone go a little too far. "She's a brave explorer, and someday she is going to be able to take actual photographs, so I guess she's about as smart as any pigeon ever was, and probably smarter than—OH, NEVER MIND."

Silence fell on that hill for a moment. The breeze reached through Gusta's hair and tickled her scalp.

"Are you telling me that a gang of *foreigners* is using *specially trained pigeons* to spy on our new Springdale airfield?" asked Molly.

It was so absurd that they gaped at her, which of course she took as confirmation.

"Well!" said Molly. "Well! Wait until I tell them about *this*!"

Who was this *them*, wondered Gusta, feeling somewhat sick to her stomach. How had things managed to go so wrong?

"You go right ahead, Molly Gowen," said Georges. "You go on and shout about it up and down Main Street, if that's what you want. Everybody in Springdale knows who the Thibodeaus are. We are the SPRINGDALE DAIRY! WE were milking cows before Sharp's Ridge even had its first barn. And Gusta's a Hoopes. You know that perfectly well. So just stop going on and on about foreigners."

Molly looked like she would gladly have swatted him, but she shook her fist in his direction instead.

"You think about it yourself, Georges Thibodeau! You shouldn't be messing around airfields without any business being there. And you two really shouldn't be sending German pigeons up in the air to spy, because if you're not foreigners yourselves, you almost are, and if you're Americans, you're acting pretty treasonous, I'd say. And I'd think anyone in Springdale would rather drink loyal, American, Sharp's Ridge milk than whatever questionable foreign milk you Thibodeaus produce—"

"Come on, Georges," said Gusta. "It's getting cold. Let's go. There's no point getting into a fight. Molly, you're taking this all wrong. The pigeon is just flying, not spying."

Danger, danger, her head was telling her. Her heart was pounding, and her feet just wanted to get away from those terrible, angry words.

"You're not getting away with this, you two!" said Molly to their backs, as they scrambled away from her down the little hill. "I'm watching you, and *everybody's* going to be watching you when I tell them what you've been up to. You wait and see."

They walked away, letting that angry voice of hers bounce off their backs like hail: Molly Gowen was a human-shaped bout of bad weather.

"Oof," said Georges eventually, when they were already quite far away. "Ouch."

And there really didn't seem to be anything much better than that to say.

❦ 28 ❧

Hard Times and Greek Myths

Gusta spent the rest of that week braced inwardly for some terrible thing to happen — for Molly's *them* to arrive at the classroom door, maybe, with uniforms on and dark glasses where their human eyes should be, and holding out handcuffs to clap on the wrists of the fifth grade's *almost-foreign spies* — but although Molly sent her quite a number of narrow-eyed, frowning glances, uniformed men did not appear, not Tuesday, not Wednesday, not Thursday, not even Friday.

That Friday Mr. Bertmann sent Gusta home with a pigeon again, and Bess joined them on Elm Street, and the arrival home of two honorary orphans and a pigeon gave Josie ambitious ideas.

"Oh, girls, let's take ourselves out of here!" said Josie, taking her apron off. "Another round of music in the woods! We'll take Delphine, too, Miss Marion — don't you fret."

The days were getting longer. It was truly spring, however chilly the air might mostly be. There would be time enough to get out past the cemetery, play a few songs, let Delphine run around a bit where it wouldn't bother Gramma Hoopes at all, and come home for a slightly late supper. They didn't even have to beg and plead, once Josie had laid out the plan that way. Aunt Marion said, "Oh, yes, please — go, take her, go!"

Josie (with her ukulele), Gusta (with the horn bumping along on one side and Mabel's little travel cage on the other), Bess (with bean jar), and Delphine padding alongside, darting away for a moment and returning ("Chase me!") all convulsed in giggles: four children, several instruments, and a pigeon.

"Parade!" said Delphine, and who could really deny it?

Who knew? Someday maybe there would be actual, real parades in which the Honorary Orphan Band would be striding along, making music.

Because the surprising thing was, they were already sounding better. Almost even . . . *good*. Josie was so clever with her hands and had such a good ear that she could find a strum on the ukulele that sounded good with whatever note from Bess or from Gusta needed a strum.

And shy Bess added two kinds of magic: the rhythm of the bean jar, keeping them all on track, and then at the oddest little pause-y moments in any song, she might even throw in some kind of whistled bird warble, and that was "good as biscuits," said Josie.

Inspired by biscuits, they sang a round of "Angeline the Baker," which sounds about a million times better than you'd think with a French horn kind of pretending to be a high-voiced tuba doing oompahs and a ukulele pretending to be a guitar and a jar of dried beans just bravely being itself, and occasional bird whistles.

Says she can't do hard work
because she is not stout!
She bakes her biscuits every day,
and pours the coffee out!

Angeline the baker,
Angeline I know
Should have married
Angeline just twenty years ago!

They filled the whole woods with that wild music, and Delphine darted around the edges, chuckling and hollering.

"Your poor pigeon!" said Bess, because they had gotten so loud, and so they paused to send Mabel flying home.

"Where'd you learn all this music, anyway, Gusta?" said Josie.

"Well," said Gusta, remembering the men from the union coming through their house, sometimes with their battered guitars. "The people my father worked with, they all knew a lot of songs."

So Gusta taught them all "Hard Times in the Mill," which is almost as catchy as "Angeline the Baker," but a good bit less silly, if you listen to what the words are actually saying:

> *Ain't it enough to break your heart,*
> *Have to work all day, and at night it's dark,*
> *It's hard times in the mill my love,*
> *Hard times in the mill.*

"Well, that's a true enough song," said Bess.

And then they tried "Casey Jones, the Brave Engineer," because Josie liked a song that told a story. And then they played around with a song that would be their very own, and that was pretty fun, too.

"We're going to give those Kendall Mills Band fellows a run for their money for sure, this year!" said Josie. "Ribbons and glory are on their way, girls!" And when Josie believed something, *that* was a parade you could hardly help joining.

"We should play for my papa someday soon," said Bess. "I bet he'd like to hear us."

Oh! Gusta's heart gave a little twist in her chest. All the papas, with all their troubles! If she had only found that Wish—but she hadn't.

"Chase me!" called out Delphine from up the little path a way.

"No chasing," said Josie firmly. "You come on back here now, Delphine."

And Delphine just giggled and ran on into the woods. "Chase, chase, chase!"

"Delphine!"

Any of the boys would have rather been eaten up by lake leeches than face a truly displeased Josie, but from the scruffy trees came the thin ripple of laughter, already sounding surprisingly far away, as if Delphine were changing into a forest creature, an escaping bird, as she danced away.

"Oh, for Pete's sake," said Josie, and the three of

them dropped their instruments and coats in a heap around the empty pigeon cage and went loping off after her.

You would think they would have had that child in hand again in about ten seconds, but Delphine somehow managed not to be found.

At first they were annoyed and amused, and then after a couple of minutes, Gusta found herself feeling very faintly worried.

They split up as they went up the hill, calling out her name: "Delphine! Delphine!"

But there was only the woods, everywhere the woods—and no laughing child.

Maybe she really had turned into a tree, like the poor girls sometimes did in the old Greek myths?

Gusta paused for a moment and listened hard to the woods, but she couldn't hear a trailing giggle anywhere. Nobody was saying, "Chase me!"

Just Josie and Bess, calling that name: "Delphine! Delphine!"

Gusta's heart went *thwomp* and fell into a hole: inside her everything froze for an instant, became still, and terrified, and dark.

How was it possible? How could a child manage to vanish, right there practically before their eyes?

❦ 29 ❧

What Delphine Found

D elphine!" Gusta called out, up the slope of the hill. "Delphine, can you hear us? Oh, please, just say something!"

And, farther away now, she could hear Josie and Bess calling, too.

Where could Delphine have gotten to?

As long as she could hear the others calling, she was pretty sure she herself would not get lost. But she tried to peer closely at the trees and rocks as she went past them, just in case, so she could pick out the strange-shaped ones as markers.

Suddenly she found that she was on a twisted part of the hill, an old, unfamiliar, primeval stretch of woods, facing a rough wall of rock that rose up among all those trees like the gates of an ancient city.

Very much like gates: there was a gap in that rock. And from beyond that gap, as if from very far away, some small person was clicking her tongue and whispering, "Hellooo?"

"Delphine!" Gusta said, and she nearly sobbed with relief when she said it. "Are you in there?"

And quick as a snake, Gusta sidled her way into the dark gap of the rocks.

"Hi! Hi!" Delphine was saying in a small clear echoing voice. "Found the cellar!"

In fact, it sounded just exactly like she really *was* in a cellar.

"Delphine, you stand still now, wherever you've gotten to!" Gusta said to her, trying to sound as stern as Josie. "I'm coming!"

And she pushed her way deeper into the cleft, feeling ahead into the darkness for a small person.

The cleft spilled her suddenly into a space she could not see, but could *feel* opening up all around her.

"Delphine?" she said very quietly, and the sound of that word ran all around that space.

"It's the cellar!" said Delphine from right next to her, and the sound of *her* words also traveled across the blackness of that space and back again.

"I know it feels like a cellar in here," Gusta said

to Delphine. "But I think—I think this must actually be a cave."

Something rustled above their heads.

She grabbed for Delphine in the dark, found her hand.

"We're going back out now. Hush."

Gusta pulled Delphine backward, back the way they had come in, but she did notice her eyes were beginning to adjust to the darkness. It wasn't absolutely pitch-black in here, not really. No. There was some light filtering in from the crack in the rocks behind them. And another crack up ahead and to the right letting just enough light in that really this cave place was not the pit of blackness she had first thought it was. It was a place of shadows and whispering sounds—and a thousand dark leaves hanging from the rock ceiling. Only of course those weren't leaves at all. . . .

"Out *now*," she whispered to Delphine, pulling her very quickly toward that sliver of light.

They were bats.

On the way back down the hill, the girls didn't talk very much, being all shivery still from the thought of what *might* have happened—what had *almost* happened.

Delphine chattered about her adventures for a while, and then let her head bob peacefully against Josie's shoulder.

"Hiding in a cave!" said Josie in wonder. Bess shook her head.

Gusta was trying very hard not to think about Delphine being lost. She tried to think instead about Delphine being found, and about the bats in that surprising cave.

She had seen that cave before.

In the old captain's notebooks.

And what had it said by that picture?

Here I have found treasure. . . .

❧ 30 ❧

Woolen and Worsted

The following Tuesday the girls had more to carry than usual on their walk into town. They were going to follow through on that good idea they'd had in the woods: of playing for Uncle Charlie.

But when they stamped up the frayed porch steps of Bess's house that afternoon, Bess's stepmother met them at the door, looking more worried than usual (if such a thing was possible).

"There's some man here, girls," she said. "Wanted to speak to Charlie. Don't know what it's all about."

"Audience just almost doubled, then!" said Josie cheerfully. "Don't worry, Mrs. Goodman. We don't mind."

But Mama-Liz shook her head in doubt. It wasn't the girls minding that *she* minded, that much seemed obvious.

"What kind of a man, Mama-Liz?" asked Bess. "Do you think he's going to stay a while?"

Bess's stepmother shook her head. "Dunno," she said.

"Then I'll just go on in," said Bess, "and ask Papa whether he still wants us."

"I dunno what the fellow's here about," said Bess's stepmother, stepping to the side so Bess could slip on in through the door. "He's full of all kind of questions, I'll tell you that much."

Questions!

It was never good news, when men showed up to ask questions. All those times when Gusta's papa had been picked up during a strike, when they were waiting for some kind of knock at the door . . .

Fear is such a strange thing. Fear hides in crevices in our brain, just waiting for a chance someday to leap up and grab us and make us want to leave our skins and run away.

"What if it's the police?" she asked.

"Oh, now, Gusta, don't be *ridiculous*!" said Josie.

"Why would we care one single teaspoon's worth of moldy wheat flour who it is in there? Now look—there's Bess back."

"Papa says we should come on in and play, all the same," said Bess to her stepmother, who shrugged and opened the door wider again.

"In you go, then," she said. "All the warm air's about gone from this house already."

Josie, with a slight but audible growl of impatience, dragged Gusta up the steps and through that door.

Gusta blinked as the world came into focus. Even fancy eyeglasses didn't make your eyes adjust any faster to the dark. The room was like a cave, but there were people in it instead of bats. Last time she'd been in this room, she hadn't been able to see the details, like the calendar on the wall—too old and raggedy to be for this year, surely—with a covered bridge in the picture.

There was a second chair dragged right up next to Uncle Charlie's chair, and a man in that chair, leaning toward Uncle Charlie. The sweet, stuffy smell of someone having recently smoked a cigarette hung over everything, thickening the already thick air of that closed-in room.

"Here's quite a crowd!" said the strange man, turning around to look at them. "Who have we here?"

"That's my Bess," said Uncle Charlie, gesturing in Bess's direction. "And her cousin there."

He didn't say anything to explain about Josie, but that didn't bother Josie very much. "We're the Honorary Orphan Band now," she said.

"An orphan band!" said the strange man. "Well, now, how about that!"

"Not real orphans," said Bess in a rush, because of course, there was her own father sitting right there.

"This is quite something," said the strange man, and he turned to Uncle Charlie. "What do you think, Mr. Goodman? All right if I stick around to hear a song or two?"

Who was this fellow? The voice was oddly familiar to Gusta. Maybe it was the rhythm of it. A sort of crispness that reminded her of people she had known (or her parents had known) in New York.

And Uncle Charlie didn't have the air of someone dealing with the cops.

Gusta began to feel just a little less anxious.

"Go on, girls, why don't you?" said Uncle Charlie. "Play us something."

So they got out their instruments and rubbed their hands together to warm them up some, and then they went ahead and played a couple of their songs.

"Not half bad!" said Uncle Charlie when the Honorary Orphan Band looked up shyly after the second song. What's more, he was smiling a little, and that changed something about the shape of his face. Some of the shadows had backed off for a moment. Bess grinned.

The strange man slapped his knee with a surprising amount of enthusiasm.

"Wherever in the world did you girls learn those tunes?" he said. "That surely does beat all! 'Hard Times in the Mill'! They won't believe me when I tell them."

It turned out to be quite satisfying, having an audience.

"Mr. Smith is up from New York," said Uncle Charlie.

Gusta jumped a little. Oh! *Mr. Smith! Up from New York!*

Could it be?

Of course, there were lots of Mr. Smiths in the world. Almost more than any other kind of mister. And a lot of them surely lived in New York. It only made sense.

"Listen, girls, what would you say to earning a little money?" said the enthusiastic Mr. Smith. Now Gusta could hear it in his voice: he was definitely a New Yorker. In fact —

"Sure," said Josie. She said it right away, as if it were the most ordinary and expected sort of thing, to be offered money for playing songs on a ukulele, a French horn, and a jar full of dried beans.

"What do you have in mind?" asked Uncle Charlie with a frown.

"Come play for the big union vote we're holding for the Kendall Mills. It'll be in the town hall — lots of folks to vote. We'll pass the hat and make it worth your while. Five dollars, guaranteed."

And suddenly, just like that, Gusta closed her eyes and was completely confident about which Mr. Smith this Mr. Smith was. It had only taken her this long because her new eyes had so flatly disagreed with her ears. Her eyes saw all the details in that face — the two moles on his cheeks, the angled eyebrows — and the details were all unknown to her. But the voice was not just familiar because it was a New York voice: it was a voice she *knew*.

"You work for the union," said Gusta, and again she missed the warm brassy voice the French horn gave her. Her letter! That's what she was thinking. Her letter must have worked some kind of magic, after all.

"Surely do, little girl," said the man. "Elmer Smith, up from New York City."

Gusta sucked in a lung's worth of air so fast she started coughing.

It was indeed *the* Mr. Elmer Smith. She had sat on a little chair in the corner in his union offices a dozen times, probably. But for a moment there her new eyes had blinded her.

"You all right?" said Elmer Smith. *He* didn't recognize *her*, but then he would never even have glanced over at the Neubronners' quiet, scrawny daughter— why would he? And he wouldn't have guessed in a hundred years that that same quiet, scrawny, forgettable daughter was up in Springdale, Maine, now, living in her grandmother's children's home. He didn't have to blame any fancy new glasses for his misrecognition. He would certainly have misrecognized forgettable Augusta even in Manhattan, without her parents in the picture.

Gusta just nodded. She was fine.

"Mr. Smith got a letter about the Kendall Mills," said Uncle Charlie. "That's why he's come up here."

A satisfied thrill ran up and down Gusta's neck. She couldn't help it: she was holding her breath.

"Not just any old letter," said Mr. Smith. "An appeal from a local workingman, up here in southern Maine. Thought it was Mr. Goodman himself who penned that eloquent appeal, but apparently not. Letter described some lamentable instances of exploitation and injustice, as for instance what has happened to Mr. Goodman here. 'High time we lent the mill workers of Springdale a hand up,' we all said when we read that letter. So up I've come, to support the fine work of the Federation of Woolen and Worsted Workers and to organize our brothers and sisters in the mills and the shoe factories. And Saturday in two weeks, it'll be the big vote. Can't waste time now. There's a race in this country, between the war, you know, and the rights of the Working Man."

"What do you mean by that?" said Uncle Charlie. "We're not at war."

"Not yet, we're not," said Mr. Smith. "But they're already using it as an excuse for all kinds of mischief. Look how they've been trying to nab that old crusader Harry Bridges! They passed a whole law just to try to bring him down and get him deported."

Oh, yes, thought Gusta. *Oh, yes. The Smith Act.*

Not the same Smith as Mr. Smith from New York.

She remembered her father's voice, the tension in

his shoulders, the way he punched one tense fist into the tense palm of his other hand. "There it is! They're coming after us for sure. They're after Harry Bridges, and they'll be after me. Alien Registration Act! Smith Act! Ha! They can call it whatever they want, but they're not really worried about Nazi spies — they're worried that people might start organizing in their factories. They'll do anything they can to deport us organizers. That's all that Smith Act is really about: it's about how much they want us *gone*."

They were going to charge August Neubronner with being an *alien* and a *Communist*, that's what he had said, and they changed the laws so that they could deport you, if you had *ever* been in some too-revolutionary group. Look at how they kept trying to deport that courageous Harry Bridges, who had come all the way from Australia to help the dockworkers of San Francisco get a fairer deal! At least being sent back to Australia was better than being sent right back into the gnashing teeth of Germany.

That was what her papa had said.

But Josie had already headed back to the crux of the matter. "Five dollars, you said, Mr. Smith?" she said. "Sure thing, we'll be there. I mean, if it's all right with you, Mr. Goodman, of course."

Josie had almost forgotten to add that last bit in her enthusiasm.

"Will there be any trouble?" said Uncle Charlie. "I don't want my Bess mixed up in any trouble."

Mr. Elmer Smith smiled. "Everything's as legal as legal can be," he said cheerfully. "Shouldn't be a stitch of trouble. You come along and see for yourself."

"But Charlie . . ." said Mama-Liz.

Her worries didn't have a chance, though, up against the confidence of Mr. Elmer Smith, or the magic of the words *five dollars*.

Five dollars was to Uncle Charlie what a ribbon at the fair would be to Gramma Hoopes: something real.

～ 31 ～

The Lighthouse

It was a Saturday in May. By decree of Gramma Hoopes, it was also Potato Day, 1941.

Gramma Hoopes had consulted the almanac and had poked an inquisitive finger into the soil of the kitchen garden, and her voice was law, in the area of potatoes. Uncle Jay drove the tractor over on Thursday and plowed up an acre's worth of the kitchen garden, ready for planting; then he raked it smooth with the harrow, and after school Thursday and Friday, the older children started hoeing the earth into proper rows, to get a bit of a lead on Saturday's planting.

It was all pretty hard work, but the boys were excited. They liked potatoes, and they liked doing something different with their Saturday (the uncles would have to do without their help for a day), and they really, really liked the early morning pancakes and bacon that Gramma Hoopes considered essential fuel for potato planting.

You didn't grow potatoes from seeds, like other plants. You started off the new potatoes with pieces of old potato. Bess showed Gusta how to cut the potatoes into useful chunks, not too big and not too small, each with not too many sides and — most important — an eye.

"Don't mangle them!" said Bess, watching Gusta early in the day. "That's the main thing. They won't grow right if the cuts aren't clean. It's just like people — Mama-Liz says ragged wounds always heal slower —"

"Bess, ick!" said Gusta, whose knife would never be able to keep up with Bess's, no matter what. "Don't you go making me think of them as little people! These are just potatoes."

"Well," said Bess reasonably, "I'm sure that even potatoes don't want to be mangled."

Gusta couldn't help thinking about all the ways wounds could turn out to be ragged — like Uncle Charlie's mangled hand. He had been mangled, all right. Not all damage can be fixed, but maybe some can. . . .

"Grow strong, little potatoes!" Bess was saying. "Be brave and grow!"

When the potatoes were all safely in the ground — except for the traditional scalloped potatoes, which were all safely tucked into the many bellies of the Hoopes Home boarders — Gramma Hoopes declared a general period of repose, meaning naps for the littlest (Delphine) and the oldest (Gramma and Aunt Marion), and either absence or utter quiet for everyone else. Bess went walking home, to see whether Mama-Liz needed anything from her. The older boys trickled off in various directions; Gusta caught a glimpse of Larry lugging a book out the back door, to go do some reading in the cozy warmth of the pullet house. Josie did the dishes, and then fell uncharacteristically asleep in a big chair in the front room.

Gusta could hear the old clock ticking away in the hall, a sound accompanied only by some light snoring from the direction of her gramma's room.

She couldn't help it — she found herself wondering where her papa might be, just at that very moment. In a jail cell somewhere? In an airplane, flying toward danger? She had looked and looked and looked, and found no Wish in this house to save him. And was her mother at work right now, or sitting in a chair and wondering where her August and Augusta were? It made Gusta feel raw and off-kilter, not knowing any of these things. It was like a great knife had come down out of the sky and hacked their family into pieces. *Ragged wounds heal slower.* That was probably true — about people and potatoes both.

Gusta shook her head, trying to get out of that dark space.

It was so odd to be the only one awake and alert in that house — so entirely peculiar to be standing there in the middle of silence, when there was never silence at the Hoopes Home — that it made her feel quite odd indeed. Nervous, maybe, even. She remembered the fairy tale about the palace put under a sleeping spell for a hundred years. And then her mind jumped nervously to another place where every creature was more or less sleeping under a spell: that cave filled with bats, up on Holly Hill.

What had the old sea captain called it in his notebooks? A *hibernaculum.* Which must mean: a place where things hibernated. And then he had said something else, hadn't he? *Here I have found treasure.*

The old captain had said that! In his notebook! In ink!

She hadn't seen anything other than shadowy

bats, when she had stumbled into that cave, but of course she had been distracted then by the worry of finding Delphine.

It wasn't likely, but it was at least a teeny, tiny bit possible, wasn't it, that *treasure* might mean an actual chest of jewels and gold?

Or maybe even (if he had gotten confused later, when he started talking about those *boxes on shelves*) a Wish?

And so, with a shiver, she opened the front door and slipped out onto the Holly Hill road.

Outside there was a faint wash of green in the trees, the buds busy turning themselves into young leaves. And birds occasionally calling out to one another, probably gossiping about the latest trends in nest building or something.

Gusta walked briskly up the hill, waking up as she went. It didn't take her very long to get to the cemetery. The road was a lot shorter without a horn weighing you down—or a pigeon cage.

But the bat cave turned out not to be such an easy place to find, even when you had been there once.

Behind the little cemetery, Gusta did pick up that thin track of a path leading up the hill. What she wasn't entirely sure about, though, was where she (following Delphine) had left the path and stumbled into that wrinkle's worth of wildness, where the cave was tucked away so cleverly into the rocks of the hill. She decided to be systematic about it, to keep following this path as far as it went, just to see where it led to, and then to turn around and walk back down slowly, trying to guess where you might want to angle around to the left, if you were looking for bats in caves.

The path climbed the hill in a leisurely way, sometimes threatening to fade out and now and then forking (she went uphill at forks) and finally curling around under what must be almost the very top of Holly Hill and suddenly spilling Gusta out onto a sunny lip of grass and rock, on the side of the hill, overlooking endless rolling tops of trees. Probably this lip was not far from the summit proper, but at that moment Gusta had no thoughts to spare about the top of the hill or the side of the hill or really anything about the topography of the hill, because what she was staring at, right there in front of her, was, instead of a cave full of bats, perhaps the very most opposite thing to a cave full of bats: a *lighthouse*.

The sea captain's lighthouse! She recognized it instantly from the picture in his notebook. She couldn't wait to tell Josie she had actually found it.

Real lighthouses were tall, sturdy, massive, giant things, but this one was remarkably short and squat, a miniature (vertically) of a lighthouse. The opposite of a giant. For another thing, the storybook lighthouses were always perched on rocks overlooking the crashing waves of an angry sea, and this one looked out over the rolling Maine woods. Because of the rocky lip here, you could see a long way, but nowhere were there waves and seagulls. So that was strange.

And yet, it was clearly a lighthouse all the same. The squat tower part tapered as it rose. A narrow set of steps led up about seven feet or so, where there was a platform with a clever iron railing around it, and a black cap of a roof on top.

Carved into the stone tower on the side facing the path were three very large words, *The Beckon Beacon*, and then four lines of smaller words, harder to see. They had been carved in very deep, and someone had painted them black at some point, but many years of weather had worn them down. By using her miraculously sharp new eyes—and by running the tips of her fingers over the carved letters—Gusta figured out that the poem went something like this:

> *A lighthouse cries out "Danger,"*
> *And sometimes it calls us home.*

True hearts be a beacon that beckons
to wanderers, wherever they roam.

It would win no prizes for poetry, but Gusta's heart was pounding in her chest.

Why would a person build a lighthouse so very far from the sea?

Gusta climbed up the very steep steps and swung herself onto the platform there, where in any ordinary lighthouse you might expect a light. There was no light here, but there was a thick old glass vase, holding the place of that light, and in that vase were what looked like little scraps of paper, the occasional dried flower, and a heap of glinting rocks, brought up, seemed like, from the dirt road through the woods.

She was still in her scientific explorer mode as she sent a hand reaching into the vase. The first couple of pieces of paper were so old that whatever writing they had on them was completely faded, and then the third and the fourth both had the same two words on them: *Come home.*

And that was when Gusta's conscience smote her, and she saw that she was reading the longings that had been secretly held in other people's hearts. She ceased to be a scientific explorer and let the pieces of paper fall back into the vase with all those shiny rocks.

She couldn't help feeling that she had just narrowly dodged becoming a much worse sort of person than she wanted to be.

And the sun was sinking in the sky, so the message might as well have been for her: *Come home.*

She wasn't sure anymore what those words actually meant—where home was or whether to get there was a matter of coming or going—but before she could remember how home-less she was, she was already hurrying back down the hill, toward the big yellow farmhouse on the corner of Hoopes and Elm.

❦ 32 ❧

The Honorary Orphan Band

For a few days it looked like the inaugural performance of the Orphan Band on the great occasion of the Kendall Mills union vote would not happen after all. Uncle Charlie didn't feel up to attending an event where there would be so many reminders of his awful days at the mills after the mangling of his arm. And he was adamant that without someone along to look out for her, his daughter, Bess, was certainly not going to be heading off to any town hall for any union election. No, sir.

Josie tried to talk Uncle Charlie into seeing it her way, which was that five dollars was a lot of money, and she, Josie, was all the protection Bess or Gusta needed to have.

Uncle Charlie shook his head: still no.

Then when Gusta was at Mr. Bertmann's workshop the next afternoon, keeping track of the results of some would-be Air Cadets' eye exams, a small miracle happened.

The last of the would-be cadets had banged the door shut behind him, and Gusta was checking over the numbers she'd written in the big Air Cadet notebook, when she thought about those five dollars Mr. Elmer Smith had promised them, and how that would have been the equivalent of nearly *seventeen whole hours* of work for Mr. Bertmann, and a small sigh had escaped her.

"What is wrong, child?" said Mr. Bertmann.

Gusta did her best to explain. They had formed a band, they had learned their songs, and now Mr. Elmer Smith from New York City wanted them to perform, but Uncle Charlie said without a chaperone, no, et cetera.

Mr. Bertmann listened, and then waved his hand in the air as if calling all the pigeons in the world to a meeting.

"Well, this is a situation of great simplicity!" he said. "*I* will come with you and be your chaperone! Any other action, child, would be unworthy."

So on the day of the union election, and with

Uncle Charlie's relieved approval, the three members of the Honorary Orphan Band swung past Mr. Bertmann's workshop on the way to the town hall. He had an umbrella with him, which he was using as a walking stick.

"So I am ready for any weather," he said, even though, to look at the sky that day, you would have said the weather would surely be fine.

By the time they got to the town hall (which itself was an elegant old wooden building), there was already a crowd of men flowing in through the doors. The girls, being distinctly shorter than the rest of the crowd— and also distinctly more weighed down by lumpy objects, like for instance the French horn—found themselves hanging back for a moment, feeling shy.

"Probably that Mr. Smith didn't really mean to hire *us*," said Bess in a whisper.

"Now, really, Bess!" Gusta felt a responsibility for boldness settling down on her shoulders. After all, who had been to a hundred union meetings in her day, starting in merest babyhood? Augusta Hoopes Neubronner, that was who. She stood very straight and looked like she knew what she was about. "Follow me," she said. "What we need to do is go in and find that Mr. Elmer Smith. The union man."

And she charged up the stairs to the town hall door. At the door she noted with satisfaction that the girls and Mr. Bertmann were still right at her heels.

There were a lot of staring happening, of course. It was still an open question for Gusta, whether staring was worse *without* glasses, when it can sometimes feel like the whole universe is staring at you without letting you see it stare, or *with* glasses, when every last detail of every single pair of staring eyes demands to be noticed and counted. Now, though, to set a good example for the other girls, she absolutely forced herself to ignore those stares.

"This way, this way," she kept saying. The union man would be up at the front of the hall, would he not? There was a table set up there, and up above the table, set apart from the main level of the hall by a short set of steps, was—oh, Lord—a stage.

And she had been right, of course: Mr. Smith was at that table. He came bounding over to them as soon as he saw them, shook everyone's hand, and said he was pleased as could be that they had come out this afternoon to help him with this meeting.

"I'll bore them for a little while with a bit of speechifying," said Mr. Smith, "and then we'll bring you folks on to wake us all up again. Sound like a plan?"

Mr. Smith found them a spot to wait near the steps that led—oh, Lord—up to the stage, and the girls got their instruments ready and tried not to catch one another's eyes.

They didn't listen particularly closely to Mr. Elmer Smith's speech about the benefits that would accrue from joining the Federation of Woolen and Worsted Workers. Gusta, of course, had heard speeches of this sort many times over. She thought Mr. Elmer Smith seemed to be doing a pretty decent job with the basic pattern of such talks, but she was distracted by how dry her lips were getting. She kept licking her lips, and then remembering all over again to stand tall. The others were quiet, too. Josie probably had other, bigger things on her mind still—and, to judge from the unique aura of her nervousness, might even be actually *looking forward*, at least a little, to performing. Josie was like that. And Bess was emitting a faint hiss-and-crackle, like one of those rattlesnakes they have out in the West: it was her jar of dried beans, in her trembling hand.

Then Mr. Elmer Smith paused and cleared his throat. "And now, friends, while you cast your vote right here in this free election supervised by the fine people of the National Labor Relations Board, we are all going to be entertained with a few tunes from the struggle, by your own homegrown talent, the Honorary Orphan Band of Springdale, Maine!"

That was their signal.

The steps —

oh, Lord!—

THE STAGE.

"Pretend we're just out practicing in the woods," said Gusta to Bess. It was perhaps the stupidest thing she had ever said. No place was ever less like the Maine woods than this oh-so-crowded hall.

"And be loud," added Josie more practically. "This is a big place. We better be loud."

"I will be right here with my umbrella!" said Mr. Bertmann, as if that were a comforting piece of information. And in fact, it kind of was.

Afterward Gusta couldn't even remember how they had managed to do it, but they had. They played their songs, all five of them. The crowd of faces out there — the crowd that had started off looking so curious, distant, and amused—warmed up and started smiling different, brighter, nicer smiles. Applauded after each song. Why, by the third song, there were actually some cheers and shouts. The fifth song was "Hard Times in the Mill," and the cheering was so loud and insistent, they had to sing it over again right then and there. It was a miracle—it was amazing—Mr. Elmer Smith was coming up the steps to the stage right now, the hugest of grins running right across his face—

And then a ruckus interrupted.

There seemed to be an upset rumble growing around the door of the hall, back over the heads of the crowd. The sound of a human thunderstorm, still off beyond the horizon. Angry words being exchanged, like the collisions of overheated clouds.

"What's going on?" said Mr. Bertmann to the men around him. He sounded rather alarmed. Then he called up to Mr. Elmer Smith: "I thought you assured us there would be no trouble!"

"There oughtn't have been any trouble," said Elmer Smith, the light of battle in his eyes. "We've given them no *reason* for trouble. But you know how local authorities sometimes are."

"They're complaining about the band!" said someone in the crowd. And indeed, they could hear now some of the angry shouts from the opposite side of the hall, something along the lines of, "Is this an election or a circus?"

Mr. Bertmann, surprisingly nimble for a man of his age, sprang up onto the stage, with Gusta's case, his umbrella, and their coats in his hands.

"Ach," said Mr. Bertmann. "Come quickly, quickly, you girls. There must surely be a back door. This way . . ."

Gusta had to give Josie, whose face glowed with the fascination as she eyed the brewing trouble, a sharp tug to start her moving in the right direction. "Come *on!*" she said to Josie. Gusta had heard a lot of stories about meetings that went wrong. "We'd better get Bess out of here!"

That was clever thinking on Gusta's part. Josie blinked and grabbed Bess's hand, and with Mr. Bertmann urging them on, they all made a break for the back door.

Which turned out to exist, which was a good thing.

But which, perhaps less fortunately, was already occupied by one of the sheriff's deputies.

"Hold on, kids! What have we here? And who are you, grandpa?"

"My name is Bertmann, and these girls were innocently playing folk songs. I don't know what has gone wrong here, but I'm sure you'll agree it's time we get these children well away from this place, if there's going to be any trouble."

"We had a tip-off there might be some incendiary political statements being made in this venue," said the sheriff's deputy. "Under the guise of a fair and neutral election. Thought we'd better come take a look. Nothing wrong with legal organizing, of course, but I hear some of these outside men may have links to the Communist Party, and we can't have that. There's been some ruckus recently, ever since that fellow, August Neu—"

Then he yelped, because the horn had slipped right out of Gusta's hands and caught him—*bang*—on his toe. It was partly accidental: Gusta had been aiming for her own toe, but the horn had jumped like it had a mind of its own.

"Oh, I'm sorry, I'm so sorry, oh, please, please, Mr. Bertmann, let's go home!" she cried out, as if it were the horn's misbehavior making her so upset, and not the name of her own father starting to slip out of the mouth of the sheriff's deputy.

Josie and Bess were staring at her because she wasn't behaving like herself. But she was desperate to get out of there.

"What you got in that case, girl? Bricks?" said the sheriff's deputy grumpily. "Oh, now, don't cry. I'm all right. I'll just take this Mr. Bertmann's name down, official-like, and then you're free to go."

He had Mr. Bertmann spell it out for him: M-A-X B-E-R-T-M-A-N-N. And then he did let them go.

But Mr. Bertmann was shaking so hard that when they were only a little bit away from the town hall, he had to sit on someone's front steps, just for a moment, to pull himself together.

"Don't be ill!" said Gusta, trying to fan more air into his pale face, because she'd seen someone do that sometime, perhaps in a moving picture. "Please be all right, Mr. Bertmann. I'm so sorry."

"It is I who am sorry," said Mr. Bertmann. "I should have guessed there might be trouble. There, there, there, I am feeling better now."

He climbed back to his feet.

"I am better now," he said again, though he still seemed a little wobbly. "Don't you worry about me, dear girls. They took me by surprise, asking for my name that way. It reminded me of bad things, else-where and long ago. But I am better now. It is all bet-ter. Let's go."

They went, but they didn't feel as though every-thing were all better. It felt as though a shadow had fallen across them and chilled their hearts.

"And we didn't even get our five dollars!" said Josie, shaking her head. "Well, all I can say is, better not breathe a word of this to Mrs. Hoopes, girls! Not a word!"

And the heaviness inside Gusta, where all the secrets festered, thickened and increased.

ఇ 33 ఏ

Molly and the Bad Dog

I t was a beautiful afternoon, and Gusta was walking home from Springdale High School by a different-from-usual route.

Any route home from the high school was going to be a somewhat-different-from-usual route, of course, because Gusta didn't belong at the high school at all, being only a fifth-grader at Jefferson Elementary, up the road. But this afternoon, after school, she had had a new and thrilling experience: she had come over to the high school with her French horn, in order to rehearse with the very grown-up kids in the string orchestra.

Miss Kendall had given a melodious and heartfelt little speech before they started playing.

"My dear musicians, I want you to meet Augusta, who is going to be our French horn soloist. She is a guest artist for us, visiting from Jefferson Elementary School. Augusta, dear, are you ready?"

Gusta nodded, while all the high-school students gaped at her. They did nothing worse than gape because they all loved Miss Kendall so, but she could guess the kinds of things they must be thinking. If Miss Kendall wanted to bring in an elementary-school baby to play the French horn, then, well, they were willing to see how it went. Plenty of time for high-school sarcasm later, if the baby messed everything up.

Miss Kendall was smiling at Gusta, a warm smile that was like having a lovely quilt draped over your shoulders by someone who would care about you no matter how many notes you might drop, under the pressure of having to play the French horn in front of a room's worth of high-school musicians.

"It is completely normal to be nervous, Augusta!" she said, and then she turned her head to the string players. "What have we learned to call our nervousness, musicians?"

"Anticipation!" said the orchestra, all at once.

"That's right," said Miss Kendall. "Anticipation.

We are all anticipating a lovely performance, and we are all so very glad you are here."

And under that kind of encouragement, how could the rehearsal go but wonderfully well? The high-school students (who were so surprised they actually applauded her after her solo) sent Gusta off afterward in a happy cloud of good feeling.

Which was why Gusta decided to take the slightly unusual road home. She wanted to stretch out the sweetness of this moment for a while, and replay it in her memories a few extra times before returning to the everyday Hoopes Home hubbub.

She let herself be a little careless in her wandering. If she arrived home a little later than she would have otherwise, that didn't seem like such a terrible thing. And the day was so pleasant, and her heart, for a change, was so floaty and glad.

Then there was a bossy *ding-ding-ding* behind her, and she turned to find a beautiful green Schwinn bicycle catching up to her. She had to jump to the side of the road to make room for it — and as she jumped she saw that the person riding that bicycle was none other than Molly Gowen.

It figured.

What a beautiful bicycle she was on, though! It was still new enough to be shiny. Even Gusta, who would never in a hundred years have dreamed of getting on a bicycle when she lived in speedy, dangerous, blurry New York City — even Gusta felt a momentary pang of jealousy when Molly Gowen floated by on her brand-new Schwinn.

About five seconds after Molly flew around the next corner, however, there came a series of disturbing sounds:

The bark of a dog that was clearly a big fellow who meant business;

A shout from Molly and a screeching of bike tires;

Another shout from Molly, this time as part of a terrible chord of crashing noises;

And more barking from the dog.

It was enough to make a person want to run very fast in the other direction, but Gusta overcame that urge and ran forward instead, to see what had happened.

She came around the bend and saw a sorry sight: Molly Gowen on the ground, the bicycle nearby and not nearly as straight and sleek looking as it had been just ten seconds before, and a big black dog barking furiously at Molly, as if berating her for having the gall to fall off her bike in front of the dog's particular territory.

Gusta knew that showing fear (which Molly was presently in the midst of doing) was the wrong way to manage dogs. Her mother had told her that several times, when they had run into crabby dogs in New York parks or on the outskirts of the New England mill towns where they had lived before New York. So Gusta swallowed her own fear and walked forward, trying to look confident and large.

"GO HOME," she said in her deepest, most confident voice, to that dog. "YOU. GO. HOME!"

And maybe it was her confident voice, and maybe it was because there were suddenly two girls to contend with, instead of one frightened one, and maybe it was just that the black dog had never seen anything as odd-looking as a French horn case before, but it blinked, backed off, and then turned tail and ran. Thank goodness!

"Oh, gosh," said Molly, pushing herself up from the ground to a sitting position. "Oh, gosh, Gusta, how did you even do that? Oh, I just *hate* dogs!"

"Are you okay?" said Gusta. "Here, let me help you up. Can you stand?"

"I'm all right," said Molly. Her knees were a mess,

and her palms were scraped up, too. "But oh, what am I going to tell Daddy about my bicycle?"

The girls looked at the bicycle. One of the wheels was bent out of shape, and its gorgeous, shiny green fenders were scratched up. It was no longer the proud vehicle that had swooped past Gusta a minute before.

"I bet someone can repair it," said Gusta, but she couldn't manage the same degree of confidence she had wielded in the face of that dog. "It's really just that one wheel that's badly banged up."

"I was so stupid," said Molly. "I let that dog spook me. Daddy gets so mad when I'm scared of dogs. Or cows."

She limped over to the corpse of the bicycle.

"Here, I'll get that," said Gusta. Who would ever have thought in a thousand years that she would find herself feeling sorry for Molly Gowen? "Is your ankle twisted, too?"

"Yep, guess it is," said Molly. She winced. "Gosh. Just because of that dog."

And she shook her curly hair as she watched Gusta pick up the bicycle, battered and twisted.

"Look," said Gusta. "Where do you live? I can help you get home."

"We're way over the other side of the main road," said Molly, trying a few unsteady steps. "It's pretty far."

"All right, don't worry. We can get you to Gramma Hoopes's house, and then maybe one of the uncles can give you a lift home in the truck."

Because now that Gusta had looked around and taken stock, she knew where they were. They weren't far from the place where Chestnut Street ran into Elm Street. Josie had always said that Chestnut Street had a bad dog.

She managed to fit the horn case into the bicycle's basket and figured she could wheel the thing along, mostly on its good wheel. Molly would have to hobble, but at least she wouldn't have to hobble too terribly far.

"So you like milk, but you're afraid of cows?" said Gusta. She was really just trying to make conversation, because otherwise helping someone with a twisted ankle limp even only half a mile can feel endless.

Molly looked over suspiciously.

"You mustn't tell anyone," she said. "They'd laugh and tease, just like Daddy and Byron always laugh. You can't be part of the family that runs the Sharp's Ridge Dairy and be afraid of cows. It's an awful shame. It's practically un-American."

Gusta figured Byron must be her brother.

"Anyway, dogs are much worse than cows," Molly said. "They come jumping out at you and have sharp teeth. It's just that cows are so big."

"I know it," said Gusta. "I'm not really fond of cows, either, but then I didn't grow up on a farm."

"Miss Hatch says you came here from New York City, but I've been wondering about that. My Daddy says with that name you have, you might have come from Germany," said Molly. "He says we have to be really cautious these days, with all the countries over in Europe fighting each other and aliens everywhere."

The previous version of Gusta would probably not have said anything much in response to this: she would have kept her eyes down and limited her voice to a mumble and felt bad later about all that hiding. But Gusta was tired of always covering up what she thought about things. It didn't seem to be what a brave and truthful person should do *in the light of trouble.*

"Honestly, Molly Gowen," she said, stopping short. "I don't know why you always have to be talking about aliens that way. Shouldn't what a person *does* matter more than where he came from? And just look at what I'm doing now: I'm wheeling your poor broken bike to my own grandmother's house, down Elm

Street. Right? And I think you know that my Gramma Hoopes is not any kind of alien from anywhere."

"Of course she's not," said Molly, who, like the bad dog, found it very hard to leave things once she had gotten hold of them. "Not your grandmother. But what about your father nobody knows, with that funny name? Rumor is *he's* German. Why wouldn't I worry about that? Have you heard what the Germans have been doing? They're invading all sorts of countries over there! Only makes sense that we have to be careful. That's all. I'm just trying to be careful. We don't want Nazis in Springdale. It's scary thinking people are hiding here in town, and we don't even know who they really are. I'd think anyone would understand that."

Some conversations are like two people picking their way toward each other across a swamp. Gusta took a cautious step, and then another.

"Well, now, look," she said, as she and Molly wobbled and hobbled down Elm Street. "Even if my papa came here from Germany, haven't you ever thought for one minute that some people might leave Germany *because* they don't agree with what the Nazis are doing? Haven't you thought for a moment how dangerous it would be, to be someone who disagrees with what the Nazis think? If someone like my father put his foot into Germany, you know what they would do? They would lock him up! And then they would probably kill him."

Gusta had to stop and gulp there. She couldn't help thinking about how her father had been running toward Canada because, if the Americans captured him and put him on trial like they were threatening to do, they might actually have decided to deport him to Germany, where all the terrible things she had just said aloud might actually happen. And she found it all overwhelming, when stated aloud that way.

She wished she knew: Had he been captured, back on that awful day in Portland? Was he safely in Canada? Was he off fighting the European war? Where, oh where was he?

"You don't have to get so upset," said Molly.

"I'm only upset because it's upsetting," said Gusta. "I'm just saying, that it's not *where you come from* that determines *who you are*. Right? Think about it. You're from a dairy farm, but you don't like cows."

There was a significant pause.

"Well, but," said Molly, "we still have to be careful. And at least our cows are American cows."

And Gusta couldn't quite tell whether or not

Molly was kidding. They were right in front of the Hoopes Home now, at least. Thank goodness.

"Gusta," said Molly, grabbing her arm. "Promise you won't tell anyone how this accident happened. Promise you won't tell. I don't want them thinking I'm afraid of dogs."

At least this secret was pretty small.

Gusta looked into Molly's eyes, and for a miraculous moment she and Molly Gowen, despite everything, understood each other.

"*Or cows,*" they both said. Secret shared.

Courage and Disaster

One morning Bess's usually cheerful face had all the cheerfulness simply ironed right out of it. Josie didn't even notice, she was so full of chatter about the spring concert—which was already *tomorrow!*—but Gusta kept stealing glances at her quiet cousin, and there was really no doubt: something was wrong.

Bess waited until Josie had gone on to the high school, and then she tugged Gusta to one side.

She said, "That man from the union came by again yesterday. You know, they got voted in at that election we had to run away from."

"Oh?" said Gusta. "That's good, right? What did he say about helping your papa?"

"That's the problem," said Bess. "He said he didn't think they could do anything for him. My papa's not working at the mills now, right? So he's not covered by anything. That Mr. Smith said the union'll be helping future Charlie Goodmans, but that's no good for us now, is it? And now my papa's sad and sick again. He didn't talk this morning. Didn't say a single word."

"Oh, no," said Gusta. Her heart sank and sank and sank, right to the bottom of the deep blue sea.

Because in the stories her heart had been telling her, the union wasn't just supposed to come in and save Uncle Charlie's hand—it was supposed to save Gusta's horn from having to save Uncle Charlie's hand.

"You think he's getting bad again? As bad as he was before?"

"Maybe worse," said Bess, and then she stopped in her tracks and grabbed Gusta by the wrist. "What can we do, Gusta?"

Oh, that went right through Gusta's drowning heart. It was a call: she had to help.

Her well of good ideas was pretty close to dry, however. And at the bottom of that well was the one thing she knew was worth enough, in all its brassy wonder, to pay for Uncle Charlie's operation. To fix his wounded hand. If she had to, she would reach all the way down into that well and do the hard but necessary thing. If she had to, yes, her voice would have to go.

That thought, however, made her heart tear into messy little pieces.

So all that day Gusta tried to think of something—something that wasn't the obvious thing, which was going to Miss Kendall and offering to sell her the French horn after all.

While Miss Hatch was explaining the intricacies of adding fractions again, Gusta's mind went around and around the loop: Uncle Charlie—Miss Kendall—the horn. Uncle Charlie—Miss Kendall—the horn. Charlie—Kendall—horn. Charlie—Kendall—

And then she found herself having a wild and desperate idea: What if she tried to go right to the source of the trouble?

Miss Kendall was such a good egg; could her brother be so absolutely, putridly rotten? If he was faced with the Right Thing to Do, would he really refuse to do it?

And if Mr. Kendall could be persuaded to do the right thing, then Uncle Charlie's hand and the horn might both be all right.

Gusta dragged Bess to the side at the end of the day and waved the boys on home without them.

"Listen," she said. "You don't have to come with me, but here's what I'm going to do. I'm going down to the mills this afternoon. I'm going to have a word with that Mr. Kendall fellow himself."

"No!" said Bess. Her eyes were wide. "What will Gramma Hoopes say? What would my papa say? What will *Josie* say?"

"None of them will say anything good, Bess," said Gusta. "That's for sure. But I've decided. It's got to be done. It's not right, what Mr. Kendall did to your father. Even if the union can't fix this, Mr. Kendall should do the right thing. He should pay the medical people and get your papa's hand fixed. And I'm going to go and tell him so."

Bess was silent for a moment, and then she nodded.

"All right, then, Gusta," said Bess. "I'll come, too. If you're there, I think I can be mostly brave. I can try."

Some part of Gusta's drowned and damaged heart mended a little at that moment.

It makes a difference, having a friend willing to come into danger with you, just so you don't have to be all alone.

Her father used to use a big word for it: *solidarity*. He used it to explain why he had to do what he had to do, on behalf of all his brothers, who were not literally his brothers, but were workingmen who just wanted what people everywhere want: decent work for a decent wage. And fairness. And not being thrown out into the street with doctors' bills to pay when the factory's own machine chewed up their hands.

Gusta looked at Bess and decided she was adding another layer to her father's slogan: *Solidarity forever . . . and cousins!*

They turned away from the school and walked down to the Kendall Mills buildings, both girls several notches quieter than usual. They were both a little in awe of what they were actually about to try to do.

"They may not let us in, you know," said Gusta, to keep Bess's expectations realistic. "They'll do pretty much anything, the owners, to keep union types out of their offices."

But of course Bess and Gusta didn't look like "union types." They looked like a fourth-grader and a fifth-grader from the local elementary school. Mr. Kendall's secretary didn't even grill them about what they wanted to see the mill's owner *for*. She just looked up at them from her desk and smiled over the top of her reading glasses.

"Sure, I guess you girls can see Mr. Kendall! He's

got a meeting in twenty minutes, but why don't you two hop on in."

And into her intercom she said something about them to Mr. Kendall—Gusta distinctly heard the word *sweet*. She took Bess's hand and gave it an encouraging squeeze.

Solidarity forever!

Mr. Kendall turned out to be a medium-size man without much hair left—not really Gusta's image of what a mill owner should look like. He looked sort of like an ordinary person, with bushy red-gray eyebrows, someone who maybe had even been decent-looking long ago, but who had gotten used to sitting behind a big desk and telling people what to do, and as a result, had lost most of his hair and acquired a sort of slumpy look around the shoulders and the midsection.

"Well, now, what can I do for you young ladies?" said Mr. Kendall with a smile. "You two collecting for the Women's Patriotic Society, maybe?"

"Oh, Mr. Kendall," said Bess, completely softening in the face of that smile. "I'm sure you must not have known about the laws—tell him, Gusta!"

"What?" said Mr. Kendall.

To be fair, Gusta would also have said exactly the same thing, had she been the one behind the desk.

It was time, definitely time, to *stand up straight and look like you knew what you were about*!

"Mr. Kendall, this is Bess Goodman," said Gusta. She took a deep breath and said it all fast, before her courage could shut itself up and go away. "Her father is Mr. Charles Goodman. He worked in your mill for . . . a long time, and then one of the mill's machines mangled his hand, which was not his fault. Because the foreman told him to fix something without — without shutting down the line. And it has, um, come to our attention that even though it was not his fault in the slightest, the mill just fired him and refused to pay his medical bills, which we are pretty sure is against the law. So we would like to ask you to make things right."

"So they don't take away our house," said Bess in the bravest of whispers. "Or Papa's radio."

Never had Gusta seen an expression quite like the one now spreading in quick red splotches over Mr. Kendall's face. It was like watching angry red countries appear one by one on a secret map of the world. He did not even glance to the side, at the bravely whispering Bess. His narrowed eyes were staring like cannons right at Gusta.

"Who are *you*?" he said.

Gusta hesitated for a moment.

"I'm Augusta," she said.

"Augusta Neubronner," added Bess. "My cousin. She's a Hoopes."

And that was when something extraordinary happened to the map of blotches covering Mr. Kendall's face: he went completely pale, all at once, fell back heavily into his chair, and then flushed red all over again.

"So that's what this is all about!" he said, and every word was ice and acid. Gusta had been in rooms with plenty of angry grown-ups, but this face here was the angriest she had ever seen. "A *Hoopes* girl, sent my way! A *Hoopes* girl, sent to threaten and beg!"

Bess's hand was trembling, literally trembling from the shock, under Gusta's. Gusta stood even straighter, because she couldn't think what else to do. And she squeezed Bess's trembling fingers very firmly, as if she knew what was going on here with this angry man, which she did not.

"Talking about what the law says isn't threatening anyone, Mr. Kendall," said Gusta, trying to keep her voice kind of conversational and calm. "It's just talking about the law. Mr. Goodman just needs the mill to pay his doctor's bill, like the mill's supposed to do, because of the worker's compensa—"

"The *gall* of you!" said Mr. Kendall, interrupting. "The stinking gall! Just like a Hoopes! Sauntering in here, thinking you can shake me down. Breaking all the bargains we ever had. Well!"

He was rising right out of his chair as he spoke— he was looming over them now, like a tidal wave of rage.

Gusta did not understand. What was he even saying?

What bargains had Gusta ever had with this red-faced Mr. Kendall? Why was he talking this way? She could feel herself beginning to lose her balance. And he was continuing his wild, looming rant.

"Well, you go tell that Mrs. Hoopes of yours, that greedy old crow—go tell that hussy Marion, too, what do I care now?—tell them they've done it. The deal is *off*. They'll not get a penny more out of me, not as long as I live and not after. I'm done with it. Done with maintaining that girl they say is mine but who could be anybody's, far as I know. Go tell Marion that child of hers is old enough to be earning her own way. What is she now, fourteen? That's an age past needing coddling."

"Fourteen?" echoed Gusta. What was he saying? Why was he saying any of this?

"That's it," he said. "I've had enough. You take my message back to those poisonous Hoopes women. Go, now. Scram!"

Gusta and Bess had already taken a couple of steps back. Being yelled at has that effect on feet — makes them want to get away. To get far away, as fast as they can.

And then some other light came into his eyes, and he actually pounced forward like a wild thing and grabbed a handful of Gusta's sweater.

"Wait — *what did you say your name was*, girl?"

"Gusta, come away, quick!" gasped Bess, and she gave Gusta a surprisingly fierce pull, considering how small a person she was. There was a small but awful sound of wool threads tearing, and then Gusta and Bess were falling back through Mr. Kendall's door, bumping into the entirely shocked figure of his secretary, who must have leaped up from her chair once he started shouting like that, and, most of all, turning to flee for real and serious.

Until they were up the hill from the mill, back as high as the main road, they focused only on running away, fast as fast, and not one bit on figuring out what had just gone wrong inside that office.

"Oh, Gusta!" said Bess finally, holding her hand

to her side as if she had a pretty terrible stitch. "What did we just do? Oh, it's all my fault!"

"*Your* fault!" said Gusta. "I don't think so. That man's horrible! He doesn't even make any sense! What was he even talking about, some sort of agreement with Aunt Marion and Gramma? Oh!"

She had finally started to add things up.

"Bess," she said. "Oh, dear. You know who's *fourteen*. Oh, Bess: it's got to be Josie. Miss Marion's child, he said. He was talking about Josie. He said, 'the one they say is mine.'"

"Yes," said Bess, and she looked pale from the seriousness of the thought that she was, like Gusta herself, beginning to have. "Oh, but no. What are you saying? It can't be. And look what that awful, awful man did to your sweater!"

Gusta was down a button and a bunch of threads—and she hadn't even noticed.

Her mind was filled with this terrible new version of everything she thought she knew about the world, this rewriting of all the family history, this catastrophic, lightning-bolt-out-of-the-sky piece of new information.

Josie, cheerful Josie, the first baby taken into the Hoopes Home, was apparently not actually an orphan after all.

❦ 35 ❧

Trying to Do One Right Thing

We can't tell her," said Bess. "We can't say anything. Oh, but we can't *not* tell her! Gusta, *what do we do?*"

They couldn't figure out at all what they should do.

And worse than Josie, even, was Gramma Hoopes. What were they supposed to say to Gramma Hoopes?

Then Gusta kicked at the side of the road.

"Makes me so mad," she said. "All of it."

"That *horrible* man," said Bess.

Then they wrestled with it some more, and the horribleness of Mr. Kendall, and the stickiness of the dilemma they were trapped in just got worse-feeling and worse-feeling.

"Oh, Gusta, just imagine: that horrible man is her *father*!" said Bess.

It was an awful thought.

"And then—*Aunt Marion*," said Gusta.

The girls stared at each other, full of wild-eyed amazement.

Imagine that! Josie had grown up all these years thinking she had nobody! Thinking she had just been dumped on the porch of the Hoopes Home as a baby, that there was no one in the whole world who cared about her in particular, and all the while . . .

"How could you *do* that, though?" asked Bess in tender wonder. "How could you live under the same roof as your own daughter, and pretend you weren't related in the slightest? Never even let her know?"

"Guess they thought they couldn't let *anyone* know," said Gusta. "A baby is an awfully big sort of secret."

They had gotten back as far as the high school, where there was the faintest sound of singing. One of the choruses must still be rehearsing inside.

Bess shivered. "Gusta, I'm afraid I think I'm going to hide under my bed or something forever," she said.

"I wish I didn't know any secrets, and I don't want to have to be telling anyone or not telling anyone. So I'm just going to hide. But what are you going to do?"

And suddenly Gusta knew the answer to that question.

"I'm going in there," she said, waving in the direction of the high-school door.

"Oh, Gusta, no!" said Bess. "You're not going to just walk up to Josie and tell her!"

Gusta shook her head. "Nothing like that. I'm going to go talk to Miss Kendall, if I can catch her."

"You're not!" said Bess in horror. "You can't. You can't say a *word* about anything to Miss Kendall. That would be—that would be—"

"It's not about that," said Gusta. Inside she had become cold, like the rivers of ice Miss Hatch said ran across the far northern parts of the world. "It's about the French horn."

Now Bess was horrified in a different way.

"But how can you even think about music at a time like now?" she said, and she wiped her leaky eyes on her sleeve. "I don't understand it. I don't understand it. I don't know what to do."

"Go on home, Bess," said Gusta, with the miserable cold rivering its way through her muscles and her veins. "You don't have to worry about me. I just have to do what I can to make things right."

And she turned away from Bess and marched up the stairs and through the front door of the high school.

It was obvious what she had to do now, since the universe hadn't been willing to bend itself in their favor. Mr. Kendall wasn't going to help Uncle Charlie. Even the union wasn't going to help Uncle Charlie! So it was up to her.

She hadn't found a Wish anywhere. She couldn't stop the wider horror of the war or even call her own papa home, even though every atom of her being longed to be able to reach out and put the tip of an index finger on the back of her papa's hand again, just to know that he really was actually there.

(And her father used to glance down when she did that. "Testing your papa, little thingling, to see if he's real?" His voice was soft when he said that, like the smudged lines of his face, a laughing voice that was also sad. She loved that sad-amused voice of his, the one that came out into the world so very rarely and that she thought of as somehow especially *hers*.)

But here was the thing about Gusta's papa, who

had so suddenly vanished far beyond the reach of her index finger: her papa had taught her that whatever you *can* do to put things right in the world, you really *must* do.

And that's why Gusta was now going in through the high-school doors and trotting down the main hall as quickly and quietly as she could.

Gusta knew the high-school building pretty well by now, knew where the music room was and where the high-school students tended not to go, on their way from the music room to the outside world. So she did a very competent job of sneaking down the long main hall, ducking into a shadowy doorway when the chorus members came out of their practice session in a laughing, chatting bunch. Josie herself was in that crowd, only a few feet away from where Gusta was shrinking into a corner, but Josie never saw her. And then, with the coast cleared, Gusta slipped in through the music room door.

Miss Kendall looked up in surprise. She was tidying a stack of music on her desk.

"Gusta! Have you mixed up your dates, dear? Concert's not until tomorrow, don't you remember?"

"Miss Kendall," Gusta started right in, before her

words could get shut down by the rivers of ice in her. "It's about my French horn, how you said you wanted to buy it, you know. For that hundred dollars."

"What is this, Gusta?" said Miss Kendall. "Good heavens! You look so worried, dear child. Please do sit down. And explain to me, please, what it is you're saying."

"The thing is, my Uncle Charlie needs an operation to fix his hand. And I know you need a horn, not just when I play it for a special concert like the one we're playing here tomorrow, but for always. So it's like my mama said in her note, 'if need arises,' and I guess it has. Arisen. The need."

Miss Kendall was silent now, simply flabbergasted, probably.

Gusta had almost never said so many words in a row to a teacher, ever. But she was trying to do one right thing, after all the things that had gone so wrong.

"So I was wondering," said Gusta. "If I give you the horn tomorrow, after the concert — would you be able to, to give me that money? Could you maybe bring the money along to the concert?"

There was a silent moment, in which Gusta got colder and colder inside, and then Miss Kendall said, sounding a little doubtful, "Why, yes, of course, Gusta.

I would be very pleased indeed to buy that horn from you, if that's what you really want to do. But are you sure? Are you absolutely sure? Because you look—"

"Thank you, Miss Kendall," said Gusta, already turning to flee. "I'm sorry. I promise I'll hand the horn over tomorrow. But I've got to go now. Good-bye."

Her horn! Her brass seashell deep singing-voiced horn!

It's done now, she thought as she fled the school. *It's done. I've done one right thing.*

And her heart broke and broke and broke.

☙ 36 ❧

Telling the Truth

Gusta had no idea what she was going to say to Gramma Hoopes, though, until she was coming through the door of the Hoopes Home and could hear Aunt Marion frying up potatoes in the kitchen, and Josie getting the boys (minus Thomas, who was down with influenza) organized for supper, and little Delphine singing "ashes, ashes, all fall down."

Then she realized, all at once, that there was something that she couldn't do.

She couldn't simply add all these new secrets to the ones that were already weighing her down. It reminded her of one of her mother's sayings, about how a camel can carry just about anything, but even for the camel there's some point where the straws become too heavy, and the poor beast's back just snaps right in two like a twig. Or, probably, sags slowly toward the ground and makes the camel reluctant to push on through the porch door and into that noisy, wonderful house.

She was going to have to let some of these secrets out into the world.

She started her new career as a reckless truth-teller by fibbing, however: she murmured something to Aunt Marion about how she wasn't feeling very well and wanted to lie down instead of eating supper. And then she lay on her cot and faced the dim wall and tried not to think too much, until she heard the boys (other than Thomas) trickling back to their rooms and the voices downstairs of Josie and Aunt Marion, busy with the dishes. Gramma Hoopes liked to have a quiet half hour to herself after supper, which she claimed was for mending—so this was Gusta's best chance.

She sat up on her bed, feeling like someone doomed to having to be brave, which is not the same thing as actually feeling brave. Her feet were a little numb, and she kept wiping her hands on her skirt, but her hands in fact were perfectly dry.

Gusta snuck down the stairs and down the back

hall and slipped in through the door of her grand-mother's room. Her grandmother was sitting at her desk; she had her funny reading glasses on and a sheet of paper in her hand.

"Gusta!" said Gramma Hoopes in surprise. "Are you ill, too, girl? If you are, you shouldn't be floating around the house like this. Come here and let me feel your forehead."

The forehead made her grandmother frown a little.

"Well! You're a tad warm, but not exactly burning up, that's one good thing. Your face is strange, though. You come sit down here."

She had another chair right by the desk. Sometimes she and Aunt Marion did accounts together in this room.

"I was just reading a letter from your mother," said Gramma Hoopes. "She's wondering how you're getting on. I'd say, pretty well, don't you think? Wait, now, Augusta, what in heaven's name is wrong with you, child?"

Whatever Gusta's inner plan had counted on, for how this conversation might go, it had not included Gusta bursting into tears. But that's what she did now anyway.

For a minute or so, she just sobbed and sobbed, while her grandmother stroked her arm and made astonishingly kind noises for someone as hard-boiled as Gusta's grandmother.

"Feeling homesick, are you, after all?" said her grandmother. "I guess that's the normal way of things."

That made Gusta pull herself together again, because she felt how easily she could just slip away from the truth toward something more comfortable. And if she did that she would be like the camel, only even worse: a pathetic sort of camel loading straws right onto his own shaky back, and that was not what she was here to do.

"Gramma Hoopes," she said, with some hiccups. "I'm so sorry. I only wanted to try to help. And now I've gone and made Mr. Kendall mad—"

"Mr. Kendall!" said her grandmother in an entirely different tone of voice. "What does he have to with anything?"

"It was against the law, what he did to Bess's papa," said Gusta. "I thought, I mean, I thought he should know, that the mill should pay the doctors—"

"We leave the Kendalls *alone*," said Gramma Hoopes, firm as firm. "You're not so new around here you don't know that, are you, Augusta?"

There was no more comfortable patting of Gusta's arm, that was for sure.

"I know that," said Gusta miserably. "I knew that. But you see, I didn't know *why*."

The next ten seconds were silent, and maybe the most uncomfortable ten seconds Gusta had ever spent. Probably there were worse seconds far off in the future waiting for her, but these ten right here were pretty bad.

"And now you will explain," said Gramma Hoopes finally. Her voice had a layer of ice to it now. "What exactly have you gone and done?"

So Gusta told her.

She left out Bess as much as she could, because she remembered just in time that although Gusta might be sent away back to New York City, at least she had a mother there to take her in, even if that mother would have to leave her rooming house and find some other place for them to live if Gusta showed up in disgrace. But Bess had nowhere else to go. So Gusta told the story, as much as possible, without Bess in it. Of course it was Bess whose father had the mangled hand and the medical bills, but Gusta focused on how it had been her, Gusta's, idea, to march on down to the Kendall Mills, and to ask to speak to Mr. Kendall, and then to go into his office, just to be yelled at so strangely, with all the threats about deals and bargains, and all the horrible description of what Gusta should tell her grandmother and her Aunt Marion. And of course she also left out the part about agreeing to sell her French horn to Miss Kendall, because that was too hard to be said aloud.

And at the end Gusta said again, "I'm sorry. I meant to help, not ruin things."

She looked up at her grandmother, and the thing about having been so upset, and having cried some, is that even through glasses the world looks almost as blurry as it used to, back before you had any glasses.

"Augusta!" said her grandmother, and Gusta couldn't even tell from her voice exactly how mad she was. Plenty angry—and also something else, both at once. "You are a heedless girl. Heedless and thoughtless and reckless. Comes from your father's side, I guess."

Gusta felt a tiny thread of resentment leap up in her at that, on her papa's behalf, but she forced herself to stay quiet, to keep her eyes on the floorboards and simply listen. She deserved all those words, every sharp edge of them.

"What were you thinking? Now Josie will suffer,

and she's a good girl and doesn't deserve it, and your Aunt Marion will suffer, for having tried to do the right thing, mind you — and yes, you and I will suffer, too, all because you —"

"I'll go pack," said Gusta, interrupting. Suddenly she just couldn't bear it anymore, the slow slipping down this slope that would end up, sure as sure, with her on another bus, all on her own. She'd rather it was all over and done with. She'd rather be already gone. "I can take the bus home tomorrow."

It became more a hiccup than a sentence, halfway through.

"Gusta, what is this nonsense?" said her grand-mother. "The bus has nothing to do with anything. You've done something harmful and foolish — yes, you have — even if you didn't mean to, and now we'll have to face the consequences, best we can. That doesn't mean I put my granddaughter on a bus!"

Those ten seconds were also memorable. Gusta's ears heard those words. Her brain rolled them around and around, thinking about them. Her heart looked up for a moment, feeling a change in the wind.

"Do you have absolutely no sense in your head at all, girl? Your Aunt Marion did something foolish long ago. Did we put her on a bus on her own back then? No, we did not. We did our best. We worked it out. And our Josie! Did we put that little baby on a bus? Of course not. Think a little, why don't you! For all that you're a good scholar, as the teacher tells me, sometimes you are as dense as a potato, Augusta Hoopes Neubronner. Now, you've messed up. Yes, you have. But don't you understand yet? We'll have to make our way through. Nobody gets put on any bus all by herself. Because you know what, Gusta? We Hoopeses are a family that does *not* send our own away. And for heaven's sake, whatever happened to your sweater?"

"When he got mad," said Gusta. "Mr. Kendall, he—I lost a button."

Her grandmother actually slapped the desk with her hand.

"That selfish, tiresome, *poisonous* man!" she said. "He's been lording it over us long enough. I thought I was doing right by Josie, not to cut her off from that little bit of money he sent over, all anonymous like, but I will tell you honestly, a great part of me will be *glad* to be done with him. Though you've still been a bad and reckless child, Gusta, and don't you forget it. And listen hard: I won't have you saying a word to Josie, not right away. Your Aunt Marion and I will have to be the ones who explain things to her. I'm trusting you to be sensible about that, for once."

Her gramma's fingers were busy examining the place where the button was missing, and the buttons below.

"That's a shame, though, the lost button. Your mother did a nice job on this sweater. Well, hand it over, and I'll see what I can do."

It was the opposite of packing her bags, obviously. Gusta slipped out of her sweater and put it on her grandmother's table, while Gramma Hoopes took a wooden box out from a drawer in her desk. Inside was a great jumble of buttons, all kinds of buttons.

"Oh!" said Gusta. It made you want to spend an hour or two poking around in that collection, wondering at the variousness of them all. And then Gusta woke up another notch or two.

"Gramma Hoopes! Did that box . . ." she said, "did that box used to sit *on a shelf*?"

"Well, yes," said Gramma Hoopes, gesturing rather gracefully. "Right over there. Why do you ask, Gusta?"

"You have a button box, and it used to sit on a shelf. Not in a cave at all, but right here on a shelf!"

"In a cave?" said Gramma Hoopes. "What has gotten into you, Augusta, I wonder?"

Gusta's grandmother was already sifting through the sea of buttons with a sure hand, and suddenly there in her hands was the very button that Gusta's sweater had just lost, with the little flower pattern stamped into it.

Gramma Hoopes held it up so Gusta could see.

"No need to look quite so surprised," said her grandmother. "Who sent your mother those buttons, anyway, when she said she was knitting you that sweater? I always keep a few back, so I have some extras on hand in the button box. But this is the last one of that set, so no more fights for you." A stern look.

Gusta shook her head, feeling like a shorn sheep without her sweater. No more fights for her. All right.

She felt trembly and cozy, both at once. The worst had happened, and she was still here, and was not, after all, going to be put back on the bus. She had been in such despair, and now *hope* was rising up in her—strange and irrational, impossible and sweet.

"Gramma, please—before you put them away, may I please, please, look at the buttons?"

Her grandmother gave her an almost-smile.

"You know, Augusta," she said. "When your

mother was very, very small, she used to dearly love this box of buttons. You make me remember those days all over again. I didn't bring it out very often, because you never can be sure with buttons—a baby might swallow them, and there always seemed to be a baby about, back in the old days. But when Gladys— your mother—was feverish and fretful, nothing comforted her like sorting through the button box."

Gramma Hoopes sighed. "And here you are now, so like her in these funny little ways. Well, I must say, life is full of surprises, and not all of them are bad. You go curl up in the big chair over there with the button box, Augusta, and I will get to work on this sweater of yours."

She already had thread through a needle—the shiny button was already shimmying down that thread toward its new home—the torn sweater was already on its way to being set to rights.

"I can't mend everything," said her grandmother. "But I can mend this."

Gusta found it hiding away in that astonishing sea of all kinds of buttons—plain white buttons, metal buttons with anchors on them, or a single blossom, a few buttons for a little child, with a blue bunny hopping across them, square buttons, shell buttons, buttons made of beads and buttons made of glass.

And yes: near the bottom of the button box was what looked at first like an ancient coin, with markings she couldn't read on front and back and a small punched-out square where an ordinary button might have its four little holes. She knew what it must be right away, because it glittered in her hand, as if catching the rays of a light she couldn't see. As if it were daydreaming about a sunny afternoon it remembered, from long ago and far away. The Wish.

"If you find one you particularly like, you may keep it for a gift," said her grandmother without looking up from her mending.

⊙ 37 ⊙

Moon Love

When Gusta woke up the next morning, she was surprised at first by the strange feeling that filled her: as if her heart had been broken open, melted down, and then patched together by kind hands into some version of its old shape again, but not without a new network of cracks and fissures running through it.

"Are you well enough for school?" said Josie. "You'd darn well better be! Ron and Thomas are both burning up now, and Miss Marion's just about frantic, but you! You've got to be absolutely perfectly well today, Gusta! It's Thursday! It's concert day!"

And then Gusta remembered everything all at once. She remembered facing Mr. Kendall, and she remembered what he had let slip about Josie—*Josie!*—and she remembered promising to sell the French horn to Miss Kendall—*the horn!*—and then crying in Gramma Hoopes's room, and that she mustn't say anything to Josie—*Josie!*—and what she had found in the button box—*the Wish? Could it really be the Wish?*—and that this evening was indeed the big spring concert at Springdale High School—*oh, the horn!*—and she and Josie—*Josie!*—both had their solos to think about—*the horn!*—and Miss Kendall! And Josie—*Josie!*—again!

"Don't dawdle," said Josie. "Don't sit there gaping and gawping, and for heaven's sake, don't forget that French horn of yours."

She kept chattering all the way to school, which was just as well, because Gusta was weighed down by this last round of secret carrying, and Bess looked so nervous and stricken when she came out from her house to join them that Josie thought she might be coming down with whatever the boys had.

"Stay away from me, you girls!" Josie laughed. "I am *not* getting sick until at least tomorrow! My solo tonight is going to go absolutely, perfectly well!"

Bess gave Gusta an agonized look, and Gusta frowned back.

"*I* was a little under the weather last night, *too*," said Gusta, trying to stare at Bess so meaningfully that Bess would buck up and start at least trying to pretend it was a normal day. "But we have to *pull ourselves together* and act like *nothing* in the world is *wrong*."

"You got that right!" sang out Josie.

As far as Gusta could tell, the only blot on Josie's happiness was that Gramma Hoopes and Aunt Marion weren't coming to the concert at all, on account of the boys being sick in bed.

"It's only a bit of singing," Gramma Hoopes had said, when Josie's face had fallen. And of course, Josie's face had fallen even farther in response to that. Gusta had seen it all, because it was amazing what faces turned out to be doing all the time, giving away everyone's secrets without a stitch of remorse.

For Gusta it was actually a relief, however, that her grandmother and aunt wouldn't be there.

From the moment she opened her eyes that morning, Gusta felt distant from herself, as if all the secrets were an iceberg, and she had floated on that iceberg out into a very cold sea. There was Mr. Kendall, and Josie, and the Wish, and the French horn. They were all tangled together now.

She wanted not to be at school. She wanted to be

quiet and alone, so she could think it all over, especially the Wish. She had hidden the Wish in the toe of a sock last night, and she had stolen a glimpse of it this morning, and it was the strangest thing: contrary to everything else she had ever learned about the universe, the Wish really did glitter with a hidden, impossible, confident light. It seemed to know what it was, and to know that what it was, was magic. In comparison, all the fool's gold on Holly Hill was merest imitation.

Of course, there aren't such things as Wishes in this world of ours. They exist only in stories.

But this Wish, as it lay sparkling on Gusta's palm that morning, seemed to be insisting that it existed nevertheless.

What should she do about that?

Just in case it was really as real as it thought it was, Gusta tucked the Wish back into the sock and hid it. She couldn't be trusted with a Wish in her hand, not before she'd had some time to think over what to do with it.

"What happened when you got home? Oh, tell me, Gusta! What happened?" said Bess to Gusta in a strangled whisper as they went up the steps of Jefferson Elementary. "I was so frightened last night just thinking about it."

"Josie doesn't know anything yet," said Gusta grimly. "We have to act like everything's fine."

Bess's face did not look like the face of someone who thinks everything's fine, but off they both went to their respective classrooms, because what else were they going to do?

While the class solved more mathematics problems, of the complicated long-division sort (*What, children, is 117.59 divided by 33.4?*), Gusta found herself scribbling question marks with her pencil and trying out fragments of impossible sentences in her brain.

I wish . . . Uncle Charlie's hand . . . and Josie, please . . . and oh, Papa! . . . but the horn, the horn, I still don't want to lose the horn . . . But Uncle Charlie . . .

The necessary verbs kept escaping her; that was part of the problem.

And her thoughts kept being interrupted by the French horn. She set it aside firmly, trying to leave it out of her practice wishes and out of her mind, and instead, it kept rising up and singing out to her.

Miss Hatch had them write a paragraph about "The Virtue of Persistence," and Gusta tried to write about anything else, but that horn of hers crawled into sentence after sentence and wouldn't leave. How hard it was to make one note roll into the next on the horn—how you had to melt right into the music and how the horn had to be on your side and how many hours it took to learn to make the horn sing—and even then it could suddenly betray you, and make a note sound like a rude noise instead of music! But when it all flowed, smooth as a river of resonant air—well, that was the best gift persistence could ever give a person, wasn't it?

Let go, Gusta told herself furiously. *You have to let it go.*

Otherwise, the horn would surely grab that Wish and make it be all about itself.

Miss Hatch handed back Gusta's paper at the end of the day with a smile: "I'm coming to hear you at the high school tonight, you know!"

Gusta had to slip away fast, so that she wouldn't crumple.

After school there was a last run-through at the high school. Miss Kendall was in her element, kind and enthusiastic and well prepared. She had even brought blouses for Gusta and Josie to wear. Probably she had also brought the money for the horn. Gusta didn't have the courage to ask about that, not yet. First things first, she told herself. First, the concert. Then, everything else.

* * *

As the musicians gathered in the new high-school theater for the concert, at the end of that day, they were absolutely chock-full of—"What do we call it, students?"—*anticipation*.

Gusta had to endure that *anticipation* a long time, because she didn't play until the end. That meant she had to sit through the other orchestra pieces and some singing by the choruses. She sat there feeling small and out of place and feeling her heart swell and crack. The horn was so comfortable in her hands. It seemed to be saying to her, with every valve and curve, *You can't really let go of me! You wouldn't do that!* She didn't want time to move forward, because every moment brought her closer to having to do what she knew she needed to do, but she couldn't help looking forward to those opening notes of hers anyway, because nothing is better than asking your French horn to give you the melody you want and having it respond.

But oh, it was a good thing she had left the actual Wish at home in its sock in the box under her bed. She saw so clearly that she might have accidentally wasted the Wish on something laughably small, on the concert ("Hope I play well!" "Hope it doesn't go badly!"), for instance, when the logical part of her mind knew she didn't actually *need* any wishes to get her through the concert, if she just stayed calm and did the things she knew perfectly well how to do. It's a funny thing, though: nervousness—*anticipation*—can make even a sensible person grasp at wishes, if they're lucky enough to have a Wish around to grasp.

And having found something as rare in ordinary, everyday life as a Wish, Gusta was determined to make the most of it: she would use this bit of magic she had found to make the most sensible, logical, effective, helpful, thorough, and loophole-free wish anybody in the history of wishing had ever wished. She was not going to let this Wish be wasted, not now when there was so much that needed fixing. Not on playing her horn. Not on anything to do with that horn. No.

Because there was a larger, less ridiculous danger: that she might fall right into selfishness, into thinking a wish might save her horn, instead of her horn saving Uncle Charlie. She knew from stories that wishes wriggle and cheat—if they even exist at all.

But unlike a wish, a hundred dollars is as real as real. That's what she told herself while the horn trembled in her hands.

She herself would not try to wriggle out of having to do the right thing anymore. Ever since she had torn off that line from her mother's letter—the horn to be sold, in case of need—Gusta had been in debt to what was right. You don't get away with things like that, not really. So now she was going to face facts and do what must be done. Then maybe she would have paid the price, and the rest of her wishing would come out, right as rain. Maybe she could even wish her papa home. . . . Oh, she was holding on hard to that thought.

But first, the concert!

And now it was time. The stage crew pulled the big curtains shut and started rushing about to set up the stage for what the master of ceremonies (Mr. Jordan, director of the school band) announced would be "Miss Kendall's 'Russian Moon: A Number with Some Musical Surprises.'" They placed Gusta in front of the semicircle of string players, and an eager subset of the high-school band over on the left.

"Okay, kid, listen up," said the lanky boy on the lighting team in the speediest, most energetic murmur. "As long as you don't go moving your chair around, the spotlight will hit on you right here. Pretty great to have a real spotlight, huh? You sit tight, and it's going to be like a ray of moonlight bangs down right onto your head. Naw, better than that. Break a leg!"

She had never heard anyone promise so many painful disasters with such enthusiasm. That must be something they taught you in high school. Anyway, there was no time for any of those thoughts now, because the lights had gone down, and the curtain was opening.

Here was what Miss Kendall, Springdale High School's most melodious teacher and all-around musical genius, had thought up for this show: The opening was quiet chords played by the string orchestra. All Gusta had to do for the first forty seconds was sit still and hope her lips weren't getting too dry from nervousness (*anticipation*). She couldn't see the audience very well, thanks to the gloom, but she could tell from the way they rustled that there were hundreds and hundreds of them out there. And then someone — maybe the lanky boy — hit a switch, and a new light, the spotlight, poured down on Gusta, and nevertheless she had to think only of Tchaikovsky and music and keeping her lips just right — or better yet, not think at all, just play.

It was perhaps the "most famous horn solo ever," her father had said, long ago. And then he had accepted the two-dollar bet that Gusta wouldn't be able to play it. That bet had been a thorn festering in Gusta's heart ever since, but tonight she felt like the thorn was melting into something else, like one of those off-by-a-half-step notes that just deepens the music in the end.

Because the music rolled out from her horn tonight like liquid moonlight. Oh, it was smooth and lovely, despite the dryness of her lips.

If Gusta admitted the inmost unsaid truths of her heart—and sometimes playing the horn felt like spilling those inmost truths, disguised as melody, out into the world—then what was leaking out now (if only the people listening knew how to hear the meaning underneath the music) was something like this: her father was gone, her mother was far away, children were so often orphans, there was so much sadness in the world—but maybe someday it could all *work out*, we could all get to all those high notes we dream of reaching. Maybe things, someday, could finally be otherwise.

Gusta knew from the stillness of the crowd that Miss Kendall's brilliant idea was working perfectly so far, that all those people were thinking a combination of wondering thoughts:

Oh, isn't that a pretty tune!

And also:

Is that little girl really playing that thing? Who is she?

(Miss Kendall had said it this way: "The audience won't believe its own eyes. It won't be able to put together what its ears are hearing and what its eyes are seeing. Can you imagine that?" Gusta, of course, could imagine that. From long experience she could imagine that very, very well.)

And the third thought, beginning to buzz around in the audience's heads:

Hey, haven't I heard this somewhere before?

This is where Miss Kendall had had her stroke of genius. Gusta's last note spilled out into the air, and then the orchestra's chords cleverly climbed down the scale into a slightly different key, and suddenly the lights came up on the other half of the stage, and there was the Springdale High School Band (with the saxophones borrowed from the Kendall Mills Band) diving right into that top hit of 1939, "Moon Love," as made famous by the Glenn Miller Orchestra.

The artificial moonlight was no longer blinding Gusta, and her lips no longer had to behave; she could sit back in her chair and watch the band, while all of her trembled a little from whatever anticipation becomes once the crisis or performance has passed.

The band might not have had the smooth, suave savvy of Glenn Miller, but they sure knew how to throw themselves into a tune. The audience cheered. Then they listened for a few more seconds, and they got the joke—*It's the same song! That's why it sounded so familiar!*—and they cheered again, twice as loud. And then Josie walked out on the stage while the band was playing, and the cheering quieted down so they could hear the next thing, which was Josie, wreathed in that magical, electrical moonlight, singing words that the crowd knew perfectly well—or had known a while ago, when this song had still been at the top of the charts. Gusta had listened a hundred times to Josie practicing this song, and as far as she could figure out, "moon love" was the kind of sneaky, awful love that steals into your heart, makes you do foolish things, and then leaves you all alone. Sounded pretty miserable to Gusta, but the members of that audience were on the edges of their seats, as if under some beautiful, melancholy spell.

And the spell seemed to be Josie's singing!

All these people here might have heard that song before, but they had never heard it sung like this, by a girl whose voice was so nightingale-sweet and honey-smooth. They were entirely won over. They were entranced. They seemed to lean forward, soaking up the beauty of it, and at the end, the whole theater erupted into cheers and applause that seemed like it would never end. Gusta and Josie had to take their own individual bows, and they also had a couple of bows together. Josie was glowing with happiness — really, she was incandescent! It had not been a long concert, but it had been glorious.

Gusta could see how happiness was lighting up Josie's face as if she were a lantern with a perfect candle new-kindled inside. Surely this was a golden moment (unless you were Gusta, about to do one right thing). All those high-school kids, the band members and the string players, were lingering on the stage and being just as sweet as could be.

"That was *so* gorgeous!" they said to Josie, "That was *beautiful*!" — and even "How'd you ever learn to play that horn like that, kiddo?" to Gusta — and the whole crowd of those musicians was aglow in the thrill of having played so well, and having made that audience so happy.

"Oh, if only Mrs. Hoopes had been here!" said Josie to Gusta. "And Miss Marion! Oh! Let's hurry home and tell them all about it. Come on, Gusta —"

"Just a moment, just a moment," said Gusta, and she made a sort of mumbling gesture in the general direction of the music room. "I'll be back. I'll be back in a minute, Josie. Just wait here a minute, won't you?"

Because first Gusta had to fulfill a bargain as hard as any in a fairy tale: she had to let go of her horn—which was just another way of saying she had to let go of her voice and her heart.

❦ 38 ❧

Paying the Price

Gusta slipped out the stage's side door and trotted through the halls of the school to the music room at the back of the building, her horn bumping against her shins — for the last time, perhaps.

To tell the truth, her hand was not very steady as she opened the music room door. Miss Kendall looked over in her direction and smiled. "Gusta! That was wonderful! How proud you must be, dear."

Gusta took a step forward, and another step forward.

Uncle Charlie, she thought sternly.

"Miss Kendall," she said, "I brought you the horn."

And she held it out in front of her, like you might bring a roast turkey to a Thanksgiving table on a fancy old platter.

"Oh, Gusta!" said Miss Kendall. "Really? Are you sure you want to do this? I know how much your horn must mean to you."

Gusta made herself nod.

A hundred dollars was so much money: enough for an operation to loosen up a scar-bound hand.

It was the right thing to do. The right thing to do.

Anything else was merely wishful thinking—and couldn't be counted on.

"But you'll take good care of it, won't you, Miss Kendall?" she added.

"Well, yes, of course," said Miss Kendall. "I'll do my utmost to see that the students treat it with proper respect. With the respect it deserves. And that you deserve, Augusta. You are a true musician and, if I may say so, a very good niece. I do hope your poor uncle will now get the help he needs."

Gusta blinked. And blinked again.

Uncle Charlie. That was right. She had to keep her mind firmly on him.

Miss Kendall was already reaching for her satchel.

It was really happening. She produced five twenty-dollar bills, which she counted into Gusta's hand. One, two, three, four, five. Gusta now had a hundred dollars in her fist.

A hundred dollars was an enormous amount of money.

Enough for Uncle Charlie's hand.

She set the horn in its case gently down on the floor.

"Thank you, Miss Kendall," she whispered, and she turned and ran blindly out of the music room.

But she didn't get more than ten feet past the swinging door before she ran right into a man in a sturdy sort of overcoat. *Oh, no!*

She was numb at this point, and her eyes, even with her glasses on, weren't seeing very clearly. But she had the terrible feeling that she recognized this person, and when he spoke aloud, she knew she did know him.

"What is this?" he said, and he closed his thick-fingered hand around Gusta's wrist—the wrist of the hand that was holding the five twenty-dollar bills Miss Kendall had just counted out. "You! *You!*"

It was Mr. Kendall, and he was so furious that his cheeks were flushing red, as if that secret map of splotches had been lurking under his skin all this time, just waiting for enough anger to bring it out.

He grabbed the money out of Gusta's hand and was examining it now in obvious rage and disgust. "More blackmail?" he shouted. "That's what you're about, is it? Threatening to tell everyone everything, if you don't get paid. Well, hear me now, you poisonous little devil-child: you won't get away with it!"

He shook Gusta with his other hand until her teeth chattered.

"Stop, stop, please, stop," she kept saying, but he didn't stop.

"Couldn't get money from me, could you? So you come after my sister instead! Of all the conniving, deceitful, wicked—"

"*Freddy!*"

Miss Kendall had flung open the music room door. She stood there, frozen like a waxwork statue for a moment in horror.

"*What are you doing?*" she said to Mr. Kendall, who turned away from Gusta (thank goodness) to sputter his rage in Miss Kendall's direction.

"Don't think I don't blame you, too, Grace," he hissed at her. "You let this happen! You let yourself be led down that daisy path—putting these venomous creatures, these vipers, in the limelight like you did tonight!"

"Vipers!" said Miss Kendall. "Freddy! Whatever can you be talking about, I'd like to know?"

"It was those *Hoopes girls'* idea, this musical number of yours, wasn't it? Wasn't it? They fed the plan to you, like feeding a hook to a codfish. And you bit, didn't you? A spectacle! To make *me* look like a *fool*! 'Moon Love'? In *that girl's* voice! Why, it's pure slander! And then I come back here to find this one has been blackmailing you—"

"What horrible things you're saying," said Miss Kendall. "I don't understand any of it. This is my annual spring concert at the high school, Fred. Of course I organized the program myself—and surely it has nothing to do with you."

He wasn't shaken at all. He was so thoroughly certain he knew what was going on. "Is that so? Well! *This* ugly little girl here"—and he gave Gusta one last shake for good measure—"this girl you had up there onstage playing that twisted tuba thing—"

French horn, thought Gusta, indignantly. He could call Gusta whatever he wanted, but he had no right to say anything nasty about her horn.

"This very girl was in my office yesterday, down

at the mills, threatening me. They're trying to shake money out of us, whichever way they can. That's what they're up to."

Gusta gasped. It was so far from the truth, what he was saying. "That's not—" she said, and Mr. Kendall gave her wrist a cruel twist.

"You going to deny it? Oh, that's how you operate, all you Hoopes women: always deceiving and threatening and denying."

"Please, Fred. Stop this! You're talking about a child!" said Miss Kendall.

"This is no child," said Mr. Kendall. "This here is a viper, *pretending* to be a child. If I don't keep paying them money, they'll spread the vilest gossip all around town. That's what this *child* said."

"What?" said Gusta. She was taken aback. She had said nothing of the sort.

"What?" said Miss Kendall (but her *what* meant something different than Gusta's). "Whatever is this all about, Freddie? I don't understand a word you're saying."

"You'd better wise up," said Mr. Kendall. "Just because I lost my head for a moment over that Marion Hoopes, years ago, now they want to shout all over town that the girl's *mine*. That Josie you're so gaga about!"

"Please don't go bringing Josie into this," said Miss Kendall. "Josie has such talent—a hardworking, good-hearted girl."

"Another Hoopes viper, that's what she is!" said Mr. Kendall. "And haven't I paid enough? Haven't I paid enough? How much more do they want from me? Coming to my office with their threats. Didn't you, you awful girl? Tell her, tell her the truth!"

Miss Kendall looked at Gusta, at her brother, and then back at Gusta again.

"Augusta?" she said. Her voice was weak.

"It's not how he's saying, Miss Kendall," said Gusta, her heart pounding lickety-split in her chest. "We only went to see him to ask for help for my uncle. To pay for his hand."

"See?" said Mr. Kendall, a triumphant bellow. "She admits it: threats and blackmail! Slandering our good name all around town."

Gusta shook her head, but what could she do against the brute force of Mr. Kendall? He was so angry, and so confident in his version of the story. And worse: horror was spreading over Miss Kendall's face.

"Oh, Gusta," she said. "So it's true? You went to the mills? Making threats against my brother? For money? But I can hardly believe it."

"Oh, you'd better believe it," said Mr. Kendall.

And Gusta could see it happening, right there before her: those awful lies and half lies were sinking right in through Miss Kendall's skin like poison. They were becoming lies that she *believed*.

That was where something broke in Gusta. She had wanted to be brave. She had wanted to make things better. But everywhere she turned, she just made things worse.

We don't always know who we are going to be when the storm breaks over us. There was nothing Gusta could think of to say, nothing she could do; Mr. Kendall would simply twist it all and make something ugly of it.

She had tried to be true, to be Gusta, even *in the light of trouble*. And she had failed.

So Gusta turned and fled.

It was only when she was already out the main high-school doors that she realized that she had come away without those five twenty-dollar bills.

Miss Kendall had kept her horn, and Mr. Kendall had taken her money.

❧ 39 ❧

A Bad Morning

J osie was still radiant the next morning as they all
walked to school; Gusta much, much less so.

"I don't know, Gusta," Aunt Marion had said,
looking at her with exhaustion and worry. "You sure
you're well enough for school? You don't look right to
me. What am I going to do if more of you come down
with the flu?"

"We won't, we won't," promised Josie, and Gusta
just shook her head. She didn't need the influenza to
feel like she was being wrung dry.

It was a strange, strange day, all around.

During mathematics, a student aide poked her
head in through the door and said the main office

needed to see Augusta Neubronner, please. She mangled the pronunciation of Gusta's name. A profound hush blanketed the classroom. Every student was wondering, as always happened when someone was called out of class, what offense had been committed and what the punishment might be.

"Perhaps it's about your solo last night?" said Miss Hatch with a smile. "You know I was there, dear. You certainly did our fifth grade proud."

The students sank back into their chairs. Mostly they were relieved on Gusta's behalf, which spoke well for them. A few were undoubtedly disappointed to have the excitement fizzle so fast.

Gusta, however, felt a knot of dread tighten in her stomach. She didn't want to talk about her horn solo. She had already forgotten all the sweet parts of yesterday. The sweetness was gone. She didn't want to think about what had happened the night before, not any of it.

The principal of Jefferson Elementary School was named Mr. Wallace Jones, and all Gusta knew about him was what the boys had told her: that he was mean and unfair, and that he had fingers missing from his right hand, like the old movie star Harold Lloyd. The boys argued about whether it was one finger or two fingers. They had apparently had enough visits to the principal's office to fuel an argument on the subject. It was "awfully disrespectful," said Josie, the way those boys talked about the principal of their school.

On the other hand, Gusta, now seated in front of the daunting figure of Principal Jones, was some tiny percent distracted from her discomfort and worry by the thought that if he moved that hand of his over another inch or two, the hand holding the copy of today's *Tribune*, she might be able to count those fingers herself.

"Miss Augusta Neubronner," said Principal Jones, and he actually gave the paper something of a shake. "I do not like to learn that a student in my school has been keeping secrets from us. Perhaps you can explain?"

Gusta was confused. Had the concert been written up in the newspaper? Sometimes that did happen. But never so fast. The concert had only been hours ago. And it wasn't so much a secret, anyway. And the principal's voice, his words, none of it seemed like what a person would say on his way to complimenting one of his pupils on her excellent performance of a Tchaikovsky horn solo.

"I—don't know, Mr. Jones," said Gusta. "The

concert at the high school—that was just because the music teacher asked me—"

"Concert?" said Principal Jones. "What concert? I am talking about secrets, ugly secrets. And misdirection. I have received a letter of complaint this morning, Miss Neubronner. Delivered by hand. From one of the town's most upstanding citizens."

It was as if he had just wandered into the drought-parched woods that was Gusta's soul, made a feint with a watering can, and instead lit a match.

Inside Gusta, everything flared up all at once in alarm.

"And this upstanding citizen tells me some things about one of my elementary pupils that I find, Miss Neubronner, to be extremely grave. Even disturbing. That you invaded his office, interrupting his work, and proceeded to threaten him, because of a family grudge against the man's business interests, which, if I may be very plain about it, form the central engine of our local economy. Miss Neubronner! Let me make one thing very clear: Jefferson Elementary does not tolerate misbehavior of *any* sort. We punish truants, we punish those who waste paper or break pencils, we punish those who pull a classmate's hair. But it is entirely beyond the pale—it is *absolutely unthinkable*—that one of our students should attempt to bring down a pillar of our little community in this reprehensible and egregious manner. I am telling you now: we will not stand for it, Miss Neubronner. Threatening local pillars? We will not stand for it. This letter will go into your school records file, Miss Neubronner. We will be watching you."

Into the pause, Gusta slipped one thin-edged phrase: "But it's not true."

She was amazed that she had managed even that much. It was almost a miracle.

Principal Jones slapped the top of his desk with the five fingers of his left hand.

"*Not true?*" he said. "Let us examine the evidence. Did you pay a visit to the Kendall Mills offices on this Wednesday, with another smaller, defenseless child in tow? Don't deny it! There are witnesses."

"I did go to the mills," said Gusta. "But I wasn't threatening anyone. I was just there to—to ask him to do what was right."

"To make threats," said the principal flatly. "Since you are an essentially deceitful person. And how do we know that?"

He tapped the folded newspaper on his desk.

"Right here. You have not been honest with us,

Augusta Neubronner. You have not been honest about who you are. But today the truth has come out."

He flipped the newspaper over. And there, staring out at her from the front page, was *Gusta's own papa.*

She gasped, of course. Her hand went out toward the paper, but not fast enough. Principal Jones had already pulled the newspaper away. She could no longer see the photograph of her father. She could only see the boldest of the other headlines: PRESIDENT ROOSEVELT: HITLER A THREAT TO AMERICAS — TIME TO PREPARE IS NOW.

"You, Augusta, are the only offspring of the notorious fugitive August Neubronner."

Forest fires can go from a spark to outright conflagration in less time than it takes for an egg to boil. The trees were burning now in Gusta's soul, almost as far as a person could see. But in all that fire, there was one cleft in the rock, one little cave a person might hide in, at least for a time, and that was the word *fugitive.*

A fugitive is someone who has not yet been caught.

She couldn't say anything aloud, though. The oxygen was being stolen by the fire inside her. She could hardly breathe, much less speak.

"I find it surprising that you would think no one

would ever discover what sort of person you are," said Principal Jones. "But we do know now, and I promise you: You will toe the line here. You will not be allowed to corrupt your classmates, to terrorize the people of this town, or indeed to misbehave in any way, large or small. Consider yourself duly warned. That is all."

Stranger and stranger: when distressed, discombobulated Gusta slipped back into her classroom, she was met by applause.

Oh, she couldn't understand anything today. She tumbled into her seat and tried not to let the fire still smoldering inside her leak out in any way. She looked very hard at the Scottie dogs on the wall, just past the head of Miss Hatch, and focused on not letting any of her turbulent thoughts show.

"I was just informing the class," said Miss Hatch, "because somebody asked—"

Georges made the tiniest little sound from the rear of the room, but from that tiny sound, Gusta knew that the somebody who had asked must have been Molly Gowen—whatever the question was.

"Somebody asked about the 'Vision of America' essays, about which two will be read by their authors as part of our Patriotic Pageant. And I said I was happy to announce, and I *am* very happy to announce, that your essay, Augusta, is one of our class's two best."

"Along with mine," said Georges Thibodeau.

"Along with yours, Georges," said Miss Hatch. "But please do try to remember not to interrupt."

❦ 40 ❧

A Worse Afternoon

After the lunch recess, however, Miss Hatch was not waiting in the classroom for them all to come back in. The room was unlocked but empty. The children couldn't understand where she might be. For the first five minutes, they sat at their desks, and then the situation deteriorated.

"What if she fell sick?" said Sally Cairns, who was famous for imagining the worst.

"An ambulance car would've driven up to the school, if they had to cart her off to the hospital," said a boy. "There hasn't been any car."

They looked at each other. Molly thought they should send someone to the office to announce they were all alone; others quietly doodled on their papers or (if they were Gusta) felt the heavy lump of dread growing and growing in her stomach. And just as the noise level in the room ticked up a few notches, the door opened, and there she was.

Those who were not at their desks scurried to sit down. Hands were folded. Silence fell over the room.

Miss Hatch looked pale, except for two angry blotches under her eyes. She looked over quickly, in particular, at Gusta, not just once, but twice, two almost instantaneous glances, and the lead weight in Gusta's stomach became all at once at least twice as large and four times as heavy.

"I'm afraid, class, there has been something of a—" She stopped. She was trying to find the right word. "A mix-up," she said, but Gusta could tell that she wasn't satisfied with that word, "about the aviation essays. I have been informed—"

Miss Hatch looked at Gusta again.

By Principal Jones, thought Gusta. *Informed by Principal Jones.*

Gusta's hands looked as pale as paper as she rested them on her desk, just waiting to see what blow would fall next.

"I have been informed that I was wrong to let . . .

someone new to our community be honored for writing the best essay on the theme of 'A Vision of America from On High.' I am very sorry about this change, since it seems to me an injustice. But I am sure our Patriotic Pageant will still be a source of pride and pleasure for all of us. The students who will share their essays with the audience will be Georges Thibodeau . . . and Molly Gowen."

A bellow from Georges: "WHAT ABOUT GUSTA?" And although he was the first and the loudest, he wasn't the only one to ask that question.

"I am asking you, class, to get out your reading books quietly," said Miss Hatch. She didn't even bother to tell Georges not to interrupt.

At the end of the day Miss Hatch held Gusta back for a moment.

"Augusta, dear, I want you to know something: in *my* classroom, it makes absolutely no difference who a pupil's father may happen to be. The things I have been told about you today, by someone who has not been your teacher and has not seen your hard work, your quick mind, and your community spirit—those things have absolutely nothing to do with the Augusta Neubronner I have come to know and value. You will always be treated like any other student while you are in my classroom."

Then she took a breath.

"But you see, Augusta, the thing is, the Patriotic Pageant is not limited to our classroom. It is for the entire school, and I do not run the school. So I'm very sorry indeed about the injustice being done to your essay, but I trust you will be sensible about this . . . *sad error*—and cheerfully let it go."

"Yes, Miss Hatch," said Gusta, her lips numb as if she had been practicing her horn for hours and hours and hours. (*Oh, her horn!*) "Thank you, Miss Hatch."

She was feeling in a very great hurry to get herself out of that place, away from that school, away from everything.

But outside Georges was waiting. He was standing on the walkway and fuming on Gusta's behalf. "Gusta!" he said. "It's NOT FAIR. Why are they doing this to you?"

That was a question Gusta could only have answered properly on a day when all the secrets everywhere had come out to dance in the sunshine—and today was not that day. She stuck to the part of the answer that could be found in incontrovertible print.

"There's something about my papa in the paper today," she said. "I guess it made everyone upset."

Georges looked at her. "In the PAPER?" he said. "He's famous? Like an AVIATOR? Like AMELIA EARHART?"

"Well," said Gusta, "I think the paper didn't say very nice things about him."

"Oh!" said Georges. "Then you mean, famous like Al Capone! Wow."

He fell silent for a moment, awed.

Gusta said stiffly, "Not at all like Al Capone. My papa wants the world to be a better place. He wants justice. He's not a gangster."

"Oh," said Georges again, and Gusta could tell he was wondering why having a father who wanted the world to be a better place could be the source of so much trouble, at school, for that father's daughter.

Gusta said good-bye and left him standing there, wondering. Mr. Bertmann wasn't expecting her that afternoon. Her head was aching. She did not feel quite right, not in any part of her, mind or body.

When she got back home, her thoughts all in an uproar, she found turmoil there as well.

"Something's wrong with Josie," the boys told her

almost as soon as she came in through the door—the boys that weren't Ron or Thomas, of course, quarantined with the influenza.

"She was crying," said Larry, in awe. Josie never cried. "Guess maybe she's sick, too."

Gusta should have asked why, but she couldn't really get the word out, and anyway, the boys' words were tumbling over each other, trying to convey to Gusta how awful the last half hour had been.

Josie, they said, had come home in tears, because of something someone had said at the high school.

"Not just anybody—that music teacher of hers. The teacher said something that made her cry," said Donald. "And you know how Josie loves the music teacher. So it doesn't make sense."

"Teacher's a Kendall. What do you expect?" said Clarence, with his usual sneer.

Donald plowed on with the story: "And Miss Marion said, 'but you said the concert went well!' And Josie said it wasn't about the singing at the concert, that it was something else. Something that Kendall fellow said, the one who runs the mills. Guess he said that Josie had asked for money or something—"

"But Josie didn't," said Larry. "She didn't do whatever that is. Did she?"

Clarence shrugged, but Donald said with conviction: "No!"

"And then Mrs. Hoopes came swooping in," Donald went on. "And she made Miss Marion and Josie go with her into her room, and they've been there ever since."

A desperate, confused hush fell over the hall for a moment, all the boys looking at Gusta as if she could untangle these mysteries for them. It was awful. She felt a little sick. It was hardly ever quiet like this in this hall.

That made her think of something else.

"Where's Delphine?" she said. "Is she asleep?"

"Bess was here earlier—she took Delphine off to see Mr. Bill's cows," said Donald. "What's going on, Gusta? Bess was all upset, too, I could tell. You don't look great, either."

"I'm sorry, sorry—I've got to—" said Gusta, and then, completely unable to imagine how she could ever finish that sentence, or, for that matter, any sentence ever again, she slipped by them all and up the stairs.

She shut the door of the little bedroom behind her, telling herself she must not cry. Everything had gone wrong; everything was falling apart. She had been tested by the storm that was Mr. Kendall—and she had failed. Nevertheless, she must not cry.

When all has failed, then a person must do whatever she can with whatever is left, even if what is left is impossible, like a Wish.

So she gave herself instructions: Pull the box out from under the bed. Find the sock with the thin, round, coin-shaped lump in it. Put her mended sweater on, and then her jacket.

The lump went into the jacket pocket. It wasn't so cold outside, late in the spring as it was already, but it would probably get colder soon enough. She could hardly tell, just at that moment, whether she was hot or cold, but she put a scarf around her neck. She would gladly have wound herself up in a hundred sweaters and a million scarves if it meant she wouldn't have to feel anything, ever again.

"Where are you going, Gusta?" said Larry when she pushed past him on the stairs. The boys had unclumped and scattered into various gloomy corners.

"There's something I have to do," said Gusta, almost running now, escaping through the hall, past Clarence saying "What?," and out across the porch, down the steps, down to the road.

She turned up the road and fled to the woods, up into the wilds of Holly Hill.

✑ 41 ✑

Wishing

The world was surely coming apart at the seams. What had Gramma Hoopes said as she sewed Gusta's button back onto that sweater? *I can't mend everything, but I can mend this.*

I don't know whether I can mend anything at all, thought Gusta, as she climbed the dirt road up the hill with the Wish clutched fiercely in her fist. *But I guess I have to try. I have to try. I have to try. Even if it's just fairy-tale nonsense, still I have to try.*

She stumbled over a rock in the road, but didn't fall, didn't fall. Although her feet were being careless, inside her head Gusta was trying to be very careful. She was making a list, as she rushed up the hill, of everything that had gone wrong in her world:

Josie! She had not meant to break that secret out of its shell. Now Josie was crying, and Josie never cried.

And Bess's father was still in trouble, still without a job. She had tried to do one right thing, and it had all gone wrong.

She had lost her French horn. She had sold it for a hundred dollars, but in the end, she had nothing, not the money and not the horn.

And her own father gone, too, a *fugitive* — if they caught him he would be in prison.

Or if he had made it to Canada, he might soon — might already — be fighting in the European war.

And the war might not stay in Europe. That headline in the paper today: PRESIDENT ROOSEVELT: HITLER A THREAT TO AMERICAS — TIME TO PREPARE IS NOW.

When you added it all up, it seemed a lot for any one Wish to fix. But you have to add things up, nevertheless, before you start planning.

Insight into necessity, as her father would say.

She was passing by the cemetery already. The Wish tingled in the palm of her hand. She left the dirt road here and took the path up the back of the hill. It seemed like the natural place to go.

Even if she was going to try to use a Wish to mend the world—*fairy-tale nonsense,* whispered her papa— even if she was using *fairy-tale nonsense,* she was determined to do it in the most logical possible way.

She was feverishly determined: she would be careful. She would not mess this up. Probably you had to say something out loud to make a wish. But just in case, she slipped the Wish back into her pocket, to keep it safely away from her planning thoughts.

She had to walk more carefully here, where there were tree roots and surprising outcroppings of stone to catch your feet, but she kept only a third of her mind on the path. The other two thirds worked away at the question of the best possible wish, kneading words into place, tinkering, rejecting, reshaping, despairing. Not any old sentence would do. She needed everything bundled up into something terse, ironclad, and loophole-free.

The first version that came floating into her head was silly: *Please make Mr. Kendall and Principal Jones and Hitler change their minds and become kind, generous people, and in particular give me my hundred dollars back.* She rejected that right away, as all loophole. It left all the people she cared about unmentioned, and who knew what a Wish might do with "kind and generous"! Maybe someone as wicked as Hitler might think it was *kind and generous* of himself to conquer ever more countries. No.

Then a very different sort of thought: *Please make Miss Kendall stay fond of Josie, no matter what.* For a moment that seemed perfect: selfless and simple. But in the second moment she realized that a wish like that did absolutely nothing to help anyone. Probably Miss Kendall was still "fond of Josie," even now, but being fond of people didn't necessarily mean you would go against your bossy brother's orders. Or even let talented Josie back into the high-school chorus. No, that was a bust.

Third, a bright, clear bubble: *Keep my father safe.*

But . . . only her father? In all that war? She shook her head: her father, who didn't like the very idea of wishes, would hate the selfishness of this one.

So: *Keep everyone safe.*

Alarm bells! Alarm bells! Alarm bells in her head!

Because just think how magic — sneaky, loophole-seeking magic — might interpret that term, *safe*! Gusta had a quick image of the whole world falling under some sort of Sleeping Beauty spell, falling asleep, wherever they were, so that they could never hurt any-one else ever again, or be hurt themselves.

An icy prickle ran suddenly up her arm, and she found that her hand had somehow made its way back into her pocket and was actually scrabbling around there for the Wish. No! She raised both her hands very fast, right into the air, far from any pockets. And stood there, feeling dizzy. She had to stop walking a moment so she could shake her head clear.

Had she really just been about to—to—to risk shutting down all of the human world? With one poorly phrased wish?

Her head was so hot and achy. It felt about twice its ordinary size—it made even walking up the path feel like an endless slog.

On Holly Hill, the woods were made up of a tangle of many kinds of trees, pitch pine trees and paper-skinned birches and old spruce, pointy-leafed maple and broad-leafed beech. As the path around the back of the hill skimmed the edge of a neighboring pasture, Gusta could see, through a gap in those mixed-up, tangled trees, mountains rising in the far distance, maybe as far away as the next state, which was, Gusta knew from school, New Hampshire. Gusta put a testing finger on the rim of her glasses: it was already a kind of magic, she thought, to look up with your own eyes and see mountains that were a hundred miles away.

One last rise up through the trees, and the path spilled her out on the rock where the sea captain's stubby, wonderful lighthouse rose up before her, with its funny name chiseled into its side, *The Beckon Beacon*. That seemed like the right place to bring a (possible) Wish, she guessed. Gusta clambered up to the little platform there, where the vase filled with fool's gold shimmered a little in the late-afternoon sun. It was time. She fetched the Wish back out of her pocket; it seemed to tingle in her hand. Far away to the east, she knew, over there where the clouds were thick and dark, was the sea. You could not *see* the sea, but the lighthouse looked out and remembered it was there. The old captain had wanted to keep the lighthouse always looking out toward that ocean.

She opened up her tingling palm and looked at the Wish sitting there. It glittered differently from the mica in the road: it sparkled as you looked at it, as if it were thinking bright, secret thoughts.

The glittering Wish and her pounding head made it so hard to think properly. She looked at it, and she wished . . . she wished . . . she longed for everything to be—oh, how could she say it? What were the words? Everything was getting tangled up in her mind: her father, her mother, Josie, Gramma Hoopes and Aunt

Marion, the war, Bess's family, the principal, the mills, back to the war, and Josie again, and everyone hurting, sweaters with their buttons torn off, oh—

"I wish," she said right aloud, and then she clapped her hand over her mouth, because she had spoken without meaning to, and the Wish had become warm and very bright and almost slippery in her hand, and she realized she was already, without meaning to be, in the middle of making her wish, and oh, if only she knew what she was doing! But she also saw, suddenly, already halfway into using the Wish, already too late, that of course she had no idea how to solve all the world's problems, that she had no more idea than a squirrel about how to make this wish perfect and fail-safe and fine.

In the end, she wasn't capable of making a wish, some wish in particular—all she could manage was *wish*ING.

Wishing, wishing, wishing. A gust of wishing wafted through her, without logical structure or carefully avoided loopholes or direct objects or even words—just a great wordless tidal wave of longing. Wishing. Wishing. She had set it off with those two little words, and now could not speak even a single word more. Her hands were shaking.

And perhaps because of the tremble that now ran all the way down her arms to the very tips of her nervous fingers, the wishing spilling forth from Gusta became so great that the Wish itself tumbled out of her hand into the vase, hit the shiny rocks kept there, and for a moment Gusta had the impression that the lighthouse had burst into light, as if the vase held bits of actual stars.

She seemed to be surrounded by light, almost too bright for her merely human eyes — she blinked — and the light was gone.

In the vase, the Wish rested between two of the shiny rocks, and it looked as dull and gray as any ordinary coin. It looked empty.

A bird in the trees behind her said, "Tooweet! Wit tooweet!"

It was not fair. Not fair. But there it was: Gusta had had her chance (maybe) to wish the world well, to wish everything mended, and instead the last Wish was gone, all used up, and nothing to show for it. *In the light of trouble*, Gusta turned out to be so full of wishing that she couldn't even manage to make use of one single actual Wish.

She had wasted it. That was the plain truth. The world was still torn all apart, and Gusta had not mended it, not a single stitch's worth.

❧ 42 ❧

Lost and Found

USTA!" said a brisk voice nearby. "For Pete's sake. Wake yourself up!"

Gusta had just closed her eyes for an instant, but now she found herself pushing up from an oddly unforgiving surface in a world without sunlight. Why had she been sleeping on the floor of their room? That was foolish. No wonder Josie—because that was the person the voice belonged to—was yelling at her.

Then she realized she wasn't in any room. Her head was spinning, and all of her body ached, and she was outside, where the air was much cooler than it had been, and around her everything was dark except for a bright star of lantern light swinging in someone's hand.

Actually, she realized a whole domino-row's worth of things at once: that her hip bones were sore because she had been asleep on the platform of the sea captain's lighthouse, that her head felt approximately like an overheated balloon, and that Josie was right now swinging herself up the lighthouse ladder with the lantern.

"Honestly," said Josie. "Augusta Hoopes N.! Haven't you caused enough trouble? Whatever possessed you to run away like that?"

It all came back to Gusta then, all the reasons she was out here in the dark, and why she was tucked up next to a vase filled with stones (and one used Wish) in a lighthouse from which you couldn't, even in daylight, actually see the sea.

"I fell asleep," she said. "I feel very strange."

Josie put a hand on Gusta's forehead and then pulled it back again with a frown.

"Yup," she said. "Burning up with fever. Mrs. Hoopes was worried you might be out here sick somewhere. Guess only a person burning up with fever would be able to fall asleep *here*. Well, let's see if we can get you back down this hill, sick though you may be."

Gusta rubbed her eyes. Nothing seemed quite real, but she was so glad Josie was there.

"How did you find me?"

"Seemed like the sort of place you might go in a pinch. You were so excited about finding it! Anyway, everyone's out looking for you, the ones who aren't sick in bed. There are folks looking for you in all sorts of places, I guess. Why not here? Oh, that reminds me—"

She brought a chunk of shiny stone out of some pocket and tipped it into the vase.

"Gotta add a little mica to the lamp every time you come," she said. "That's what Mrs. Hoopes always told me. It's tradition. Calls you home, some folks think. Not that fool's gold calls anyone in any direction, of course, not for real. But let's get *you* on home, now, Gusta."

Josie helped Gusta back down the ladder. She had to leave the lantern behind for a moment, because Gusta was all wobble. Then Josie went back up and grabbed the lantern again while Gusta swayed in the shifting light.

"I know you're sick and all—hang on to me here!—but I still can't believe you were foolish enough to run away. No, not just that: foolish enough to get us all into hot water, and *then* foolish enough to run away afterward."

Gusta's legs were stiff and awkward, but somehow, with Josie's help, they managed to move her along the path, spattered with the unsteady swinging blobs of lantern light. Josie was holding the lantern, and she went slightly ahead, with Gusta hanging on to her arm and trying to put the words together that might say what she needed to say.

"I'm so sorry, Josie," she said. That was all she could think to say. "I'm really, really sorry. I didn't mean to cause so much trouble. Especially not for you."

"Of course you didn't mean it," said Josie. "Watch that rock there! No point in your being so ridiculous."

Gusta didn't feel ridiculous: she felt plain bad.

Josie stopped and turned, the lantern shining in her hand and lighting her face from the bottom up, which made her look mysterious and full of fire.

"All the same, Gusta. It was *ridiculous* to go bother that awful Mr. Kendall," she said. "That's like pitching stones at a hornet's nest."

"I'm sorry," said Gusta again. Her head was aching.

"Want to know something?" said Josie. "That's

what *everyone's* saying. Miss Marion said that. She's sorry. And even Mrs. Hoopes. Mrs. Hoopes, saying she's sorry! Everyone's sorry, I guess, about their big old secret leaking out this way, unexpected like."

"How," said Gusta. "How? How'd they stand it, all that time?"

After all, she, Gusta, had only had to carry that particular secret for a day or two, and it had been almost too heavy to bear. So how Aunt Marion and Gramma Hoopes could have kept that weight on their shoulders, all those years . . .

"Don't know," said Josie. "It was what they thought they had to do; that's what they keep telling me. I guess because they wanted to keep me, is the thing."

"Of course they wanted to keep you!" said Gusta, and for a moment she had to stop and rest, while the night woods spun all around her in the lantern light. Josie gave her a moment and then prodded her forward.

"There's no 'of course' about it, though, is there?" said Josie, back to her practical self. "Look at the state kids who come to live with Mrs. Hoopes. That little Delphine is plenty cute, right? Why do you think she's not with her own family, somewhere else? Well, I know why, because I remember the day some girl came to our door in tears, and she had a belly about as big as a blue-ribbon pumpkin. She was 'in trouble,' that's what she kept saying. So of course I said out loud, stupidly, 'Why? What kind of trouble?' And they hushed me right up, Miss Marion and Mrs. Hoopes did. But think what they must have been thinking! And they were kind to that girl. They were. She had her baby, who turned out to be Delphine, in one of the spare bedrooms, and she didn't take her away with her when she left. Maybe that girl wished she could, but she couldn't. She couldn't go home with a baby. She had to leave her. And I thought"—she kicked a rock away in the dark—"I thought: oh, I see, that's how it was with me, too. Some poor woman came here and left me behind. Maybe she was sad to leave me, but I'll never ever know. And then it turns out, *she didn't leave.*"

Josie swung the lantern.

"She didn't leave!" she said, and her face in the lantern light was the oddest combination of angry and glad. "She just hid the truth away, and she and Mrs. Hoopes brought in all the other children, the state kids, the boarders, the real orphans, and that was the story—all so's I wouldn't have to go away."

"They don't put their own on a bus, the Hoopeses," said Gusta. "Gramma Hoopes said that to me."

"A bitty baby on a bus?" said Josie. "I don't think so! Well, anyway, the truth's out now, and it'll take some getting used to. I don't know how I even feel anymore. Whether I'm happy or sad or mad as hornets about it or what!"

But being Josie, she actually laughed aloud about this.

After a moment, Josie added, "But Mrs. Hoopes—I mean, I guess, *Gramma* Hoopes, golly—said, 'Doesn't change anything, not really,' and in a way of course she's right."

Except of course it *did* change things. Both Gusta and Josie knew that. It changed everything. It changed "Mrs. Hoopes" into "Gramma Hoopes," didn't it? It changed the names of everyone. It changed who they *were*. It made Miss Kendall angry, and Miss Kendall was never angry. But most of all, it turned Aunt Marion—golly!—into somebody's mama.

"Oh!" said Gusta.

A new thought had risen up in her mind all of a sudden.

"Josie," said Gusta, leaning heavily against her. "Think about it. You and me and Bess—we're not random people to each other at all anymore—we're all *cousins*!"

Even unsentimental Josie made a surprised sound then as she chewed on that thought. "How about that?" she said. "Look at your feverish head, coming up with these ideas! You got that about right, I guess. Cousins. Well, ha!"

And then soon, despite everything, they were hobbling down the last part of the road to the house, where there were lights in so many of the windows that Gusta's heart quailed a little: all the people who were out looking for her! All the trouble she had caused!

"I don't want to go in," said Gusta. "They're all going to be so upset and mad."

"Don't be *extra* foolish," said Josie, making a dismissive swoosh with the lantern in the general direction of the front porch. "You're burning up with fever, and you need your bed. And nothing here is going to be as hard as school on Monday. Everyone will know everything by then—you know they will. Once a secret's a little bit out, it's all over town. The talk will be all about why I'm out of the chorus and whose child I am and whose child *you* are—yep, I heard about that article in the newspaper, too."

"They said today I can't read my essay at the Patriotic Pageant, because of that thing in the paper." Suddenly that little bit of memory had popped back into her head. It made her teeth chatter a little.

"Oh, really? So it's already started. Are you cut out of being the Statue of Liberty, too?"

Josie had taken an interest in the Statue of Liberty thing, since it required organizing a costume.

"N-n-no, I don't know. Statues don't say anything, right? So I don't think the principal cares."

"Oh, well, all right, then. Up the stairs now. One at a time. We'll have to talk Mrs. Hoopes into letting us have a sheet, that's all." Josie squared her shoulders, readying herself for that battle as well as all the thousand other battles that were surely coming their way. "Listen up, Gusta," she said. "You and me, we've got to walk around like we're a mile above all this nonsense. That's the only way. Stand tall and walk proud."

Gusta took a moment to stand tall, right there on the porch stairs in the dark. There was a lump in her throat—a lump about the size of that wasted Wish.

"You sound like my papa," she said to Josie.

"Do I? Well. Then he and I agree on something,

even if he *is* running from the law. And going into this house of ours right now is a chance to practice. You hear me, Gusta? In we go. Practicing for school on Monday and for that pageant next week and for all of it. Onward. Sick, but proud. Stand tall, cousin!"

"Solidarity forever," said Gusta, with half her fever-shattered voice but the whole of her heart.

And, standing tall, in they went.

∝ 43 ∾

A Vision from On High

Time and fever passed. It took some days before Gusta was well enough to go back to school, and even then she felt less than herself: thin, somehow, and watered down.

But almost as soon as she got back, it was time to worry about the pageant.

Josie and Bess were adamant: there was only one necessary and appropriate costume for the Statue of Liberty — a sheet, cleverly draped. A sheet that would not, as they all assured their grandmother, be damaged at all. Not cut with scissors or sewn up recklessly or anything — just draped and pinned.

Gramma Hoopes held to her "no" until the very last night, when Josie promised she would personally come over from the high school for the pageant and do all the necessary draping and pinning herself.

"Too bad it's that Molly Gowen who's going to be up there speaking!" said Bess. "I guess it's going to be all about milk, milk, milk the whole time."

The Dairy Wars were famous even outside the bounds of the fifth grade.

"And then the Thibodeau boy will have to remind us all about the virtues of Springdale Dairy," said Josie.

"When he's on his own he doesn't always talk about the dairy," said Gusta. "He's much more interesting than that, believe it or not."

Bess and Josie shared a meaningful look. "Oh, is that so?" they said.

In fact, good old Georges Thibodeau, who carried the principle of "just say what you need to say, whenever and however you feel you need to say it" right over into the writing of contest essays, had confessed to Gusta that he had written "an actual poem" as his entry. Now, Georges was not what Gusta would ordinarily have considered poetic-looking, but it turns out that looking poetic, or not, does not determine the kind of composition one produces.

On the day of the pageant, Georges was cool as a cucumber, up there in front of everyone. Gusta was very impressed. Miss Hatch had decided he should go first in the fifth-grade part of the program, while the rest of the class stood quietly clustered under — yes — the Statue of Liberty. The class as a whole would recite the Liberty sonnet, and then Molly Gowen would recite her composition, and then it would all be done. That was the plan, anyway.

Because she was up on her pedestal being the Statue of Liberty, and because she was a Statue of Liberty *who wore eyeglasses*, Gusta had an excellent view of the audience, both the children seated in neat lines in their chairs, class by class (some of them in costumes because they had already performed their pieces for the pageant — but the fifth grade went last), and the parents in the rows behind, and the late-arriving parents standing against the walls. Gusta also had an excellent view of the top and back of Georges Thibodeau's head.

"Away! Away!" said Georges now, in his ever-so-slightly foghorn voice to that room full of intently listening people.

"Away! Away! Above the clouds,
The silver airplanes fly away!
They will defend
Until day's end.
They waste no time. They cannot stay . . ."

He was doing a fantastic job. He mentioned Amelia Earhart and the brave crew of another lost plane, *L'Oiseau Blanc,* and he managed to squeeze those names into lines that rhymed. Miss Hatch was standing to the side of the stage with her hands clasped, smiling. The Patriotic Pageant was turning out to be an enormous success.

Here, however, is where odd things began to happen.

Gusta, who was carefully being the Statue of Liberty, started thinking, by accident, about people who fly airplanes, and then slipped from that thought to thinking about her father, who might even this very minute be flying an airplane for Canada or headed across the sea to help fight the Nazis in Europe. He hadn't written a single letter, of course, so she did not know where he actually was. He was far away. He had left them. He was beyond the call even of the French horn's clearest, truest note, or of the sea captain's beacon, or of any wish.

And now there was no more horn, and no more Wish, and even the one hundred dollars, which had seemed so much like something solid and real, had come and gone.

Like her father, gone.

Tears built up in her eyes all at once, without warning, and a few of them spilled down her face. She could feel them spilling, and it was awful, because *she was the Statue of Liberty*, and could not put down her torch or wipe her eyes.

The crowd cheered for Georges Thibodeau! That meant his poem must be over.

Even now she couldn't move, of course, because now began the actual Statue of Liberty part of the program.

The whole fifth grade was on the stage, reciting the Emma Lazarus poem together.

Stand tall, stand tall, keep, oh keep standing tall! Gusta told herself. She blinked fiercely. She tried to think about other things. She looked at the adults standing in the far back of the room, lined up against the walls. She could see their faces looking up at the students onstage, some of those faces filled with particular love, because perhaps their own child was a fifth-grader.

And then it turned out that one of those faces *belonged to her mother*.

There was not the slightest doubt in the world. Her own mother (!!!) had turned up for the end-of-year Patriotic Pageant, all the way from New York. She must have arrived a little late, because there she was, slipping into place against the back wall by the doors. Gusta would never have spotted her in the old days, before the eyeglasses. But now she could see it was her mother, even from way up here, and at the end of the last line of the Liberty sonnet, in the momentary pause before the applause broke out, she saw and heard her mother put her hand to her mouth and, looking up at Gusta, way up there, give a smiling, gasping, heartbroken, proud little sob that traveled right up to Gusta as fast as a pigeon and as bright as the brightest note of any horn.

"Oh!" said the Statue of Liberty aloud—and she dropped her torch.

Some people didn't notice, probably, because it was time for applause, and nobody was hurt, thank goodness, because, fortunately for them, torches that are actually pieces of painted cardboard don't do as much damage as the metallic, flaming kind.

Gusta hardly heard Molly Gowen's name being announced. She was too busy trying to figure out what had happened to her torch and trying to spot her mother again, at the back of the crowd—all while not moving an inch.

She saw (without much paying attention to the

details) that Molly was walking to the front of the stage. Gusta just wanted the pageant to be over by this point. So Gusta wasn't paying very much attention to Molly taking a deep breath, tossing her curls back, kneading her fingers together nervously, beginning to speak.

And then Gusta heard her own name, and felt the crowd out there shift in their seats, and as distracted as she was at that moment, Gusta understood that something peculiar was happening.

"Actually, it shouldn't be me standing here right now; it should be Augusta Neubronner," Molly Gowen had just said. *That was really what she was saying!* "I'm telling you this now because we all know how important it is to be honest. That's part of being American, or at least it should be. Our presidents are supposed to be honest. Our senators and our town leaders and also our captains of industry are supposed to be honest. For instance, I know for a fact that Sharp's Ridge Farm has been producing completely honest, American milk for more than ten years. And I think even people in the fifth grade in America should be honest, too. So: the honest truth about this aviation essay contest is that the two best compositions in our class were written by Georges Thibodeau, whom you just heard, and by

Augusta Hoopes Neubronner. And not by me. That's the truth. So I think Augusta should come up to the front here now and recite her composition for us. And you can come up to Sharp's Ridge Farm and read mine if you want, because I'm proud of it, and it's about the importance of milk to the American aviation industry, and it will be tacked up on the wall at Sharp's Ridge next to the ice-cream freezer. And that's all I'm going to say. Let's be honest, true-blue Americans now: let's listen to *Augusta*."

And Molly stepped to the side, turned around so that all the amazed students onstage could catch a glimpse of her flushed face and her very determined, Molly Gowen eyes, and she beckoned with a grand gesture to the Statue of Liberty—*Gusta*—who was at that moment so stricken with surprise that she was almost as unable to move or think as a real, genuine statue.

It was only because Georges started cheering that Gusta began to unfreeze again. His bellow was so friendly and encouraging that a scattering of people in the audience were infected by it and began to clap their hands or even cheer themselves, although they must all have been mightily surprised, and maybe even amused, by this twist in the Patriotic Pageant.

Molly was still making bossy gestures that definitely meant *Come down here right this minute, Augusta Hoopes Neubronner!* But of course it wasn't a simple thing, finding a way to gracefully descend from her pedestal, when Gusta's mind was all in a muddle of shock and surprise. Stepping down from her perch under all those eyes was plenty scary, especially considering that she knew Gramma Hoopes was sitting out in the audience, watching carefully to make sure no harm came to her bedsheet.

She took a careful step, and another step, and then she felt herself losing her balance nevertheless, knew she was about to fall, knew she was already falling, and curled up in a ball as she fell because she was trying so hard, so very hard, not to put any rips or tears in her grandmother's sheet.

Wonder of wonders: she rolled, and came back upright again, and the sheet was fine!

The crowd went wild, because no one there had ever seen the Statue of Liberty turn somersaults before. Nor would they likely ever see that happen again, all the long years of their lives.

The rest of the fifth grade had been herded off the stage by then. Only Gusta was still standing there, and she was blinking from the miracle of the unexpected somersault and the untorn sheet.

And then the next unexpected-but-predictable thing happened, which is that as Gusta now looked out at those smiling, waiting faces, one of which belonged to *her own mother,* she could not remember a single word of that essay she had written in what seemed now like the awfully distant past.

Stand tall, she told herself. *Look like you know what you're about!*

She felt a cold shiver all through her — probably the same shiver someone feels when they are about to fly up in an airplane, on their own, for the very first time — and she opened her mouth and even though she didn't remember a single word of her actual essay, she began to speak anyway.

Gusta couldn't exactly remember, afterward, the details of what she had said. She remembered little bits of it, like snatches of a dream: she remembered saying something about how many people shared Georges Thibodeau's dream of flying up in an airplane high in the sky and looking out the windows down at the fields like squares way below you, but that when she had written the first version of this essay on "A Vision of America from On High," she hadn't really been able to picture very clearly in her mind's eye what that would even be like, looking down from an airplane, because her own eyes had been so bad that she wouldn't have been able to see the whole length of that airplane, much less the fields down below. But that she had learned since coming to Springdale, Maine, that vision is about more than what even a very good pair of eyeglasses allows you to see. That there are all sorts of ways of seeing from "on high," and all sorts of very different ways of looking at the world.

And then she talked a little bit about bats and pigeons, the pigeons always seeing the world as *the way home*, and the little bats feeling about themselves with their bat sounds and bat noises, the shape of the echoes painting them a picture of their world almost as if they had tiny invisible fingers hundreds of feet long that they could run over the fields and forests below them, like we might feel the grain of a carpet, maybe.

Each of us has a vision of America, she said, like the way each of the flying creatures — the pigeon, the bat, the flying man in his metal airplane — sees something different when they look down at Springdale,

Maine. She hadn't known that before, and she was glad to know it now.

And that was all. Probably if she had had the written essay in her hands, she would have had another sentence at the end there, something to wind things up with all elegantly, but it was what it was, and the words had spilled out of her under their own power, and now they stopped spilling, and she was done.

The room was applauding—her grandmother was smiling—the Hoopes Home boys cheering so loudly that their neighbors had to lean away—Miss Hatch, over there to the right, looked rather pale and stunned (but also distinctly proud, pleased and proud)—and Gusta's mother (her mother!) was not just grinning ear to ear, but was pushing forward through the crowd to where Josie and Gramma Hoopes were sitting, was embracing Josie in a great, enormous hug (Josie looked rather surprised), was turning now to come to Gusta—but Gusta was already there, trailing the untorn sheet, her arms around her mother's neck, and glad, glad, glad!

☙ 44 ❧

Growing Underground

Well," said Gusta's mother, with a sigh of contentment, as she and Gusta looked out over the field, dusted with the pale green of new shoots and first leaves. "It's a great comfort to see you and the world mending so well. When that letter came from your grandmother, saying you were sick"—she gave her head the kind of sharp shake that sends the past back into its corner—"well, I had a bad time of it. And then I jumped on the bus, as soon as I could manage, and came up here. And here we are! Look at those potatoes sprouting up already! It'll be time for hilling them soon enough."

They had already helped with the frying up of breakfast, and the cleaning away after breakfast, and the caring for the chickens, and even some weeding of the vegetable garden. Gusta's mother seemed to have an insatiable hunger for all the old farmhouse chores, and Gusta stuck by her and helped, and it was like having all the hurt places in her heart weeded and cared for and fed, going through that lovely long day of chores with her mother.

Hilling, though! Gusta liked the sound of that word. For a moment she set the potatoes aside in her mind and imagined instead Holly Hill, where the forest was thickening every day about the old bits of stone wall.

"You and I could go *hilling* later, couldn't we?" she said to her mother. "I've found so many wonderful things on the hill. The old captain's lighthouse and glittering rocks."

"Ha, Gusta!" said her mother. "Maybe when I come back, beginning of August, blueberry season, we can go up the hill and pick for a pie. But you know that's not actually *hilling*: you hill potatoes so more potatoes will grow. Shovel earth on top of them, so more potatoes grow underground."

"Oh," said Gusta. She was savoring the words *when I come back*. Then another odd thought came into her head and slipped right out of her mouth:

"The baby potato plants must think you've given up on them, then, when the dirt gets shoveled over their heads."

Gusta's mother put her arm around Gusta's shoulders for a long moment. "Maybe they do," she said. "Hadn't ever thought about it from the point of view of the potatoes. Come to think of it, maybe it's even like being sent away to live in a place you don't know, with a grandmother you don't remember, and a new school and new teacher to get used to. That's a lot to have shoveled over anyone's head, even someone as hardworking and capable as you, Gusta. I know. I do know."

Gusta couldn't say anything to that for a minute or so. She just leaned against the warmth of her mother, come at last to visit her in Maine, and she felt all sorts of little jagged pieces inside her settling down comfortably into a pattern that meant something, even if she didn't know quite yet what that something was.

Even if there was still no news from her father. No sign from Canada—no sign from any prisons or jails in this country. They were still in the dark about what had happened to him, Gusta and her mother. That was a still-sharp disappointment, in the midst of so much joy.

And of course there was the problem of the horn. She hadn't told her mother about Mr. Kendall pocketing those five twenty-dollar bills. She hadn't said anything about the money, because she also hadn't said anything about tearing that line off her mother's letter, way back on that cold day when she had walked up Elm Street for the first time.

"But look how much you've grown, underground!" said her mother, with a twisty, half-glad, half-sad smile. "You're an inch taller and a mile smarter. Wish I could just stay up here and watch you grow."

"Oh, why *can't* you stay, Mama?" said Gusta in a rush. "Now that you're here, why don't you just stay?"

But those were unfair questions, and Gusta knew the answers to them already. Gusta's mother *couldn't* stay for very long—not this time. Not yet. She had her job in New York, and you didn't just walk away from paying jobs.

But here she was now, and that was a pretty good sign that she would come back again.

And part of why she could be here now had to do with Josie. Gusta's disastrous visit with Mr. Kendall might not have been entirely a disaster, after all. It might be part of the reason her own mother could now come home and do chores for a day or two, instead of always staying so far away. Her mama had explained, and it was almost like a fairy tale, when she described it—a fairy tale that had had to wait a very long time for any kind of happy ending.

Long, long ago there had been a big fight, apparently, over the difference between what Gusta's mother thought was the right thing to do for Josie, and what Gramma Hoopes and Aunt Marion had decided to do.

Gusta's mother thought if a child was not an orphan, she needed to know that, come what may.

Gramma Hoopes thought that you should not be so reckless, when there are people's lives and reputations in the mix. But on the other hand, of course you had to keep family close. If need be, then, you brought in all those other children, orphans and half orphans— you started a Home in your home—to disguise the fact that one of those orphans, the First Girl, was actually your own, the child of your child.

"So I said," Gusta's mother had said, hooking a loose strand of hair behind her ear (they were out in the soft evening air together then, looking across the fields toward Holly Hill), "that I wouldn't be part of their falsehood, and I wouldn't come back until I could call Josie my own niece. I was hotheaded, wasn't I? But you know"—she had had a little fire in her eyes when she said it—"*I still think I was right.*"

Honestly, Gusta was rather amazed that she had never realized, all these years when her father was rallying people to the cause, that her *mother*, too, was a person who, like the Statue of Liberty, held a light up high and wanted truth to shine into all shadowy places. A stubborn person, when it came to justice and love.

But we discover things about our parents all our whole lives long.

There were things Gusta's mother had forgotten about her own sea-captain grandfather, for instance.

So when Gusta brought down the big notebook from the attic, with all its pictures of snaggletoothed bats, Gusta's mother clapped her hands in amazement and turned the pages with careful hands. She thought that the professor in New York for whom she had been doing so much editing and typewriting might be very interested to see those pictures, too. Professor Jones worked at a museum where they studied all kinds of animals—even bats.

So with Gramma Hoopes's permission, Gusta's mother packed up two of the notebooks very carefully and took them back with her to New York City.

And just before she climbed up the stairs onto

the bus and rumbled away, Gusta's mother bent and whispered a fairy-tale promise into Gusta's ear: "And remember: blueberry season, Gusta! I'll come back for sure, in blueberry season. Apart and working through July — and then I'll come home and we'll both eat pie!"

☙ 45 ❧

Josie Puts Her Foot Down

"L et me get this straight," said Josie. "You went and sold your horn, but you didn't get any money for it?"

Gusta had finally been cornered. Literally cornered: in the kitchen, at the end of a bout of washing dishes. Josie corralled her with arms and dishcloth and wouldn't let the question go: Why hadn't Gusta ever bothered to go over to the high school and *pick up her horn?*

Didn't she even *care* about the Honorary Orphan Band? (said Josie) Whose chance at a legitimizing ribbon from the county fair was plummeting every day, without their horn player? Wasn't that horn supposed to be all special and dear to Gusta's heart? So why hadn't she ever brought it home? Didn't Gusta even *care*?

Oh, how Gusta cared! But the horror of Mr. Kendall's hand grabbing the money—his threat about calling the police—the shame of having let him take that hundred dollars away—the feeling of failure Gusta sank into whenever she thought back to that music room at the high school—the fear that if she said too much, Josie would get herself into yet more trouble—

"It's the Kendalls," Gusta had said, keeping it all vague, though the pain in her soul was pretty much the exact opposite of vague. "I can't go back to Miss Kendall, not after everything."

Josie shook her head.

"Nope, not good enough, Gusta. You are explaining this to me now: Why can't you just march over to the high school and pick up your horn? Miss Kendall may not like us anymore, and it might not be the most pleasant hour of your life, but she's not going to steal an instrument from a kid. I tell you honestly, if you won't go get it back, then I'll go, and I'm sure that's worse, where the Kendalls are concerned."

Gusta stared into Josie's determined eyes and saw that the game was up.

"Miss Kendall didn't steal it," she said. "She bought it."

Josie blinked. "You sold your horn?" she said. "You really did? Why? And whyever wouldn't you tell us afterward, anyway? I thought you were bound and determined never to sell that horn until your dying day or longer."

"Because of Uncle Charlie," said Gusta. "The horn was worth a hundred dollars, and that's enough to fix his hand. I couldn't not sell it, then, could I?"

"Oh!" said Josie. For a moment even Josie could say nothing at all. Then she said, "So he's getting his hand fixed up for real? You got all that money? And Bess never even said a word!"

Gusta gulped. She hadn't known before that shame could bubble up in a person like a tarry, viscous fluid, burning every part of your throat and soul.

"That's because there didn't end up being any money. He grabbed it away," she said. "Mr. Kendall. I couldn't stop him. I should have run away faster, before he grabbed it. But I didn't, and it's gone."

Josie asked about five more questions, pulling the whole story out of Gusta's poor shame-ridden gut.

Her last question was, "Are you sure Miss Kendall knows he took that hundred dollars away?"

That took Gusta by surprise. She hadn't done a lot of thinking about what Miss Kendall's view of it all might have been.

"She needs to know," said Josie finally. "It's simple logic. I guess I'll have to go talk to her after all. I know she's in the school on Wednesdays—there's summer rehearsals for Regionals going on."

"No, don't," said Gusta. "I'll go. I won't look so much like a frightening blackmailer if I'm all on my own."

Josie laughed, probably because Gusta was still pretty scrawny around the edges.

"You sure?" she said. "All you have to do is go in there and tell the simple truth, you know. You should have the French horn or the money, after all. It's only fair."

And that was how Gusta ended up back at the music room door, after almost being run down by a few grown-up-looking girls with violin cases.

She took a deep breath and went in through that door as if she were actually brave.

There was Miss Kendall, straightening music, as usual. She looked a bit different, though—older and tireder. And when she saw Gusta, her face went pale, which was very different from days gone by.

"Augusta!" she said. "What are you doing here?"

"The thing is, Miss Kendall, there's something I need to ask you," said Gusta.

"What can that be?" said Miss Kendall. She sounded so very sad. "I will tell you the truth, Augusta. I've never been as perplexed and disappointed in all my days. I was so proud of you girls, of your talents and your hard work. But my trust was misplaced. And now you come back again? Whatever for?"

Gusta took a deep breath.

"The thing is, Miss Kendall—it's about the French horn," said Gusta. "It's just, I only wanted to sell it to help my Uncle Charlie. But without the money, it doesn't do any good. And I don't know—I'm not sure—but maybe you don't know . . . that I didn't end up with the money."

Miss Kendall pulled back. The sadness in her face froze immediately, into something harder. "But Augusta! I put the money for it right into your hand, in this very room. How can you say otherwise?"

"So I guess Mr. Kendall didn't tell you after all?" Gusta was so nervous and so frightened and so angry by now that she wasn't quite sure how her sentences were managing to come together. But she had backed down too many times, and she was not going to back down today. She figured she must have learned *something* from her stint as the Statue of Liberty! She stretched her now-sixth-grade self as tall as possible—*a mighty woman with a torch*—and told the truth, the truth, the truth: "Because, Miss Kendall, he *took* that money away from me, right outside that door! Two minutes after you gave it to me. I thought he would have told you. But maybe he didn't tell you. So it did no good for Uncle Charlie after all. He still needs that operation. So I thought I would come ask you about it, since you have the horn and Mr. Kendall took the money. . . ."

Without the horn, her voice seemed like such a puny thing. She ran out of words, there at the end. But she had spoken the truth, and that had to count for something.

Miss Kendall was staring at her. "How can you say such a horrible thing about—about Mr. Kendall?" she said.

"I think you should ask him," said Gusta. "Ask him, Miss Kendall. Please just ask him. He didn't know about the horn. And he was so angry. Please ask him, that's all."

And that was about all Gusta could manage. She slipped back out into the hall and ran out, out, and away.

"Well, that's that," said Josie when Gusta got back home. "Don't be so disappointed. You've done what you could."

And they folded sheets together for a while, slapping the air out of them so the folds would stay crisp, so that this one small corner of the universe would be, at least in this one small way, orderly and rational and fair.

ᚖ 46 ᚔ

Aliens

Gusta had just about reached the end of her twenty-three hours' worth of work for Mr. Bertmann, but from hints he had dropped, she hoped he might be willing to keep her on even after the eyeglasses had been paid for, fair and square.

She sat in his office-workshop now, making neat columns of numbers in his account books, while at his tall worktable, Mr. Bertmann tinkered with all the tiny little parts of a future camera, to be worn someday by Mabel or Nelly. It was a quiet Wednesday afternoon.

Then suddenly it was no longer so quiet. There was a brisk knock at the front door, and men's voices. But there were no Aviation Cadet exams on the schedule. Gusta looked over at Mr. Bertmann, and he shrugged and went out into the hall to see who it was.

"Oh!" he said at the door. Something about the way he said it made Gusta sit up straighter.

"Hello there, Bertmann!" said a voice. "Some bits of official business to clear up. May we come in?"

They came clunking into the room, the sheriff (with his star on, so you knew who he was) and two other men. Gusta swept the desk clear as she stood up—nothing like a sheriff's star to make you feel everything should be tidy and you should be standing up.

"Run on home, Gusta," said Mr. Bertmann.

"No," said the sheriff. He didn't say it with any meanness, but somehow it was a little frightening, all the same. "Let's just all stay here, for a moment."

There was a silence.

"There's this thing about the registration, you know, Bertmann," said the sheriff.

Mr. Bertmann looked hunted and awkward and proud, all at once.

"I don't like *registrations*," he said. "I don't like lists being made of good people and bad people."

"Well, but there's a war brewing," said the sheriff reasonably. "And the bad guys are Germans, aren't they? And here you are—and you, too"—he took Gusta entirely by surprise, turning to her—"And you're Germans," he said. "So it just doesn't look so good, does it, not putting yourself on the registered alien list? I don't want to cause you trouble, Bertmann. But when there are complaints that come in—"

"Complaints? What complaints?" said Mr. Bertmann.

"Look here, Mr. Bertmann," said the sheriff. "Let's not get all riled up here. Maybe you just misplaced the registration form. I'll bet that's what happened."

Gusta looked at the emotion crackling across Mr. Bertmann's face, and she looked at the stubborn blandness that the sheriff was wearing like a mask, and she found herself speaking right out. Apparently she was no longer as good as she used to be at keeping quiet or backing down.

"Then I'll find his form," she said. "You don't need to be troubling Mr. Bertmann about it. I've been helping with his records. I'll find whatever the form is, if it's missing."

They all stared at her, of course, but she stared right back. With the new glasses, she could stare much better than in the old days.

"Well, now," said the sheriff.

"What complaints?" said Mr. Bertmann again.

The sheriff shifted his feet back and forth a little.

"Those pigeons of yours, carrying messages —"

"Oh, well, the pigeons!" said Mr. Bertmann. "What harm do they do? They always only fly home! Messages from myself to myself! But if you're worried about my *pigeons* . . ."

"It's the combination, Bertmann," said the sheriff. "It's not just the pigeons; it's the being *German*, together with the pigeons. You can see why people might think —"

All of a sudden Mr. Bertmann simply ruffled up with anger, spitting mad. "*You people*," he said. "Do you know what you are saying? Do you know what I am? Do you know why I'm here? You think I am German? You think maybe I would work to help the Nazis? Well, but *they* wouldn't call me German! I am a *Jew*! Do you know what that means? A Jew! Do not tell me about the Nazis. Nobody here can tell me anything about the Nazis. Nobody here can possibly hate them as much as I hate them."

Gusta could see that the sheriff hardly knew what to say.

"Anyway. I filled out your forms," Mr. Bertmann continued. "Years ago. When there was hope, I did file them. The I-intend-to-become-a-citizen papers, what-ever it is you call them."

"Oh, now!" said the sheriff. "That's good. The Declaration of Intention. When did you do that, Mr. Bertmann? Should be a record somewhere."

"Don't know," said Mr. Bertmann. In fact, he shrugged. "In the last decade, some one of those years. What does it matter?"

"Now I'm surprised at you, Bertmann," said the sheriff. "Of course it matters. Otherwise, looks like you are avoiding lawful alien registration, but if you're in line for citizenship —"

"No," said Mr. Bertmann. "By the time they wanted more papers from me, it was too late. There was no hope anymore. What good was your citizenship to me then? So I stopped with the papers."

"Oh, come now, Bertmann!" said the sheriff, but his heartiness was beginning to sound a little hollow. "What are you saying?"

"I will tell you, since you ask," said Mr. Bertmann. He straightened himself up, but his expression was all shadow. "It is because of a human being, a dearest human being, with the name Rachel Ada Bertmann. Yes, I had a wife. Why did I come all this way, so long ago? Because I saw what was happening in our country, and I thought, in the United States of America there is room for a good man, a Jewish man, to make a life for himself and his wife. But my wife, who was much younger than I was, still had an elderly father, clinging to his old home. She said, 'I will stay a while, so he is not alone. Maybe I can convince him. And you go on ahead to America and make a new home for us and send for us when you can.' So I came here. I came to Springdale, in Maine. I have worked hard. There is room here for a wife, yes, and even a wife's father. I had hope then, and yes, I put in the first paper. I thought to become an American, to help my wife. And then came November 1938, the terrible night between the ninth and the tenth. You may know it."

The sheriff looked puzzled.

"The Nazis went out in the streets of the towns to murder us that night in November. They broke down the windows of my wife's father's shop. He could not withstand the horror of it. His heart just broke — broke into pieces, stopped working — and he died."

The sheriff shifted his weight from one foot to another. He was looking more like a human being, at that moment, and a little less like a sheriff.

"Very sorry to hear it, Mr. Bertmann," said the sheriff. "But then, if her father is gone, why doesn't your wife come over here now, to live with you in Springdale?"

"Because, sir, when she applied for the document, the visa, to come to the United States, *she was not accepted*. They turned us down! They do not understand what it means to be a Jew in a land run by Nazis! They said, 'We see you have this man Bertmann willing to sponsor you, but who will be your other sponsor?' they said. 'Where are the documents from the bank, for this man Bertmann and the other sponsor you do not have?' And they did not give her the document, the visa. She wrote to me, and the ink was, I tell you the truth, half ink and half tears. And of course I wrote to everyone I could think of. What else could I do? I even wrote to the president of these United States, but he is very busy and did not respond to the desperate letter of one little foreign man in Maine. And then one day comes another letter from Germany, in handwriting I do not know, and I learn I do not have a wife anymore. A kind person who knew us wrote: 'Your wife, Herr Bertmann, has sickened and died in these sad times.' And maybe that kind person has herself sickened and died by now, in that awful place. And now, you come to me and you call me an *alien*, you threaten me, and you say my pigeons must be spying for the very ones who killed my wife, because yes, even if they did not shoot her or hit her on the head, they surely destroyed her spirit so she could not continue to live—"

He broke off then. All those words had tumbled out of him, and it was as if there was nothing left for him to say.

And in the room, everything was frozen into a stunned silence.

"Well, now," said the sheriff after a while, sounding a little pale, sounding like someone trying to feel his way back into sheriff-ness. "Now, then. That's a sad story, and I'm truly sorry for your loss. I guess it's not so much your pigeons we're after, Bertmann, anyway. Everyone in this town knows about you and your pigeons! Get the registration letter in, old man, and we'll do what we can. We know your service to the U.S. Recruiting Office. Anyway, that's not the point. It's *Miss Neubronner* we're after."

"What?" said Mr. Bertmann.

Gusta would have said the same thing, but she couldn't get a word out.

"Augusta Neubronner," said the sheriff. "Daughter of August Neubronner?"

"Yes," said Gusta.

"Well, now, see, that's serious. *He's* an alien and a

German and a Communist and a fugitive from justice at this point, young lady. That's a powerful combination of trouble. And we understand from the school that you have been unwilling or unable to furnish a birth certificate. Questions have been raised about your nationality and your loyalty. We'll need to have a conversation with you."

"Don't be absurd!" said Mr. Bertmann, coming back to himself somehow. "This girl is a child. She is not just a child: she is a good child. She is the *best* of children. I tell you, you will not—threaten—this— child. If you have questions about her, you will of course discuss these matters with her grandmother, Mrs. Clementine Hoopes. Gusta, go on home."

Fugitive from justice! Gusta was thinking, and her heart was galumphing on in her chest like a crazy thing. Her papa was still a fugitive from justice! But that meant—they STILL hadn't caught him yet. *Oh, Papa!*

"We'll all go together," said the sheriff. "Got my car out front there waiting."

Gramma Hoopes Speaks Up

They all crowded into the sheriff's car; Mr. Bertmann kept a protective arm around Gusta all the way down Elm Street.

When they pulled up in front of the old home, one of the boys was out front, took one look, and ran around to the back fast as a blur, carrying the message: "Sheriff's car! Right out there in front!"

So when they stomped up the steps of the porch and knocked on the door, Gramma Hoopes was already there to meet them.

She looked like a queen in the hall of her house, Aunt Marion beside her, and the hint of boys watching from the shadows, all the way as far as you could see.

"What's the trouble, Darnell?" she said to the sheriff.

The sheriff lost a whole dollop of his grandness right there.

"It's about this Augusta Neubronner you've been harboring here," he said.

"That would be Augusta *Hoopes* Neubronner, of whom you're speaking," corrected Gramma Hoopes. "My granddaughter."

"That's the one," said the sheriff. "We need a look at her birth certificate, please. She's the daughter of a fugitive from justice who's also an alien and a Communist, so you'll understand the need for some concern."

"She's the daughter," said Gramma Hoopes, "of my daughter Gladys Hoopes."

"Her father, though—the criminal, on the run—"

"He's not a criminal," said Gusta, because she just couldn't help herself. "He's a *labor organizer.*"

"Well, now," said the sheriff, and Gramma Hoopes said, "Gusta, child, hush."

"It's just *he's not a criminal*. They were going to deport him back to *Germany*," said Gusta, instead of hushing. "Germany, where he would have been *killed.*"

"And that is quite true," said Mr. Bertmann.

"They are not kind to labor organizers now, in the fatherland."

"Probably not," said her grandmother. "That it, Darnell? You finished?"

The sheriff wiped his forehead with his handkerchief. "There's still the birth certificate, Mrs. Hoopes. People saying the girl has no right to be here."

"Who says such a ridiculous thing, I wonder?" said Gramma Hoopes.

"Now, now," said the sheriff. "People with a certain weight in our community."

"Mill-owner types," said Gramma Hoopes, and there was so much ice in her voice that the sheriff actually flinched.

"Now, now, Mrs. Hoopes," he said, but anyone could see he was losing this battle.

"I'll have you know, Darnell," said Gramma Hoopes, "that this granddaughter of mine was born *in this very house*. Yes. Upstairs there. You know how I know?"

"Yes, Mrs. Hoopes," said the sheriff.

"Because I was there," said Gramma Hoopes. "Because that's what I do, isn't it? When I'm not raising children, I'm helping them get born. Is that right, Darnell?"

"Yes, Mrs. Hoopes," said the sheriff.

"In fact, as I recall," said Gramma Hoopes, "when you were born, Darnell, the people in the room that day were your mother, and you (eventually), and me — have I got that right?"

"Yes, yes, Mrs. Hoopes," said the sheriff. "That's what I'm told. All right, all right. But why didn't you put in for a birth certificate for the girl?"

"Didn't get around to it right away," said Gramma Hoopes. "Gets busy on a farm. Guess I'll get around to it, when I have a moment. Are you quite done here, Darnell? Because I was working on supper."

And the sheriff and his men slunk right back out of that door and back to their car.

Mr. Bertmann turned down the offer of another ride, and then he turned down Gramma Hoopes's offer of supper, too, although he was grateful for it. He wanted to get back to his pigeons, and he wanted some fresh air and quiet on the way.

He did put one of his old hands on Gusta's shoulder before he left, though. And he said, "This, Mrs. Hoopes, is a *good child*."

And Gramma Hoopes said, with a sniff, "Yes, Mr. Bertmann, she is. I would say that they are *all* reasonably good children, in this house."

Praise from Gramma Hoopes! A shimmer of happiness sped around the crowded shadows of the hall: the boys were pleased.

"Stop gaping at me, Gusta," said Gramma Hoopes, but Gusta was in awe.

Her grandmother had just told a whole bushel of lies on Gusta's behalf. Hadn't she? *Born in this very house?* Gusta was quite, quite sure that none of that bore the slightest resemblance to the truth. Well!

That thought warmed Gusta's soul right up. She figured that to tell lies as wide and deep as that must take more than just a quick and wily mind. It must take something a lot like *love*.

❧ 48 ❧

Return

The thing about summer: on the one hand, all that extra time when you're not in school and therefore could be out in the woods or sitting on the porch. On the other hand, canning.

"If I never see another pea," said Gusta, shaking out her stiff fingers, "I'll be happy."

"It's not the peas that are the problem, silly," said Josie. (Her fingers never seemed to get stiff.) "It's the pods they come in."

They had already been shelling peas at the worktable in the kitchen for approximately three million years, and there was still a huge green heap left waiting for them, and when were they ever going to go walking in the woods, ever again? Of course, it would be wrong to complain. They could have been Aunt Marion, for instance. She was at the stove, handling the jars and the pressure cookers, her face glistening from the work and the heat and the steam.

It was the start of the canning season, the time of year when Aunt Marion came into her own. The strawberries from the garden had come and gone in a blink of an eye—turned into jewel-red jars of jam. And now it was the turn of the peas.

"You'll be glad enough for the peas, come winter," said Aunt Marion from the stove. There was a kind of feverish intensity to her, and not just because of the heat. Some of the fever could be chalked up to enthusiasm.

Aunt Marion was very enthusiastic about canning.

"Blue-ribbon peas!" she said. "Remember that's our aim: no squished peas allowed, and no pebbles or anything else to which the judges might object."

"Or rusty lids," said Josie, giving Gusta a wink.

Gusta had already heard that sad story, and more than once: about the year when Aunt Marion's strawberry jam had been kicked out of contention at the fair due to a single streak of rust on a lid.

"How many different canned goods can one

person enter in a single year?" asked Gusta. She was wondering, secretly, how many more days would be spent in this kitchen, preparing fruits and vegetables for their mason jars.

"As many canned goods as the canner can can, I suppose," said Josie, and she gave a little bark of a laugh.

And just at that moment there was a clamor out in the main hall: a knock on the door, followed by the staccato pounding of boys' feet racing to open up and see who might be there.

That was intriguing, but stranger yet was the silence that fell next. Whoever was at the door, it must be someone the boys didn't know. Josie and Gusta looked at each other, and even Aunt Marion paused to wipe a wisp of steam-dampened hair back out of her eyes and listen for a moment to the sudden hush out in the hall.

Larry poked his head in through the kitchen door.

"There's someone here for Gusta!" he whispered.

"What, now?" said Aunt Marion.

"For Gusta!" he said in his normal voice. "A lady came!"

They all left the peas behind and crowded into the hall.

And there, with an awkward object dangling from her right hand, and a look of determination (mixed with a little distress) on her face, was Miss Kendall.

There was a silence, which was especially silent on Josie's part. Josie was right next to Gusta, though, so Gusta could *feel* her shoulder start to tremble.

"Hello, Augusta," said Miss Kendall, and it was clear that she, too, was having some trouble keeping her breath steady. "I've brought you something that belongs to you."

And she set the French horn case down in the middle of the hall.

Everyone looked at the French horn: all the boys, Josie, Aunt Marion, Miss Kendall, Gusta, and even Gramma Hoopes, who came into the far end of the hall from her office.

"Grace Kendall," said Gramma Hoopes, frowning and standing very straight, the general effect being that of a short, human-shaped icicle.

"Good to see you, Mrs. Hoopes," said Miss Kendall. "I hope you've been well. I'm just here to return Augusta's horn. As you can see."

"You kept it a mighty long time," said Gramma Hoopes.

"There was a sad misunderstanding," said Miss Kendall, her voice low and melodious again, as it used to be. "Augusta, my dear child, I'm so sorry about that. I have spoken with my brother, and from what he said, I understood, I gathered—anyway, I saw that keeping this instrument would be a grave injustice. And it seems to me a French horn like this should be with someone who loves it very much. I'm so sorry about the . . . misunderstanding. I want to make things right, whatever way I can. If I can't return the money, at least I can give you back your horn. And you have so much talent, Gusta. I do hope you'll play and play."

Oh, it took Gusta by surprise: her love for that horn just swelled up and filled her heart and then spilled right over into that hall. She had missed it so much. There was still the problem of Uncle Charlie, and her father was still endlessly far away, but the horn sat in that hall, silently telling everyone that sometimes the world does what is right, and lost things come home.

Gusta couldn't say a word.

Miss Kendall had hesitated there for a moment, too; she was looking now slightly past Gusta's shoulder and up.

"And you, Josie," she said, softly. "I'm beginning to see how I have . . . been misled—about this whole situation."

But Gusta noticed that Miss Kendall's eyes stayed carefully away from Aunt Marion, who was wiping her hands nervously on her apron, front side and back side, front and back, as she hung back in the hall.

"All right, then," said Gramma Hoopes. "Very kind of you to stop by, I'm sure. Gusta, say thank you to Miss Kendall. And then we'll not keep her any longer, will we?"

But before Gusta could speak a word, Miss Kendall reached out across the last foot or so of air between them and took Gusta's hand in both of hers.

"Thank *you*, Augusta," she said. "Your advice was excellent. And you, Josie. Good-bye, now, everyone."

And an instant later she had let go of Gusta's trembling hand, backed out of that hall through the front door, and vanished.

"Well!" said Gramma Hoopes grimly.

"My peas!" said Aunt Marion, and dashed back into the kitchen where the peas were growing mushy on the stove. There was almost surely no hope for those peas. Even Gusta knew that much about peas. They are delicate creatures and don't like being forgotten.

But Gusta's mind was busy thinking about Josie, not peas. She looked at Josie, and she looked at her horn, and her heart ached from both hurt and happiness, and she wasn't sure what she should say, actually, other than "Jo—"

Josie interrupted her by clapping her hands together.

"Aaaaand the Orphan Band's back in the picture!" she said. "Just let them try to stop us now!"

✂ 49 ✎

Fair-Well

Then there was the great Saturday in early July when it seemed like half the residents of Springdale came spilling out into the park near the mills, to hear the traditional preliminary round of competition for the upcoming Seventy-Fifth Annual County Fair. So many people! Georges Thibodeau ran up to tell Gusta he was crossing his fingers for her, for sure. A smiling Mr. Bertmann pressed a small cardboard square into Gusta's hand: "For you, for luck, dear girl! *It's Nelly's first photograph!*" Aunt Marion and Gramma Hoopes and all the Hoopes Home kids had come along to hear the music, too. So had a small army of hungry mosquitoes, but that didn't dampen any enthusiasm. If you can't stand a mosquito or two on occasion, Maine is not the right state for you.

Kendall Mills had had its own band since the early years of the century. They had fancy, real uniforms with braid on them, and absolutely no member of that band was either female or under the age of fifteen, so while the Kendall Mills Band was noisily warming up on that bandstand—by tradition they would be playing first, in honor of their blue-ribbon win in the previous year—the upstart members of the Orphan Band of Springdale had to work hard to keep from thinking about how much shorter and younger and fewer they were than the band from Kendall Mills.

There were other groups milling about nervously, people with harmonicas in their hands and even a trumpet or two, but they were also all adults.

And then it was getting closer to the moment when it would be time for the concert to start, and Gusta couldn't help but notice that Josie's face was full of a wild and anticipatory happiness. Josie, unlike most people, felt as comfortable on a stage as on her own front porch. Maybe more comfortable.

"Come on, let's get ready," said Josie, and the girls were about to start moving up toward the grandstand steps, to be ready when the Mills Band had finished, when a nervous-looking man with a fancy hat on his head, a big piece of paper in his hand, and sweat beading up on the sides of his face hopped up on the stage.

"Well, hello, folks," he said to the crowd. "I think a lot of you know me. I'm Rufus Green, supposed to be your master of ceremonies today"—sprinkling of applause, which Mr. Green damped down by waving his hands at them—"but see, I'm here to tell you— there seems to have been a bit of a turn of events."

What did that mean? Gusta and Bess exchanged glances, but neither of them had any idea. All they knew was what anyone even without glasses would probably have been able to figure out: Mr. Green was mighty worried and troubled about something.

"Guess I'll go ahead and let Mr. Kendall of the Fairgrounds Steering Committee make his announcement to you now."

Mr. Kendall!

The girls looked at each other and (much more surreptitiously) over at Gramma Hoopes, who was seated with the boys and Aunt Marion.

The crowd was murmuring. The part of the crowd that was Georges Thibodeau wasn't going to settle for merely murmuring, of course.

"LET THE BANDS PLAY!" he shouted from way

over by a big tree. It gladdened Gusta's heart to hear him, still interrupting even though school was out for the summer.

And then Mr. Kendall himself came up from the other side of the grandstand. Gusta felt her brow furrowing, just seeing him there. Josie made a slight hissing sound. Gusta wasn't brave enough to turn and actually look at her face.

Mr. Kendall skittered up the steps. He avoided looking anywhere near the Orphan Band, but that didn't surprise Gusta one whit.

"Good evening, citizens of Springdale," said Mr. Kendall. "As part of the Steering Committee for the Springdale Fairgrounds, I'm here to announce a major change of plans for this year's county fair."

Then he did look in the Orphan Band's direction, and there was poison in that look, which was not a nice thing to see.

"In this year, 1941, we are looking to modernize and professionalize our use of the fairgrounds and to bring in some needed revenue to the Fairgrounds Committee. Therefore, instead of the traditional amateur competitions at the county fair this coming August, we have arranged for a fine group of New York City performers to come up to the fairgrounds and put on a first-rate stage show, with matinee and evening performances August eighteenth through the twenty-third, for a nominal fee. That's ten vaudeville acts booked directly from New York, plus the usual midway attractions that you know and love. And I guess our fine men of the Kendalls Mills Band will just have to continue their reign as champions through to 1942."

There was a stunned silence in the park.

"What did he just say?" said Bess to Gusta and Josie.

That was the end of anything like a hush in that park, because about a hundred people asked their neighbor something pretty close to what Bess had just asked Gusta and Josie.

"It means no Blue-Ribbon Band this year," said Josie, her lips very tight and grim. "Nor any Red-Ribbon Band, either, what's worse for us. *That's* what it means."

Questions were beginning to be shot up at Mr. Kendall on the stage—how much the tickets would cost, what this meant for all the other competitions, like the heifers and the jams and the cakes and the pies, and why nobody had announced any of this earlier. The men in the Kendall Mills Band had the decency, at least, to look like they were sweating the sweat of embarrassed discomfort in their gold braid–trimmed uniforms. Had *they* known this was happening? Gusta couldn't quite tell from their faces, but she guessed maybe not, from the surprise written in their tense shoulders and elbows.

Mr. Kendall stared at the crowd like he was just daring them to say the Fairgrounds Steering Committee could not out-and-out cancel the fair — and next to him, poor Rufus Green stood mopping his brow, and stammering out nonanswers to all those questions.

"In the paper," he kept saying. "There'll be an announcement in the paper tomorrow."

Gusta had been distracted by surprise or looking in the wrong direction, or she might have been able to stop the next bad thing from happening. The next bad thing was that Josie suddenly went striding up the grandstand steps, ukulele in hand.

"Mr. Kendall!" she was saying, and there was something almost Gramma Hoopes–like in her voice.

"Oh, dear," said Bess, tugging on Gusta's sleeve, and when Gusta saw Josie climbing those steps, she just instinctively followed her up, horn and all. She had the faint impression that all the Hoopes Home kids had just jumped to their feet at once, off there to one side, and Georges was on his feet, too, over the other way, but Gusta's attention was mostly riveted on Josie and on the angry figure of Mr. Kendall on the stage just beyond Josie.

"Josie, wait," said Gusta. "Wait!"

"You!" said Mr. Kendall, and Gusta, despite her glasses, had trouble telling whether he spat that word mostly at Josie, or mostly at her, Gusta. Probably at both of them. She caught up to Josie, balanced the horn in her left hand, and put her right hand on Josie's waist: *solidarity forever* . . . even when your cousin is doing something that may be awfully ill-advised.

"Mr. Kendall!" said Josie. "Are you telling us you just sold out our whole county fair to some New York folks for money?"

Mr. Kendall glared at her. *His* glare and *her* glare did (Gusta had to admit) look a little alike, around the edges.

"I said nothing of the sort," he said. "I said we're modernizing. And bringing in professional talent. And in any case, if you think you and this child of a criminal *fugitive* can just get away with your indecent slander, if you think—"

"Papa is not a criminal, though," said Gusta. It just burst out of her. Then she remembered she was only up there on that stage to drag Josie away or protect Josie or—well, anyway, not to start shouting herself.

"Your *father*—" said Mr. Kendall, making that word sound like the most poisonous and vile thing in the whole entire world.

Although he himself was probably the most poisonous and vilest person to be saying anything, just then, about *fathers*!

"No," said Josie. "Stop."

And the strange thing was, he did stop. He made the mistake of looking away from Gusta, looking at Josie's angry, glaring face, that was (you had to admit) not entirely unlike his own, just at that moment. And you could see him remembering something, maybe a lot of things, including what it meant for him to be shouting at Josephina Hoopes, here in public on the grandstand in the park. He was still mad, Gusta could see that, but in that split second he backed into being almost an actual human being again.

"We're the Honorary Orphan Band of Springdale, and we came here to play some songs, and that's all," said Josie, and now she wasn't just talking to Mr. Kendall. She was looking around at that whole crowd's worth of upset people, who had come down to the park to hear some music. And then she turned to look right at her cousins, at Bess and Gusta. "Didn't we, girls?"

They nodded. What else were they going to do? And in any case, a bright and floating sort of feeling was beginning to rise up in Gusta's chest, the feeling of something shadowy you've feared for a long time suddenly being hit by a piercing ray of sunlight and fading away.

Mr. Kendall was backing away from Josie, from all of them.

"So what I think is, we should play anyway," said Josie. "Even if we can't hope to be the Red-Ribbon Band. What do you think?"

She was sort of asking Bess and Gusta, but a lot of people in the crowd all around shouted friendly noises up in their direction in response.

"Yes!" said those friendly noises. "Go on, now. Play us some music!"

So they did.

They played "Angeline the Baker" and "Hard Times in the Mill" and a couple of cheerful, quick-moving songs they had made up themselves, and it's safe to say no band composed of French horn, ukulele, voice, and bean jar ever had a more enthusiastic reception anywhere.

At one point Gusta looked out over the brassy

curve of her horn at that smiling, clapping crowd and saw something her own eyes could hardly believe: *Gramma Hoopes*, nodding her head in time with Bess's beans!

And when they climbed back down from that bandstand, with the flush of having been onstage still warming their cheeks and their insides, the Hoopes Home clan came pushing joyfully through the crowd: Gramma Hoopes taking the lead, with the boys and Delphine and Aunt Marion trailing along after, and all of them smiling wide as frogs.

"Well done, you three harridans," said Gramma Hoopes. "Though, really, that name has got to go. 'Orphan Band'! Outlandish! But the lot of you can find your way around a tune, I'll grant you that."

"It was great! You were great! You sure told him, that Kendall! That was great! And then you sung great!" said Larry, so excited he had lost half his words, and the boys all nodded—even Clarence.

To everyone's surprise, Gramma Hoopes didn't scold Larry for mentioning the forbidden name. Far from it. She gave a satisfied sniff instead.

"*That man* basically just announced he has sold out his own town," she said. "What good can come of something like that, I'd like to know?"

Aunt Marion was a few feet behind the rest of them, because she was shifting the weight of Delphine from one arm to the other. She heard what Gramma Hoopes said, though, and she shook her head. "Why, there's been a fair every year since forever! This was going to be the seventy-fifth, that's what the paper said. Whatever are we going to do?"

"Rise above, Marion," said Gramma Hoopes. "What we will do is rise above. And eat our own preserves. Tell me, though, you girls: Whatever inspired you to take up singing and playing that way? To think you could compete with those Kendall Mills men?"

"Well, to be honest, Mrs. Hoopes—I mean, *Gramma*," said Josie. "To be completely honest, we just wanted a chance to be the Red-Ribbon Band. So you would know that singing can be as, as"—and she flashed a grin at Gusta and Bess, which was a cue.

"As real as jam!" they sang out together, that band of not-really-orphans, that chorus of cousins.

⧼ 50 ⧽

The Sneakiness of Wishes

Light fingers, light fingers!" said Gusta's mother, laughing, because Gusta's fingers were already streaked with blue.

It was a true summer day, the air very warm, birds occasionally commenting from their perches in the trees. Gusta was learning how to pick blueberries on the far side of Holly Hill, where a rocky slope had kept the trees properly discouraged.

Blueberries like to grow low to the ground, in places where the sun can sweeten them.

It was like gathering treasure, working across the slope of that hill. All those thousands and thousands of berries! Gusta discovered she didn't even have to

lean down all the time, which was good because leaning wasn't awfully comfortable; she went ahead and
plopped herself right down on a little rock and turned
very slowly from one side to the other, picking the
little purple-blue spheres and dropping them into her
bucket, fast as she could go.

As fast as she could go wasn't very fast, as of yet.
She was working on that. Her mother's light fingers
worked as quick as a blur, somehow stripping whole
bunches of berries into her bucket at once.

You had to pull on the berries without pinching
too hard—without pinching at all, actually—because
they were wild, young blueberries, and a little tender-
skinned. It was like your fingers were just brushing by,
inviting the blueberries into the bucket. Not demand-
ing, not insisting: *inviting.*

When her mother's bucket was almost, but not
quite, full to the brim, and Gusta's holding about an
inch's worth, they switched pails and kept going until
both of them were full.

"There!" said Gusta's mother, taking off her sun
hat to flap some air across her cheeks. "That's two pies
accounted for, plus some extra. Let's go up that way
and sit a moment."

They climbed up the hill to the captain's old

lighthouse, which turned out to be the perfect place to share the bottle of tonic her mother had smuggled along. Once in a blue moon, Gusta's mother liked to drink a root beer. (No, more than that: she liked to produce a bottle of root beer as if it were a wicked indulgence and sip it with gusto.) So now she and Gusta tasted a few more of the berries, just to make sure they were still as tangy-delicious as they had been ten minutes before, and they passed the tonic back and forth, bubbly and sweet.

Tonic, berries, mother . . .

It was good to be alive on a day like this one, with the crickets singing out of the grasses and the mosquitoes only coming around just enough to remind you how lovely it was that mostly they were staying away.

Gusta's mother reached into her pocket and pulled out a piece of mica to plonk into the old jar.

"Tradition," she said to Gusta.

"I know," said Gusta, and then of course she couldn't help but remember that other time when something had fallen, midshine, into that jar. "Oh, Mama, I didn't even get a chance to tell you before — but I went and wasted the old sea captain's Wish."

Gusta's mother passed the tonic over so Gusta could have another sip.

"My grandfather's Wish? You found something that really looked like a Wish? So where did you find it?"

"It was in the button box!" said Gusta, and her mother slapped her own knee with satisfaction.

"The button box! Of course. Where else would it be?" she said.

"And now it's in here somewhere," said Gusta, pointing into the jar, where the mica twinkled so quietly. "It was that horrible day, when everything went wrong and I was sick. I wanted to make a wish that would make *everything* better, that would fix up Uncle Charlie's hand and end the war and make the Kendalls be nice to Josie and save the French horn and bring Papa home . . . and instead I wasn't thinking straight, and I messed up, and I dropped it. I'm so sorry."

Her mother was quite silent and still for a moment. Gusta felt like a stone on a teeter-totter, not yet knowing whether its fate would be to roll *this* way or *that* way.

Listing everything out like that made Gusta remember all the things she had meant to fix and had messed up instead.

But her mother made a sweeping-away gesture, and it turned out Gusta wasn't on a teeter-totter at all.

"Oh, goodness, Gusta," said her mother. "Don't feel bad. Wishes are such sneaky things. You never can tell how they're going to go, wishes. Plus your Uncle Charlie's headed off to Portland tomorrow, and that's something."

Yes, it was true: Uncle Charlie was going to the big hospital in Portland.

They were going to work to free up his hand from the scars binding it. It was the kind of fine-honed medical work that couldn't have been done even twenty years ago, they said, and all that fancy doctoring was surely going to cost even more than a mere hundred dollars—more than even a French horn could pay for. But Uncle Charlie was going to have his hand worked on anyway, and that was all thanks to the sea captain's bats.

"I certainly never expected to owe so much to a bunch of flying mice," said Gusta's mother.

"Thank you, bats! And thank you to your magical typewriting machine," said Gusta.

That, too.

When Gusta's mother came back up to Maine, she had brought a great clunky gray box with her, and in that gray box was an actual typewriter, such as they had in some of the training classes at the high school (Josie was very impressed).

There was news to go along with that typewriter: the Museum of Natural History, where Professor Jones worked, turned out to be very interested in the notebooks of old Captain Griffiths. They liked his sketches from the forests of Madagascar, and they liked his sketches from the woods of Maine. They really, really liked his bats, which they thought might be a new subspecies, hitherto unknown. They wanted to make a book, a printed book, with copies of those sketches, so that many people could buy it and read it, and they wanted to put the original notebooks on display in the museum, and not only were they willing to hire Gusta's mother to type up the captain's notebooks, which she could do even while living up in the faraway woods and fields of Maine, but they would pay Mrs. Clementine Hoopes a thousand dollars for her permission to turn those lovely notebooks into a real and actual book and then put them in a glass case, on display.

A *thousand* dollars!

So it turned out that the "treasure" the old captain had found in that cave was those bats themselves.

A thousand dollars was enough to pay for Uncle Charlie's hand and more besides. That money would surely help them all get through this strange time, while the war was burning its way through so many parts of the world.

Gusta's mother put her arm around Gusta's shoulders and squeezed her tight. And then she did something Gusta wasn't expecting at all: she pulled a battered envelope out of her pocket and handed it to Gusta.

"I've got something here for you, Gusta," she said.

The half sheet of paper inside that envelope did not have a lot of words on it, and they were cautious words, but Gusta read them with a fluttering, breathless heart:

My dear small thingling! I am learning to fly. I hope you are learning to sail your own little boat. Be ever brave, for these are times which call for courage, even from the smallest thinglings. Your loving Papa.

Oh! Gusta looked greedily back at the envelope — there was no stamp.

"It came from someone who got it from someone who got it from someone else," said her mother. "He is so careful, you know, your papa."

"And brave," said Gusta.

"Yes," said her mother.

"And now we know for absolute certain that he got to Canada," said Gusta, with such a whoosh of relief in her heart and her voice that her mother put her hand on Gusta's shoulder for a moment to steady her.

"You were worried, too?" said her mother. "Of course you were!"

She sighed. Gusta could feel the empty spot in her mother radiating its own complicated *wishing*. That was something they had in common, the two of them, a weakness for wishes. And an empty spot in their hearts that was roughly the shape and size of August Neubronner, husband, father, fugitive, and faraway fighter.

"I hope they can finish their war, over in Europe, and the whole world can calm down," said Gusta's mother. "And your papa can come home again. But I don't know when those things will happen, Gusta. I really don't."

Gusta was rereading her letter.

"He forgot I'm in the part of Maine where there are no boats," she said.

Her mother laughed a little; the laugh was sad, but it was a laugh.

"Said the girl sitting in a lighthouse . . . Well,

anyway. It's a metaphor, that bit! Here, let me have another sip of that lovely stuff."

Gusta's mother took that bottle of tonic back and finished it right up, smacked her lips, and looked out over the slopes of Holly Hill, rolling down toward (eventually) the invisible sea.

The dark wall of a thunderstorm was taking shape over to the north. And ahead of the storm, the light danced about, making everything glitter while glittering was still possible.

Making everything more intensely what it really, truly was.

The *clear light of trouble*, etching out the edges of things against the black backdrop of the storm.

Gusta leaned against her mother's arm, and they watched that light doing its work.

"You know, when I think about it, it's almost as if—" Gusta said, and she stopped, because it seemed like it might be silly, and then she started bravely up again, because sometimes saying things that might be silly to your own mother is actually a perfectly reasonable thing to do. "It's as if, even though I messed up that wish so badly, a lot of things *are* a little better, anyway. Do you think—do you think maybe that wish found ways to come a little bit true?"

"Wishes are sneaky," said her mother. "That's the only sure thing."

Then she laughed.

"Look at us, talking about those old Wishes as if they really could change the world somehow!"

"I just want Papa to come back," confessed Gusta, since this was the kind of place and the kind of light that made a person want to tell the truth.

"Oh, Gusta," said her mother, *"yes."*

And then Gusta's mother did something wonderful and wild. She put down the tonic bottle and cupped her hands around her mouth and shouted, "Cooooooome hooooome, Auuuuuuuugust!" so that the sound of it went floating out above the trees on the hill.

Gusta laughed with surprise.

"Don't be shocked," said her mother. "This is the sea captain's own beacon we're perched on. Beacons are for calling to people, seems to me."

So Gusta tried it, too: she cupped her hands and called her papa home, calling right out loud. It felt good to let some of her secret wishes out into the world that way.

She was sure her horn would approve.

The wind picked up a notch—the storm stepped

closer. Gusta thought about the kitchen back on Elm Street, where there must be a bustle of activity right now, of chopping and stirring and kneading and laughing.

Someone in that kitchen was probably looking up at the clock and wondering where Gusta and her mama were.

Gusta smiled: it was good to live in a place where you were missed when you were gone and welcomed when you finally came back in through the door.

Love and stubbornness, she thought. Love and stubbornness could make a family as sweet as blueberries and as real as jam.

"Come on, Mama!" said Gusta, reaching for that lighthouse ladder, aglow in the last bright rays of the sun. "Come on, let's go, quick, before the storm catches up."

It was time to get those berries home.

AUTHOR'S NOTE

"Oh, this reminds me of Maine!"
—my mother, in front of any beautiful landscape anywhere

There are stories that come from the heart, and stories that spring from the very bones that give us form. *The Orphan Band of Springdale* is one of those bone-marrow tales. It is my echo of a story that I wish my mother had been able to finish telling me—the story of her childhood, which was so hardscrabble and tough that she could only bear to give us scraps and pieces of it when we were little.

We knew that she had to go to a new school in a new town every year, because her family could never afford to pay the rent and so had to move constantly.

We knew that her father was not around most of the time.

We knew that during particularly hard times she would be sent to live in the orphan home run by her grandmother up in Maine—an orphan home that had been started in order to hide a family secret.

And we knew that out of all of this trouble and hardship, our mother emerged with some fine and enduring talents: how to tell a good story, how to bring extended family together around a table, and how to play the French horn. When summer came, she would take us back to the farming country of southern Maine, and we camped on a hill that had been allowed to go back to woods and from the top of which all the grown-ups insisted that *with a good telescope* you might be able to see sails off the Portland coast.

This was not the Maine of fishermen and salt water. Instead of the ocean, we had occasional treks to Square Pond. The mosquitoes kept us on our toes.

The cousins would gather at the end of the day, and over long afternoons my mother and grandmother and aunts and uncles and cousins would share epic stories in few words, while we kids ran around creating small kingdoms in the woods.

I would have eavesdropped more often if I had known I would lose my mother early.

My mother died too young, years passed, and all the stories about Maine kept wriggling and whispering inside me. Eventually I realized I was going to have to give voice to them. I could never know the whole truth about my mother's childhood, but I could still write it anyway — as fiction.

To make the fiction as true as possible, I spent some time at the Sanford-Springvale Historical Society in Maine, reading through old issues of the excellent local paper, the

Sanford Tribune and Advocate. The flavor of 1941 comes through those newspaper pages: anxieties about drought and the war in Europe, "alien registration" drives, union elections in the local mills, a "7-Point Health Certificate" school campaign waged with vigor against bad eyes, crooked teeth, and malnutrition, all garnished with competing hyperbolic ads from the local dairies.

So the seeds of this story are true, but the resulting crop is fiction. I changed the identities and biographies of my characters and even tweaked the names of the towns out of respect for the difference between Gusta's fictional world and the childhood of my mother.

My mother did love a good story, and I hope she would have been tickled by this one. In the heart-and-marrow of my dreams, sometimes she even looks up from the pages and smiles her wonderful, crooked grin and says, "Oh, Anne, this reminds me of Maine!"

ACKNOWLEDGMENTS

From our first conversation about this story to the final push to get the line edits done, Kaylan Adair always somehow managed to be at once ferociously exacting and lovingly encouraging. I am so grateful to her for helping me through the long labor of this book.

At a crucial moment, Mary Lee Donovan stepped in with grace and aplomb. The people of Candlewick are a truly wonderful crowd! Anne Irza-Leggat, Phoebe Kosman, Kathleen Rourke, Lindsay Warren, and Allison Cole share an inspiring love for books and benevolent care for those books' writers. Copyeditors Maya Myers and Maggie Deslaurier and proofreaders Kay McManus and Martha Dwyer turned the last rounds of edits into a surprisingly pleasant experience. Josie Portillo's cover design makes my heart happy.

Ammi-Joan Paquette has transformed the experience of being an author into something surprisingly joyous: thank you, Joan, and thank you to all the wonderful people in the EMLA community.

Writing this book meant rediscovering the hills, fields, and woods of southern Maine that I first learned to love as a small child. Cousins and siblings—Stuart, Sara, Donna, Susan, and Barbara—filled those weeks on Walnut Hill long ago with mayhem and fun, whether we were exploring the woods, admiring the cows, or pumping water for washing socks. We were so proud that our Granny Mac could chop wood like nobody's business, and we loved the stories told by all the uncles, aunts and great-aunts, and cousins once removed. I am grateful to Uncle Jim and Aunt Paula and to my sister Barbara (and her husband, Ken) for everything they've done to keep us all tied to Maine. And to Cousins Donna and Alan for welcoming us back so many times.

Thank you to the members of the Sanford-Springvale Historical Society and to my eldest daughter, Thera, who joined me on a particularly memorable research expedition. Verle Waters and Kathryn Anderson shared farming stories. Stephanie Burgis and Jenn Reese gave me hope. My family — Thera and Ada and Eleanor and Eric — encouraged me all the way through, as did my dear friends Will, Jayne (and the war tuba band), Roo, and Judy. Roo came tromping through the woods to help me find my mother's grave on what would have been her eighty-third birthday: friends are truly the bright mica in life's back roads!

This book is dedicated to the memory of my mother, Helen, who was the original nearsighted, snaggletoothed child with a French horn in her hands. She died much too young, and I miss her.